APERTURE OF THE EYE

Also by Carl Spence

The Girl from Jeparit
Thomas J Greer, PI

APERTURE OF THE EYE

Carl Spence

Published in Australia in 2020 by Carl Spence

Website: www.carlspenceauthor.com

© Carl Spence 2020

ISBN 9780648334842 (paperback)

NATIONAL LIBRARY OF AUSTRALIA

A catalogue record for this book is available from the National Library of Australia

Dedicated to the beauty of Exmoor

OPTIC NERVES

CHAPTER ONE

The image in his mind never faded, despite every attempt to forcibly dim its distinctness. It started as a source of self-imported comfort, standing at the very top of a select assemblage, but then as time passed and hope diminished, it became an enemy. It went from his daily thoughts, then to dreams in which he never wanted to awake, to nightmares from which he knew he could not escape. The same scene, with the same words, always.

Somehow it was easier to cast out the day itself – the day it actually happened. The psychiatrist had performed some trick it seemed, and who was he to question how. Fade can happen, so allow it to, he'd said. And one day you may be free. But until then, know it may never fully come and all you can do is adapt.

Logic and rationality had long since been broken. John had grown to distrust both. Every doctor had said that was natural, but reminding him that misgivings and hesitation must never cloud the benefits of preserving the very things that made us a person.

When the words were all he was left with, it was the absence of any more action that could be taken that became most ruinous.

The decay that took hold and then engulfed his marriage to Samantha left only a carapace of something that was once living and loving.

There was a time when John pretended that everything was as good as it could be, but that didn't last long. It came as a shock to some, but not all, when he said that she had left and the house would be sold. No longer would it be possible for her to live in England, she told him. Whether this was because of where it happened or that everything had changed, he was uncertain. But where it happened meant it would never be possible for him to live anywhere else.

Samantha returned to Australia to arrive in the spring, determined to plant flowers and start again, before it was too late.

Another winter would come and go and it wasn't until late summer that John's friend, Richard, took the unusual step for him, to dare mention it. Friends were wary of raising the subject, knowing full well it was always on the edge of his existence every waking, and probably, sleeping hour, and that the edge of sanity itself was not so far away that it wasn't visible to those who knew him well.

Richard started slowly. Carefully.

"I was browsing through *The Times* the other day, John, and there was this article about this fellow. I made a mental note to mention it to you."

It was true that Richard had made a mental note. It was more than one, and he felt it wise to raise it when the conversation was light and John was at home, in familiar surrounds, on a sunny day outside in the garden.

Richard had taken to visiting John on the weekends, usually a Saturday, although, as John no longer worked, it was more to suit Richard. It had always concerned him that John had chosen to give up work, to walk away from his career. There was far too much time on John's hands for his friend's liking. It was not quite true that it was only the other day that he had read the article. It was more like two months ago. What he wanted to mention had been given a working over well beforehand.

"Do you mind if we sit? And talk about this thing, I wanted to mention to you?" Richard gave him no choice and sat on the garden bench, opposite the only other chair in the yard. John sat down.

"Would you like a cup of tea? A glass of water?" John asked, as he crossed his legs.

Richard had his attention, and he didn't want John to get up and go into the kitchen, even for a moment. He'd raised the 'thing' and he didn't want there to be any opportunity to avoid it. It wasn't inconceivable that John would go upstairs to his bedroom, close the door and not return. He'd done that before, when he had attempted to talk with him, and he ended up having to go. "No, thanks, I'm fine. There's this fellow in Camden. I think you should … it may be worthwhile – I say this for a number of reasons – perhaps, make an appointment with him. He's—"

"Thank you, Richard. I appreciate your concern, I really do, but I'm done with all the psychiatrists. My last appointment was three months ago. I don't think it's necessary anymore."

Richard paused, accepting he'd been cut off before he could explain further, and smiled with half a grin. "That's good. I agree." The truth was he didn't agree. "But I meant someone else. I know you're still thinking a lot. I know you've gotten stronger."

"Yes, I have."

"That's why I haven't suggested it earlier."

"What? Suggested what?"

Richard knew full well that his friend had made small improvements, but he was stuck in a limbo of despair, and that it was only a matter of time that the rot he had allowed to set in to his marriage would take hold of his soul. His choice to not work would soon become no choice at all. Unable, mentally, was the next step.

He also knew his friend could think of nothing else than what had happened and his efforts to push it away weren't working.

"This fellow has developed a reputation in this area, in these cases. He's very good, apparently. Compassionate, but clever. He's also young and energetic. Perhaps you should read the article in *The Times* about him."

"Who do you mean?" John asked.

"He's a private investigator. His name is Tom Greer."

John uncrossed his legs, sat back in the chair and shook his head. He folded his arms. He made a slight noise, like a laugh through his nostrils, but it was clear to Richard he was anything but amused.

"You want to raise this *now*? Don't you think, for Christ's sake, I've already thought of that – seeing a private investigator?"

"John, I—"

"No, Richard! I don't need some hot shot, young … whatever, who is going to give me *compassion*. And nothing else. I can get that from …" He took a deep breath, sighed and shook his head, as if he had decided not to elaborate. "I can get that from the police, from my doctors, from you! No. I'm not going there. I can't. Not now."

"Why not? What have you got to lose? The *money*? Is that what you're concerned about?"

Richard knew full well that was not the reason, but he had to continue with this discussion somehow.

"Don't be ridiculous! You know that's not a concern. I would give every cent I have to know what happened. Just to *know*. But I don't want to pay for more agony. And that's what it would involve! To be honest, I'm surprised you would even consider suggesting it."

"I want you to be honest with me, but that means I can be honest with you, can't I?"

"Yes. You know that. But I don't see how it will help. I just, don't see it."

"There are a few things you can't see, perhaps, that others can. Why don't you just give it a chance? I'm not blaming you. But sometimes I feel … if I didn't point some things out, at least talk about them with you, I'd be letting you down. I don't want that."

"That's fine. I understand that. But, it's not about *you*, is it! Besides, like what? Like, what do you *see* that I don't? I hope you're not going to say I didn't see things with Sam."

"No. Sam's made her choice. That's not what I mean. I like Sam, you know that. But I don't even know if I'll ever see her again. She's made no contact with me. My concern is for *you*. Choices that may *get you back on your feet*. Working again. I see, as does everyone, that you continue to beat yourself up about it and you don't think you've done enough. This can be a step forward."

"I don't think so."

"Please just consider it. At the very least, it will have the effect of putting it in someone else's head, and allow you to get it out of yours, knowing someone is looking into it other than the police. It might allow you to get on with your life. Maybe something will come of it."

John stared at Richard for a moment, digesting his friend's sincerity. Richard no longer saw any anger.

"Look, I'm not suggesting getting a dog. Although, I could, if you want one. Bella is having puppies," Richard added, smiling as he said it, as if he wanted to now lighten his tone, seeing the possibility of getting somewhere.

"I don't think I want a dog. Nothing against Bella."

"If you made the appointment with Greer, I would come with you."

"What would *he* be able to do that the cops couldn't? Didn't?"

"I don't know. *We* don't know. That's just it! We could see and explore it. I know that you've felt every rock hasn't been looked under. That yes, you respect what everyone did, but you remain unsatisfied. I think you might feel better, just by hearing what he has to say."

"It's been a long time."

"Yes, it has. But to leave it any longer is …" He stopped voluntarily this time, seeing the point had been made, that John could see what he was saying and had no need to hear anymore.

The silence that followed was one that close friends know.

After a moment, Richard said, "You could tell Sam, if you like. But you wouldn't have to."

"I want to think about it."

After Richard left that afternoon, John went to the bedroom and took his shoes off and stretched out on the bed. The late sun hit the corner of his face, streaming through the window and shining its fading light into the emerging darkness of the room.

He closed his eyes and found his mind somehow content to think of her, as if he had been given permission. So, he went back there once again. He let his head sink deeper into the pillow, and he went to that place that made him so happy and that also destroys. It was not hard and he could summon it at will. But this time, *this* time, he was determined to enjoy it.

It always started the same way.

He pulled the rip cord on the lawn mower and it started up. First, he mowed the hillside. He could smell the grass. When he was at the start of the small plateau, she came running down. Her cheeks were rosy and her red hair curled, flowing down over her shoulders. Mummy had made her put on her joggers and small white socks, which looked so out of place with her pink and yellow frock. From the window of the house she had seen the butcherbird fly into the yard and perch itself in a tree, alerted from afar by the sound of the blades. By now, she had seen this a few times that summer already, and she stopped at the bottom of the little hill and watched the bird fly down so incredibly close to the mower and gobble a newly turned worm then fly back into the tree to wait for the next opportunity.

"Daddy, he got one!" she yelled.

He saw her and smiled and watched her run back up that hill and back to the house.

CHAPTER TWO

Lunch breaks. They were usually when Tom made the effort to do his memory exercises.

He couldn't remember exactly how many times Alister, his mentor, had told him just how important a good memory was to a private investigator. Whenever he had lunch with him at one of their favourite restaurants and he muttered something like not being able to remember someone's name, no matter how trivial the remark was in passing, Alister would stop him mid-sentence and remind him to perform certain tasks daily.

As Tom never missed lunch, no matter how busy he might be, that hour or so he spent on his break served as a perfect reminder to exercise his brain.

Usually it involved picking two people at a sandwich bar or a supermarket and observing four or five characteristics, such as what they were wearing, their hair colour and style, their shoes and any other feature that might stand out, then putting it out of his mind, only to attempt the next day to write each observation down.

At least a few times a month Tom would grow tired of that and revert to writing a grocery list, putting it in his top drawer in his office, then two days later attempting to write the same items. But he found that sometimes made him hungry, which led him to go out to get something to eat or an early lunch and the original exercise would start again.

Whilst he could always recall the restaurants that served the best steaks and the pubs that had his favourite ales, he couldn't remember the last time he had seen his father.

It had been more than seven years ago. The estrangement felt like it was only on the surface, for he felt a lack of animosity, even though when his parents separated, he could not help but side with his mother. Perhaps time itself had healed some wounds, he thought, as he sat on the train that Saturday, eating lunch, knowing that in less than two hours he would see his father again.

Normally, the train was Tom's least preferred form of travel. He preferred to drive whenever it was possible. But in the short phone call he'd had with his father, he allowed himself to take the suggestion that he be picked up by him at the station, and it seemed that was the easiest way to go about this whole thing. There would be no knock on the door of his house. Bruce would have to recognise his son, now a man fast approaching 30, after he disembarked from the London train.

Whether he had changed much physically, or even at all, Tom thought it best to leave for Bruce to assess. His hair was still blond and curly and he had stopped growing in his late teens. His weight had remained moderate and roughly the same, thankfully, he thought, because that other aspect of health, involving physical exercise and low alcohol consumption, didn't quite describe his current regime, or any past routine. That could be put off for later years, he was in the habit of reassuring himself, and there was no urgency to be incredibly physically fit, just yet. He knew Bruce imbibed and perhaps the old saying about the apple not falling too far from the tree applied.

He wondered whether his father would show the signs of aging, now he was 60.

Another thing Tom couldn't recall was the last time he felt nervous, except perhaps with a certain female client, whom he held a slight degree of affection towards, if he allowed himself to admit it. Invariably, he felt no nervous tension at all and could at a moment's notice deliver a speech in front of the United Nations, in the highly unlikely event he was ever called upon to do so, without giving it a moment's trepidation.

But just before he pulled his bag off the rack as the train pulled in to Canterbury, he felt something in his stomach that was a definite uneasiness. He had read somewhere – exactly where, he need not recapture – that being nervous was a good thing, as it meant one cared.

Like his son, Bruce Greer was a shortish man. Almost completely bald now and with a bit of a belly, undoubtedly it was he who had changed more in the intervening years, at least physically. A baker by trade, he had retired that year not long after his birthday.

Tom found him sitting on a bench in the area outside the exit. When he caught his father's eye, Bruce stood up and they embraced. "Have you eaten?" Bruce said. And when Tom said yes, but he could eat again, Bruce said he could too and they went to a place just nearby, after dropping the bag into the car.

On average, each Saturday, at least half a dozen people would call Tom's office and leave a message.

Cathy, who had worked for Tom for years and had moved from being his receptionist to his full-time personal assistant, never ceased to be amazed by the things people would say when leaving their details. Unfortunately, those people who left more detail than necessary would not receive a return phone call when the office re-opened on Monday. Not everyone would get an appointment with her boss.

This Saturday she was in the office catching up on some paperwork and could hear some of the messages coming through. There was something almost delicious, she thought, about not having to answer the phone. The recording she had placed was very clear that they were closed but callers could leave a message. Hearing someone talk to a message bank made for light entertainment as she went about reducing her pile of paperwork and filing. It kept her company while she moved in solitude from reception to her office to the storage room and back again.

"Hello, is that Mr Greer? … Oh, I'm sorry," the voice said, after the brain engaged, and the caller realised she was speaking to a machine. "Um, ah, my name is Mrs Beryl Cannon and I have a problem. My cat's gone missing. I can't find her anywhere. If you could please call back before 5, I'd appreciate it. Thank you. Oh, and I would like you to investigate a strange smell from my garden." She hung up without leaving her number.

Cathy was always surprised at how many people would rattle off so much information but forget to leave a contact number. Some would call on Monday and complain, only to be told it wasn't possible for them to receive a return call.

Twenty minutes later the second came through. "Good afternoon. My name is Alan. I'd like to make an appointment with Mr Greer. I'm afraid something dreadful has happened. I need help finding out what it is. I can't go into the details over the phone, only to say it's not normal and it's … now let me tell you, Mr Greer. It's definitely possible my cousin is spying on me and he's the cause. I suspect he's a pervert. Now that I think of it, I'm sure he is and he's after me. My number is 762—" and then he was cut off.

Cathy had set the length of each message space quite short, so that there was only time to leave some information, a name and number. That acted as a sort of automatic cull and saved all staff considerable time.

It was shortly before 3 pm when Cathy heard the almost weekly threat come through from some nutter, as they were fond of calling such callers. It was typical of the many that were regularly received. "I'll get you Greer, don't you worry about that! I'd be watching your back, if I was you … you little …" They had long since given up reporting the calls to the police.

Just before she left and had put the last pile of the filing away, a Mr Casper called. He left a number, spoke clearly and politely, and said he was seeking an appointment. As he gave no further information, she made a note to definitely call him back on Monday.

On the train to Canterbury it occurred to Tom, not for the first time but in greater detail, just how much his father didn't know about him. There had been no emails or letters. No birthday cards or Christmas phone calls. It was perhaps possible that his mother had filled him in, but he would never really know. Bruce was not the topic of conversation when Tom visited his mother in Norwich. This all led him to ponder about what he'd been up to, and what he might say, if his father asked. What information would he prioritise and relay over other aspects of his life? Assuming, of course, Bruce wanted to know.

"Beer?" his father said, as they sat on stools and looked at a menu.

"Thanks, sure."

There was a slightly awkward silence as they watched the man fill the glasses and place them on the bench they were sitting at, perched on high stools overlooking the busy kitchen. "How's your mother doing?"

"I last saw her about three weeks ago. She's good, I think. I've been trying to get home to visit her at least once a month, but I've been busy with work."

Bruce nodded and took a large gulp from his glass.

"How have you been, Dad? You look good. I heard you retired."

"Yes. I suppose it's official now. So not working anymore, I don't have to get down to the bakery early. I can sleep in if I want to. Old habits die hard. I'm usually awake by 4 anyway, so I take the dog for a walk. She's a good dog. Doesn't mind getting up that early. Hey, do you remember the dog we had when you were little? Elly? She looks a lot like her."

"Yep. I must have been about ten when she died. You had her before I was born, didn't you?"

"Yep, we sure did. And what about you? You had more boy in you than man last time I saw you."

Tom took that as an invitation to look more closely at his father and observe any changes in him. He had a stubble of grey whiskers and he couldn't tell if it was a three-day growth or more or less. Tom still didn't need to shave much at all and his skin was smooth and supple, more like his mother's. Perhaps he would never have the bristle even at his father's age.

"Yeah, it happens, ha! Anyway, I'm good. It's good to see you, Dad. Cheers." They touched glasses. "I'm bloody hungry and this place looks brilliant."

Tom pulled the menu towards him and studied it carefully. There were a whole bunch of trivial and not so trivial questions running around simultaneously in his head, but he figured there would be time to talk. He always needed to eat regularly to think clearly and he ordered a burger and chips and so did Bruce.

The place was very eclectic and under one roof there were many choices involving hot, cold, raw and fresh food, breads, cheeses, seafood and ales. Tom had never been to Canterbury, not even when he worked for EAC Investigations which had a satellite office there. He was looking forward to wandering into town, hopefully with his father, that after-noon. And when that came to fruition, at his suggestion, and they sat by the river with a cup of tea and scones, sourced from the nearby quaint antiques and old homewares fair run by a small army of elderly ladies, there were no rear-guard actions.

"I hear you're in investigations now. That you got your own firm an' all. That, you're pretty good."

"Don't believe everything you hear, even if it is from Mum." He didn't want to talk about work. He sipped his tea. "Why did you leave her, Dad?" It seemed best to get that question out of the way. It was impossible to be upset by anything, sitting in that idyllic spot.

"Because she left me, many years before. It wouldn't have been fair to anyone for me to hang around."

Tom sniffed and thought about saying something that came straight into his head, but instead he turned away slightly and looked at the ducks on the water. "It really is beautiful here. I can see why you like it."

In the later afternoon, after they wandered the fair, they walked slowly further into town, chatting, and Tom realised he hadn't packed his camera. When he said he wished he had brought it, he told his father about the course in photography he had undertaken at university in Norwich and that his skills behind the lens had come in handy, with what the job sometimes entailed.

He told him how, despite the university course, photography had developed as more of a hobby than a profession. His father laughed when he told him about falling asleep in parked cars when carrying out surveillance, once to be awoken by a police constable banging on the window, together with a bunch of other funny things that had happened to him, including when he went to Australia with his friend Paddo.

"I don't like to talk about work, that much. I've kind of disciplined myself not to, not only because of the confidentiality side of things, but just to ensure I'm not overly consumed by it all. It already extracts enough out of me, so I'm not prepared to let it have my weekends as well, unless I have no choice, when the job requires it or, I guess, more accurately, when I *really* like the client and don't mind doing it."

"You've given yourself good advice, Tom. I've never really had to worry about confidentiality," Bruce said. "I mean, sure, I keep my recipes a secret and would only reveal some with a serious bribe, but yeah, I know what you mean."

"Like the rock cakes you gave us as kids? Mum can't even reproduce them!"

"Exactly. I'll leave the keys to my vault to you in my will. You can take the recipes to your mother then. But not before."

They decided to pay for a little boat ride around the pretty city. They heard tales of Chaucer and Marlowe, sprinkled with the mention of a few bishops and criminals. The pang of not having his camera was partially allayed by absorbing the sites along the river and the ways of the beautiful young lady regaling them in such a splendid and professional manner. She mentioned in the course of her stewardship of the boat that she was a student of the classics at the University of Kent, part timing as a tour guide. What a delightful afternoon, Tom thought. As he alighted, he gave her his trademark wink, almost involuntarily, and said thanks.

In the evening, Bruce cooked a shepherd's pie and for dessert, he had baked an apple frangipane tart with salted-caramel sauce. A man more than a little rough around the edges, his pudgy fingers came in handy for kneading, and his son once again appreciated how sensational his father was in the kitchen. Tom was able to track down a bottle of Australian Shiraz from the Barossa and spoke further of his time there and his friends. And it was halfway through the bottle of wine that Bruce asked him something altogether unexpected.

"You're almost 30, Tom. Have you been in love yet?"

It was a question he had never considered. But he understood it was a fair question and deserved an honest answer.

"No. I haven't had a relationship that's lasted more than a couple of weeks."

Tom picked up another slice of pie and asked, "What can you tell me about it?"

Bruce ran his fingers through the stubble on his chin. "It can last forever. That's for certain. I've never stopped loving your mother. We'll never get back together, I know that and so does she. It's just … different love now. But it's still love. I wanted you to know that. And, if I can, I wanted to give some advice. Would that be okay?"

"By all means, Dad. Provided you know that I don't have to follow it."

"Of course. What would advice be, if you had to actually follow it? It would be an order, some sort of command. No." He shook his head, took a sip of wine and placed the glass back on the table. "Remember that sometimes people change. I mean, people that are close to you. It's odd really. Sometimes it's gradual and, then, sometimes it's like, all of a sudden. Like out of the blue one day. Be prepared to change with them. I guess what I mean is keep an open mind about it. That's all."

"Thanks. That's good advice. I'll try to follow it. And thanks for dinner. I'm glad I came. It has been a very, very good day."

"I'm glad you came too."

"Can I ask, Dad? Did you follow your own advice?"

"No. Unfortunately, I didn't."

CHAPTER THREE

A late arrival at the office on Monday morning coupled with a crowded waiting room and phones ringing off the hook meant Tom's usual aversion to the start of the week was sharpened to the point where he needed to be careful. Careful not to offend, careful not to allow his success to date and his exponentially growing reputation to bring down his people-loving nature.

It was hard, and Cathy knew that it was hard for him and, consequently, for her. "Mr Creighton is holding," she said, as he hung his overcoat on the back of his office door.

"What the hell's he holding? Don't tell me, I can guess," he snapped, before she had a chance to speak further. "He's a tosser! Pretend that he's been accidentally cut off, but don't call him back!"

"Tom! I have people in the waiting room! I've been here since 7.00! *What* do you want me to tell him? He called three times last week. I can't keep putting him off! Have you done that inspection he asked? He keeps asking me. I need to tell him something! I can't tell him you haven't done it, *again*."

"Tell him anything. Tell him I've died! Who's in the bloody waiting room? How many appointments have you made?"

"There's only one waiting for you. The two others have just turned up. I'll get rid of them."

"I saw four out there."

"The 9.30 appointment has brought his friend. I think his name is Richard."

Tom sat down and opened his laptop.

"The client is Richard or the friend? What's his story again?"

"No, the client is John. I'm not certain what the detail is with him. I did know, but last week was hell, so—"

"Cathy!" He looked at her as if everything wrong with the world was down to her.

She left the office in a huff, preparing her mind to tell Mr Creighton yet another fib to buy time.

Tom looked at his watch. It was bang on 9.45. He gathered himself and went into the waiting room, slowing his walk, doing his best to lower his heart rate and give the impression he was delighted to be in the office.

The weekend had been surprisingly good but now it was back to a different reality.

His father had given him a hug just before he got on the train back to London. It was the best hug he had received for a long time, from anyone. He felt like he needed another one, but the chances of getting one from Cathy were now blown for some considerable time, with only himself to blame.

His father's hug had felt restorative in some satisfying way. The whole experience had. He felt he wanted to reflect on it, and take more time to do just that, perhaps over a quiet ale or two, and to think about both the past and the future. But with the demands on his time that would have to wait. Probably until he had lost the urge altogether or forgotten what he felt.

"John?" he called, and the two men got up. "Come in, please," he said, and turned to show them through with an arm and palm out-stretched to usher the way.

Tom's office had been arranged so that he had the option of sitting at his desk with the client opposite or suggesting the other side of the room on the lounge chairs, in front of the coffee table.

On one wall stood a large bookcase, filled with a broad range of books, mostly light, popular titles, some humorous and others sport oriented. A cricket ball encased in square glass held up one side of the books. Anyone who cared and was relaxed enough could read the engraved label and engage in some conversation about the gentleman's game. He had read some of the books, but not all of them. Some had made their way there merely for show, with the promise to himself they were on his list to read, in the quieter moments, one day. It had been a long time since he simply had the time to read anything other than an occasional newspaper.

The waiting room contained some photography books, but certainly not his favourites, as there was a tendency for books in reception to walk out the door.

He motioned for them to take a seat on the lounge. That seemed appropriate. There were no papers to sign today and his instinct informed him that they were feeling just as uptight as he was, and in need of something less formal. First meetings were never joyous, and if there was any joy to come, it would necessarily never be at this point.

He grabbed his notepad and sat almost as a psychiatrist would on a separate chair. He gave the impression that he was relaxed, like he had flicked a switch somewhere in his body, crossing his legs and smiling, but not too much, as they sat together yet noticeably apart on the large couch.

But the atmosphere wasn't as calming as Tom would have hoped.

"This is my friend, Richard," John said.

Tom noticed that John's tone implied that his friend was some sort of enemy, or a scoundrel he'd found in the street and hauled in for support. It was clearly a formality at best, a courtesy he needed to dispatch as a nicety.

Tom held out his hand and they shook hands, all leaning in but remaining seated. Normally, he did that at reception, and it occurred to him, he probably should have done this then.

"I'm pleased to meet you both," Tom said.

At that point, Richard's phone rang and he pulled it out and switched it off.

"Sorry, I should have done that earlier," he said, with a somewhat worried look on his face, as he put the phone back in his pocket.

Worried looks were always a regular occurrence, even on the couch.

Tom took a moment to allow a pause, some silence. He did it as much for his own benefit as theirs. For he knew the next thing was going to be hard for them. He could tell by the look of concern on both of their faces. Were they a couple? They knew each other well, he had little doubt about that, already, despite John's initial tone. The thought entered his mind that they could very well have just had a massive argument and were now forced to keep it hidden.

"You've both left your contact details etcetera with my staff?" Tom said, after a moment. Thank God for the word 'etcetera' when one needed it, he thought, hoping they would come to the point without too much delay.

"Yes," Richard said, then looked at John.

Another moment of silence, this one a little more uncomfortable, especially for John who shifted in his seat, seemingly unable to get comfortable, despite the chair carefully being chosen, at some expense, to cater for this very experience.

"What is your full name, John? Just for my immediate purposes. I like to write some things down."

"It's Brownlan. John Alexander Brownlan."

Tom didn't know if he said Bronlan or Brownlan but chose to write something anyway and let the details come through to him later. He seemed to pronounce the surname more with an 'o' than an 'ow'.

"And I'm Richard Smith. We … I've come to support John. We've been friends, very good friends, for a long time." He placed his hand on John's knee and smiled at him, before returning to look at Tom more seriously.

It seemed to Tom then that Richard was trying very hard to be supportive, diligent about it, almost as a professional support person might be, such as a social worker.

"Very good. How can I help?" he asked, holding John's gaze.

John looked down and then towards Richard and remained silent. Tom raised his eyebrows a little, and turned his head back towards Richard. When there was nothing, Tom slowly leaned in and placed the notepad and pen on the coffee table. As he did so, Richard began.

"John is only here on my insistence. He thinks it's going to be a waste of time. I'm sorry to tell you that." He nodded his head and raised his eyebrows, as if to give himself support for getting that part out of the way, for everyone's benefit.

"It's not just that, Richard!" John said.

"It may very well be," Tom said, as he folded his arms. "It can often be a waste of time to see someone like me. But, as you're here now, you may as well get a second opinion," he added with a smile and looked at them both. "I would need to know of course what you're concerned about. I don't have any detail at all. Sometimes I do – have detail that is – prior to a consultation. But, sometimes it works just as well to see what I think, fresh, without it. In any event, I'm here to help, if I can."

"I think we should leave," John said, turning to his friend.

Another awkward silence.

"John, I'm not leaving." With an apologetic look that bordered on defeat, he turned to Tom. "I'm sorry, Mr Greer."

"No problem. You can come back, if you like. Both of you. There's no charge for today."

He was in the mood to tell them there would be a small bill for wasting *his* time, but of course he refrained. In that moment, he also regretted not having a second cup of coffee. Patience again, he reminded himself, was his weak point.

"Alright," John said, after shaking his head, then tilting it back and rubbing his eyes. They were shot, like he hadn't slept. He had a neat, tight and full beard, brown almost identical to the colour of his hair but with the odd grey strand poking out around his chin. Richard was clean shaven, tanned and immaculately dressed in a suit without a tie. Tom picked them both to be in their mid-to late-forties and professionals of some sort.

"I'm not going to pick up the pad. There's a fact sheet that you can fill out at your leisure. I'm happy to just have a chat today. Sometimes it's best that way. You can tell me anything. Anything at all. It will not leave my office, I can assure you."

"There's nothing I can tell you that's not already known. My friends know. The police know. Some journalists know. It's *all* well known.

That's why I feel ..." John paused and looked at Richard as if to say, there really isn't any point to say anything more.

"Mr Greer *doesn't* know," Richard said calmly. "That's what he's telling you, John. Tell him, or, if you prefer, I can."

When John's eyelids twitched and he squirmed in his seat, Richard lowered his voice and softened his tone even further. He leant to his side and from his lowered position, tried to meet his friend's eye. "What ... do ... you ... want ... to do?"

John threw his head back. He crossed his legs and placed both hands on his knee. He stared at the wall before taking a deep breath and beginning. "It was a little over two years ago."

Richard sat back slowly and smiled at Tom, as if he'd won a minor victory.

John continued. "I cannot," he stopped, and went to say something and stopped again. "It's ... too hard for me to get it out of my mind. We were on holiday. My wife and I. Our daughter had just turned 9."

Tom nodded. He wanted to say yes, but remained silent. Ideally, he felt it was best not to interrupt, or say too much at this point in case John just got up and left, which seemed a distinct possibility.

"It was in the late afternoon, almost dusk. We'd decided to drive at first, then walk. Just a little bit, maybe to say we'd done it. It was my idea and a stupid idea. We didn't need to do it. It was nothing more than a last-minute thought. In the morning we'd been to the Valley of Rocks."

"Exmoor?" Tom said, risking the interruption for clarity that it was the location he was familiar with along the coastal section of Exmoor National Park.

"Yes."

Richard caught Tom's eye again and, for that moment, both felt a slight bond, that this man had now relaxed a little and was talking through the pain, but perhaps to his benefit.

"She'd been difficult that morning. She didn't want to get in the car again. We were staying near Exford, so we had to. In the afternoon, we decided to leave the coast and go out to the edge of one of the trails in the national park. Get on the trail and walk for a couple of hours. Anna had fallen asleep in the car on the way."

"Anna?"

"My daughter. She seemed full of energy when we got out of the car and her mood improved for a while when we started to walk." He grabbed the space between his eyes at the top of his nose with his two fingers. "I'm sorry," he said. "I've told this so many times now."

"I understand," Tom said. "Take your time."

His voice started to change a little, as though he was struggling more and spiralling into some sort of descent.

"It was about five o'clock in the afternoon. I know because I looked at my watch, just before it happened." He almost smiled, but he shook his head in bitterness and anger, like a thought had brought back a bad feeling. He swallowed and cleared his throat.

"She had fallen behind and Sam, my wife, had powered way ahead. She was possibly a hundred metres ahead by then. I'd said to Anna that … if she didn't pick up her feet, I'd leave her. I said that. Those were my words, for her to pick up her feet. She gave me some cheek, as was her way, so *I* powered ahead. When I had done that sort of thing in the past, she would run and catch up."

He glanced at Richard, then back to Tom and scratched his eye with a shaking hand. "She would have been twenty metres behind me, before I stopped. I'm absolutely certain of that distance. There was no one else in the area at that time. It was a good thirty minutes since we'd seen anyone. I stopped. I'd lost sight of her. I turned back. I looked at my watch. I was determined to go and pick her up and just be done with her whingeing. Stop hassling her and put her on my shoulders. Carry her the rest of the way."

Richard, Tom noticed, was now concentrating on the silver ring he was wearing, twisting it around over and over on his finger as he listened.

"And I went down the trail." His voice broke and his eyes filled instantly with tears. He wiped the moisture away from his eyes and then his nose with the back of his hand. "I'm sorry," he said.

Richard started to put his hand back on his friend's leg. "DON'T, please! I'm fine," John said, only barely turning to his side, as if his neck would only allow the faintest of movements.

He retrieved his hand immediately.

John's face quivered and his mouth contorted. Without any apparent form of control, he forced it out. "And she was gone!" He paused. "Gone. Without a trace. Without a word. Without a scream ... nothing. Nothing. Just ... gone, like she vanished into thin air."

Like he had extracted a thorn from deep inside his flesh, inside his heart, he stopped shaking and stopped talking.

Tom now understood his client that bit more, as painful as it had been to witness. He approached his next words with caution after a moment of silence and reflection, if not sheer admiration for John, for being able to say what he had said.

"You're saying ... if I'm understanding it right, John. That, your daughter ... Anna ... had somehow fallen or ... was abducted?"

"I'm telling you what happened." He didn't shout it. He said it like it was just a neutral, matter of fact detail, comment, reality, where there was nothing more to add. "There was no place she could have fallen. Not there."

"There were no other people on the trail at the time?"

"I've told you. No!"

There was no room, Tom felt, to ask him to repeat one detail, just to be clear. Once was enough.

"And the police?"

"What?"

"What did you tell them?"

"I told them I went back and she was gone. That I ran back down the track for a mile. Probably more. Every direction, on and off it. That I yelled out for her. That I panicked. That I ran into the tree-lined areas on the side. I yelled for Sam at some point. She didn't hear me at first. But when she finally did, I ran ahead and met her as she came back. She was calm at first and dismissive. It was absurd, ridiculous, couldn't be happening. Then, she became frantic and started blaming me. We both looked and looked and looked and yelled for Anna."

"When did the police arrive?"

"It took about an hour for them to meet us. Some people came along the trail and ran back and summoned the rangers. They arrived about the same time as the police."

"What happened then?"

"They went over the same ground as we did. We were all weaving a bit along the river or the stream. They looked all along the water's edges and spent a lot of the time there searching. By nightfall we had gone back to the car and they brought in the bloodhounds. We gave the police every bit of clothing we had with us and the dogs found nothing. Absolutely, fucking nothing."

Silence, and then Richard said, "She's never been found."

Once it had got to this point, Tom asked some questions which he was sure he already knew the answers to. He knew, for instance, that around the ten-day mark, the police would have told John and his wife that as they had found nothing, they felt they had little alternative but to scale back the search, to the point of calling it off.

"How long did the search go for?" Tom asked.

"Twelve days," replied John. "The police said they could try for a few more days, but … but, in their opinion, to keep searching in the same area was futile. We gave them, and everyone else, permission to stop."

"And the area. What was it like?"

"The trail was clear. She wouldn't have walked off it. There was some bush. It was in an area that was quite thick. Thicker than where we started. But the trail was safe. There was no steepness or drop offs. Nothing like that. Further up, maybe, but not there. Not for a mile, either way, at least."

"Excuse me," Tom said. He got up and went to his desk and pressed the phone. "Cathy, please bring us in a jug of water when you have a moment." He returned to the chair thinking how he could only imagine how painful this must be for John and his wife.

"Your wife. Is she available to come in?"

"No. She's returned to Australia. I'm Australian. We are … no longer together."

Tom nodded but pressed no further.

And then Richard found enough confidence to speak again. "I suggested that John come and see you, as I understand you're a specialist in missing person cases. That you've developed an expertise."

"I'm far from an expert. I've probably more of a willingness than some other firms to take on the cases. But I can assure you, I have some experience and have learnt some things. There may be some common threads that you can pick up, save time as it were, if you know your way around some obstacles. The benefit of experience can help there. But, again, from what John has said …" Tom paused and shook his head. "In answer to your concerns about it being a waste of time, I'll give you my opinion now, and say, no. It's not a waste of time … with one important qualification."

Cathy entered with a tray of glasses and water and placed it on the coffee table.

"And it's this. It may be, down the line, not so much a waste of time, but if I hit dead ends, other options might be considered at that point. I don't give up easily, though, if that's any comfort."

"Can you give us your gut reaction, Tom, about where you would start with something like this?" Richard asked.

Tom liked people who asked direct, strong questions and who called him Tom, without him having to give permission to dispense with 'Mr Greer'.

"How long ago was it?"

"Two years and one hundred and forty-nine days," John said.

"It sounds like an abduction, rather than misadventure, but with elements that don't make sense or necessarily fit in with that. I'm aware of a handful of such cases worldwide in national parks. Not just with children. They're rare cases. Some have never been solved and date back more than half a century."

"There was no one there but me," John said. "No one."

"That's why it seems contrary to logic," Richard added, before Tom could do so.

It was times like these that Tom would invariably invoke the wisdom of his mentor, Alister and his casual tutorials. He could hear his voice. *Remember at times of great emotion, when the client is telling you things that'll keep you awake at night, dreadful things that might impact you, like it impacts them, if you let it, that's the time to pull out the fee agreement. Not for the money, but to remind yourself to stay apart from it all. That it is their life but for you, it's a job. Nothing more.*

After a few more questions and answers, Tom learnt that John had permanent residency in the UK and that he was a computer software developer. That's how he had met Richard, almost a decade ago. Tom said that he would be in touch once John had signed and emailed back the forms and paid £850 on account. The amount had almost tripled from what he was asking twelve months ago.

John made no comment that indicated that he was going to sign or pay. Just being there, at his friend's insistence, was enough. But he thanked Tom, as did Richard.

Tom reminded them about the fact sheet and questionnaire, also to be returned when convenient.

He did not disclose his real gut reaction. That there was something about the case that made him think he wouldn't solve it. But gut reactions could be wrong and he had been wrong numerous times before. So, it was unwise to do anything other than maintain both an open mind and a distance, for when children were involved, the pressure and the pain for everyone doubled. He would not refuse the case.

When they had gone, Cathy came in. "I got the impression it was fairly heavy. Was it?" she asked.

"Yes, it was a bit. I need to slip out. To clear my head."

"Can I tell you about an appointment I made for you this morning?" she asked.

Tom looked at his watch. "What, another one? What time?"

"Not today. I mean, I arranged it this morning. It's for tomorrow."

"Oh, good. Next week would have been better. Why the urgency? How come I don't get to talk to many clients first these days, on the phone, before they see me? You just vet them."

"You're not happy with my vetting? That's not what you said last week, when you gave me the raise."

"It's fine. Look, I need to eat and have another cup of coffee. I had very little breakfast. What's the story with tomorrow?"

"Well, he sounds very nice. I don't think it's urgent. He just sounds very nice."

Sometimes Cathy tested Tom's patience and he failed the test often. "And? What does he want?"

"I don't quite know. Something to do with a woman."

"Right. Well, I'll be back in half an hour." He got up and took his coat off the hook.

"There's something else you should know about this Mr Casper," she said.

"Yeah? What's that?"

"He's blind."

CHAPTER FOUR

Inspecting the warehouse seemed a waste of time. Tom had never said as much to Don Creighton when he first suggested it, or more accurately required it, but the more he thought about him and his badgering and paranoid ways, the closer he came to breaking the retainer. That would go entirely against his principles, for if he promised to do something, he must follow through.

Tom stood outside the abandoned building thinking. *What a dump!* That if it burnt down, it might do everyone a favour, not the least the neighbourhood. A vacant allotment would be a vast improvement.

Burning it down was the very thing, however, that Don suspected someone was planning. He wasn't quite sure who, and for Don, it was really more than a suspicion. Just exactly what an inspection was going to reveal was lost on Tom. Rarely did he decide that following the client's directive to do something as part of achieving the overall objective, whatever that was in this case, would take priority over his own recommendations. But he had caught him at a weak moment, just before knock off time on a Friday, three weeks ago. Tom had arranged to meet his friend Marzena for drinks and he was running late and was thirsty.

He wandered around the edge of bricks and rusted sheets of iron covered in graffiti and when he heard a dog bark, his instinct was to look for a space to take cover. The sound trailed off into the distance and when a man with a small removalist truck pulled around the corner and saw him loitering and shouted something out the window designed to make him jump, he did. Tom muttered, 'Bastard,' under his breath.

The windows were boarded over and 'post no bill' signs were displayed in defiance. Someone had spray painted: 'Our PM stands for Post Mortem' and he laughed. Around the corner on a section of red bricks someone had scrawled: 'This joint is not for Rent', a sarcastic statement of the bleeding obvious. It was cold and grey and a sprinkle of rain fell. It smelt bad. He'd had enough.

The smiling black labrador was the first through the door and led his master to reception with a swagger that suggested he was about to greet old friends. Cathy was expecting the encounter and looking forward to seeing the man who could not see. She stood behind reception next to Barbara, who was on the phone. Everyone was smiling, even Mr Casper. Something funny had been said by the man on the phone and Barbara laughed just as the dog sat in front of the counter. "You must be Mr Casper," Cathy said.

"That's right," he said with a smile.

What an unusual sight, Tom would have remarked, had he seen it. A smiling client, about to see him for the first time and happy, smiling staff. He'd just got off the phone from Creighton, to get him off his back. It had left a bad taste in his mouth which might spoil lunch. But job done and he'd duly inspected the place, as he'd been asked to do, and there was no evidence of possible arson planned. Why would there be? And what would it be, if something *was* planned? He'd send Creighton a bill for the trip out there with a letter recommending he engage a security patrol instead of a private investigator.

When he got to the waiting room, he found Cathy on her haunches and Barbara in front of the reception desk. Mr Casper was sitting in one of the chairs. "What's his name?" Cathy asked, running her fingers under the throat of the handsome, shiny dog.

"Bob," Mr Casper said.

"Nice to meet you, Bob," Cathy said. "You gorgeous thing, you." She looked up at Barbara. "Isn't he just beautiful?"

"Oh yes," she said. "Does he mind being patted?" she asked. She couldn't resist having her turn while the opportunity presented itself.

"Does he mind? He absolutely *adores* it," Mr Casper said.

Cathy noticed he had a very educated, if not slightly posh way of speaking and his manner was equally refined. No one had even looked at Tom, who stood looking at the scene before him.

Mr Casper then said, "You must be Mr Greer." He got up. The girls took a step back, amazed this visually impaired man knew Tom had appeared before him. Mr Casper had not turned his head. Tom approached without saying anything and Mr Casper stretched out his hand to shake, with the same smile that had not left his face from the moment he walked in.

Tom looked at his eyes. For some reason he expected him to be wearing dark glasses but he wasn't. His eyelids were slightly lowered, covering some of his eyes, one more than the other. He looked over sixty and his hair was brown and combed neatly to the side. Perhaps it was dyed. An old, well-worn, pin-striped charcoal suit hung loosely on his tall, skinny frame. It looked like he'd worn it for some years and lost weight as he'd become older.

"Lovely to meet you, sir," Tom said.

"And this is Bob," Mr Casper said.

"Good morning, Bob," Tom said. "Would you like to come in?"

"Of course, thank you," Mr Casper replied and he made a slight turn. The dog followed Tom in the direction of his office.

"Would you like me to sit in?" Cathy asked as they walked away. Normally, she would only sit in if Tom had previously requested it. She couldn't help but ask as her curiosity took hold.

"Oh, I'm not certain that would be necessary," Tom said. But then he noticed a look on Cathy's face that he'd seen before when she wanted him to seriously reconsider something. He added, "But ... Mr Casper, would you mind if Cathy joined us?"

"Not at all! By all means. The more the merrier," he said as he entered the office.

Cathy quickly darted behind the counter and grabbed her laptop before she joined them. Mr Casper positioned himself on the couch and

Bob settled at his feet. It was all as if the clever animal had been to the office before, several times, and knew exactly where everything was.

"Would you like a cup of tea or coffee? Water?" asked Tom, once they had all sat down.

Cathy had brought the chair that was opposite Tom's desk over. She held her knees together and opened the laptop on them.

"A cup of tea would be lovely," he said. "With milk, please."

Cathy got up and went back out to reception and told Barbara to bring it in, with a jug of water, then quickly returned to her seat, eager not to miss a thing.

"I suspect you need to know a little bit about me. So, Cathy," Mr Casper said, "whilst I'm very capable of supplying the information to you other than verbally, it might be easier if you just take a few notes on that laptop."

Tom looked at her and smiled and she smiled.

"Okay, then," she said.

"My full name is Stephen Roderick Casper. I'm an Associate Professor at UCL. I'm in the school of economics. I received my doctorate twenty or so years ago at the University of Toronto. I spent several years in Canada, mostly Quebec, before settling back in London. In recent years, I've developed a particular, if not somewhat esoteric interest in empirical microeconomics. I recommend my students take the time to read as much as they can in that area."

He had a truly lovely, cultured way of speaking, they both could simply not fail to notice. And the smile remained.

"I see," Tom said.

Cathy frowned at him. He blinked quickly several times, thinking that one of his standard replies to keep the conversation in motion might be a tad insensitive in this case. He must not say *I see* again, he checked himself.

"Speaking of seeing, and to save you asking, as sometimes people feel uncomfortable but curious about this sort of thing, I lost my sight partially as a child of twelve and, by my later teens, totally. Bob here is my sixth companion and I must say, one of the very finest."

At that very moment, Bob looked up at Cathy without lifting his head from the carpet.

"Mr Casper," Cathy said.

"Yes, dear?" he replied.

"UCL?"

"Ah yes, I'm sorry. University College London."

"Thank you," she said, and typed something on the keys.

"I live at St John's Wood. Not far from Lords. I'm a member of the MCC and cricket, I suppose, is my favourite sport, at least in the summer months. I've a range of interests outside of work, but I shan't bore you with them."

"MCC?" Cathy said.

"Marylebone Cricket Club," Tom said. "One of the greatest!"

"Indeed it is," added Mr Casper.

"Sorry," Cathy said.

"No mind, dear," Mr Casper said. "It's not important."

"How did you come to make an approach to our firm, Mr Casper?" Tom asked.

"Someone mentioned to me that you were quite good at what you do. I think it's best if I don't mention who. I don't wish to bore you."

"Not at all. How can we help? I'm all ears."

Cathy shook her head at Tom and yet again he realised he had said something a little insensitive, out of habit. Later she would tell him to stop with the comments about eyes and ears altogether and just listen.

"Yes, I should come to the reason I'm here, I suppose. It's not *overly* troubling me. I don't want you to think that. Or get that impression at all. It's more that I'm curious. There is also no urgency. None at all. We have been seeing each other for about a year now. That is, my girlfriend and I."

Barbara entered and delivered the refreshments. She placed the tea on the table with a saucer.

"Oh, that's lovely of you, dear. Thank you," Mr Casper said.

Barbara said the sugar sachet was on the saucer if he needed it. He picked up the cup and blew it gently before taking a sip. He took another sip before finding the sachet, putting it on the table and then tipped a little of the tea in the saucer and placed the saucer on the floor next to Bob. "I hope you don't mind," he said. "He's very polite and won't spill a drop."

"Of course not," Tom said.

Cathy looked on, with an expression of gentle wonder, as if her heart was melting.

"How clever is your dog," she said, not as a question.

"Cleverer than some people, I'm sure," Mr Casper said with a bigger smile than usual. "And vastly less demanding." He returned to the topic. "She's quite lovely, my new girlfriend. I think you would both like her. Her name is Catherine. But she likes to be called 'Cat'. I'm not certain how Bob feels about her at times. He knows I like her. But, he's undecided, I feel. And I don't think it's because of her name."

Cathy gave a little giggle.

"I'm serious," Mr Casper said. "Bob is a very good judge of character. But I think even after a year, he's not certain she's the one."

Cathy raised her eyebrows and looked at Tom.

"I did have *the one*, once," Mr Casper continued. "We were married, but she died. I've never had any children, not for the obvious reason some people think. It just never happened, I'm afraid. I'm perhaps too old now. In any event, I digress." He took another sip from his cup and Bob resumed his position after lapping up the milky tea, with his chin resting back on the carpet. "About three months ago, I noticed some things started going missing from my flat. Little things. Nothing of great value. It might be a salt shaker or the scoop I use to scoop out the washing powder. I always place it back in the box. At first I thought I was misplacing them. But, I'm usually very disciplined about such things by necessity, as you might understand. I quickly got into the habit, many, many years ago of placing items back in the same place each time. Naturally."

Tom poured himself a glass of water and wiggled the jug at Cathy. He mouthed, almost whispering, "Want some?" She shook her head.

"There's no need to whisper, Mr Greer," Mr Casper said. "I'm not insulting you by saying that. Please, don't take me the wrong way.

People often whisper around the deaf and the blind I've noticed for some reason. It's very funny, actually. But I shall continue. Several weeks ago, we had our first argument. It started over nothing, really. She had come over for Sunday lunch. A roast. It's one of my favourites. I like to have a brandy before lunch. She doesn't drink. I went to get the bottle from its usual spot and it wasn't there. By now I was getting a little tired of this sort of thing happening. Eventually I found it, but in a spot I would never have put it."

"How long did it take you to find it?" Tom asked.

"A week or so."

"Where was it?"

"It was in my kitchen pantry and I came across it by accident. I was cranky when I couldn't find it that day. She told me I didn't need it. That I could do without it. That annoyed me more and I said something foolish. She left."

"What did you say?" Tom asked.

"I said that she shouldn't treat me like a child."

Cathy, who was typing all this down as if she was taking minutes, paused and shook her head at Tom.

"She came back that evening and apologised. She brought with her a bottle of the finest French Cognac. Oh, it was just marvellous. And the evening went very, very well. She has been visiting me at least three times a week since our little tiff. But whilst I occasionally have students over, she's really my only visitor. And last week, I noticed one of my towels had gone missing and my favourite aftershave. I'm very loathe to say it, but I think she might be playing tricks on me and stealing from me."

"Right," Tom said. Not meaning he was right, necessarily, but meaning his account of this occurrence was something that should be noted as quite important to him. "I must ask, why don't you either break it off or confront her? Given what you've told us. What it's looking like. Or, even raise it somehow less ... accusatory. Have you tried that?"

"No. And I don't want to. I just want to know. To know as an absolute certainty, first. Then, I will decide what to do. If I say what I *think*, it will be over. Simple as that. I'm sure I will not see her again."

"If she's stealing from you, Mr Casper, would you want to see her again, anyway?" Cathy asked.

"Probably not. But I don't want to raise it or confront her. I would like Mr Greer to find out independently. I know it sounds silly. Perhaps totally absurd. But I'm prepared to pay to know. It's important there is the right order about this. Very important, in fact. But it's essential that she does not know I have engaged you, at all."

"I'm with you here, Mr Casper. But, are you sure? Sure, that … we should go about it this way?" Tom asked. "It's got its problems, perhaps, is all I'm saying. If you don't *mind* me saying."

"Not at all. However, I'm positive I wish to engage you."

"What does she do, for a living, I mean?" Tom asked.

"She's a clairvoyant. Although, she prefers the title, 'psychic'. She's in high demand, at least as I understand it, and is apparently very good. She has even been engaged by the police at times."

Tom rolled his eyes, shook his head and looked at Cathy.

"I know you think I might be being foolish. I can't go to the police for such trivialities, you'll appreciate. And I don't even want to. I just want to know."

"And if it's bad news, as you suspect?" Tom added.

"I will then take matters into my own hands."

"And end the relationship and demand your things back?" Cathy asked.

"As I said, dear. I will no longer need your firm's services then. I don't want my things back. Will you take my case, Mr Greer?"

"Where might I find Cat, Mr Casper?"

"Her full name is Catherine De Chambeau. Whether that's an adopted name, I don't know. I don't care. I've been to her residence once only, so I will need to ring your office with an address. Can I do that? I don't think she operates her business from home all the time, and I think she may have some rooms for consultations elsewhere."

"Yes," Tom replied. "Of course."

"And can I take that as a *yes* about taking my brief, as it were, Mr Greer?"

Tom looked at Cathy and she nodded.

"Yes. Yes, you can," Tom said.

"Very good. Then I shall leave you to get on with your day." As soon as he said that, Bob got up from lying on the floor. "Let's go, Bob."

The smile on his face had faded, just a little. He rose from the couch. "Oh, and Mr Greer. Just one other thing. I don't care how you go about finding out. You don't even need to tell me. But, there are two golden rules I would ask you to follow, if that's alright."

Now Tom was smiling. "Of course."

"One, as I have said, never let her know I have engaged you. Two, don't hurt her, no matter what you find out. In fact, there is a third rule, now that I think of it. And that's to recognise at all times that each rule is as equally important as the other."

CHAPTER FIVE

When in doubt Tom always preferred to undertake the easier of the tasks confronting him first, except when procrastination overcame him, as in the case of inspecting Creighton's warehouse. Putting off an easy task usually meant there was something about it that bored him or just failed to take his interest. Serving court documents squarely fell into that category, as did surveillance. Often he sent Cathy to serve documents which saved many an angry complaint, but he would never ask Cathy to stake someone out and Barbara's skills were not suited to either.

And when in doubt about which client to service next, he would go to dinner and figure it out over a meal before doing anything of substance at all.

Tom hadn't seen Alister for weeks, so he called him to invite him to a mid-week catch up on Wednesday evening. His mentor's experience and worldly ways always helped when he wanted to discuss the more challenging matters, particularly when he was in need of thinking aloud but in the privacy of some tucked away corner of a restaurant.

Apart from staff, it was only with Alister that he would share some of his daily routines and Alister relished being able to continue to consult with and mentor his rising star. Somewhere between the first and second glass of wine, Tom would put a feeler out to him, to gauge his reaction. The truth was, he would proudly tell Tom, that he was already highly regarded in the industry and he could indeed be pleased with what he had achieved before the age of thirty.

Yes, he had developed somewhat of a specialty in missing person cases, solving more than average and sometimes surprising the police in the process. That was never the aim, for he always treated the coppers with the utmost of respect and sympathised with them most of the time. Besides, they were on the public's pay roll, couldn't charge an hourly rate to private citizens like he could, and their resources were stretched.

There were several people he'd found who didn't want to be found, some of which were angry with him when he did, despite their family being delighted.

But equally, he had begun to develop a reputation for exposing rich, cheating husbands to their suspecting wives – a relatively lucrative area and one where his clients were extremely grateful to him.

A couple of young rivals across the metropolis had heard of him and the word was he was a maverick, who would stop at nothing, especially if he liked the client. That was always the key.

Given he was getting too busy to take on some cases, the next step was to consider putting someone else on. His office in Camden could accommodate one more investigator, now that he had convinced the landlord to let him rent the extra rooms on his floor and he wanted to see if Alister knew of anyone who might be interested, even part-time.

He also wanted to see what Alister's first instincts were in relation to the heart-wrenching case of nine-year-old Anna Brownlan. Some run-away teens had crossed his path before, but never a child so young and the circumstance of her disappearance seemed unfathomable. Just where on Earth would he start with that? While Alister had retired fully from investigative work, even from tutoring students, his wealth of experience was invaluable.

"I can't take your call just at the moment, so kindly leave a message," he heard Alister say in his almost imperceptible Scottish accent.

Tom had adopted the same message on his own phone and, like Alister, never promised a call back.

Foiled in his desire, it occurred to him by late afternoon that he had not invited Cathy to dinner for some time and, as she had been on the receiving end of some of his less agreeable moments of late, it was time for him to make it up to her, even though she was clearly not his first choice. For Alister, it would have been Middle Eastern food at their new favourite place that had been only open for three months. With Cathy, it was always Chinese, just around the corner from the office.

"I wasn't certain, you know," she said, just before taking a mouthful of her wonton soup, "that you were going to say yes to Mr Casper. He's a bit of a funny one."

"He seems to be a very interesting man. But it was his membership of the MCC and his interest in cricket that swayed me a bit. If I can get to the bottom of his problem, maybe I can suggest that I accompany him to a match at Lord's Cricket Ground. I've never been to a match there. Though I suspect from what he said about this Cat lady, he may not be that happy with the revelation that what he suspects is true."

"Don't you think it's a bit odd that he has come to us?" Cathy asked. "Why wouldn't he just ditch her? He's obviously intelligent. It just seems a dumb way to go about it."

"If all our clients went about things smartly, we'd be out of a job. That's for sure. But I agree. What shall we have for the mains? The £25 or £35 banquet? We had the cheaper one last time and I was left hungry." His eyes turned to the large menu, almost the size of a newspaper broadsheet, sealed in laminate.

"I don't care; you choose. You know, when he said *the one*, I almost burst out laughing. Not at him, personally, I just thought it was a bit funny. But I really like him, actually."

"He's got that about him; he's very likeable. Why anyone would want to do that to him is beyond me. I hope we find out."

When the first dish of the banquet arrived, Tom raised the subject of possibly employing another investigator. Scooping the sizzling Mongolian lamb took priority over Cathy's answer when asked what she thought, but she agreed it was something definitely worth considering. "Sometimes I think we're turning down cases that you don't want to do, but someone else might. That's costing us money," she said.

"You're probably right."

"It's not that I don't understand why you turn some people down. I do."

"I know, I'm fussy."

"It's not a bad way to be. But you know what I mean?" she said, as she filled her bowl with a second helping of special fried rice.

"Yep. I might look into it next week. I want to ask if Alister knows of someone."

"What are you going to do about that poor man? Anna's father. Where are you going to start? It's horrific. I read about it when it happened. The paper said something about there being more than two hundred searchers and they turned up nothing. Some people, volunteers apparently, continued for almost a month. Nothing was found."

"Yeah. I've already looked into it a bit. I don't remember hearing about it. I was mega busy at that time and probably insane. I was hoping to talk to Alister about it, but I can't reach him."

"Didn't he say he was going to visit his brother in Scotland soon? Maybe he's there," she said.

"He didn't mention it to me. He's always telling me how much he doesn't like to travel anymore. That he's content to stay home in his little flat and wander down to his local every second night. I might drop in there."

"I see you got to the inspection for Creighton. How did that go?"

"I don't know what the stupid man wants from me. It was a waste of time."

"Where was the warehouse?"

"Out near Harrow. It took me bloody ages to drive there and then find it. It's a dump! Remind me to send him a bill and tell him to get security and leave me alone!" The mere mention of Creighton caused a sudden desire to veer away from the topic of work altogether. "How's that brother of your boyfriend doing with his football career?"

"He still hasn't heard whether the club is going to give him a contract. He's hopeful, but realistic."

"That would be brilliant if he got one. I mean, you could play football for like three years and never have to work again."

"I don't think that would suit you. You actually need to work. You whinge about being busy, but you thrive on it."

"I have to work because I can't play football."

"Didn't you play cricket?"

"Yep. I can play that, not that well mind you. But I can."

"I guess Mr Casper must listen to the cricket a lot on the radio," she said. "I wonder what he does when he goes to the ground?"

"I suppose so. I bet he goes to lots of the games though, just for the atmosphere alone."

When the last of the food was fully consumed and they declined coffee, Tom walked her to the station.

Her journey home would be a little more than half an hour.

As it had always made sense to him to live close to work, he had a walk from Camden Town of just under fifteen minutes to his newly purchased two-bedroom flat. It was an expensive buy and more than he wanted to pay; however, he figured with the cash flow of the business – a growing and profitable business – he could afford it.

Ideally, he would like to live in Norwich yet that was now impractical. When he declined Marzena's suggestion that she move in with him to help with the mortgage, they both knew his days of sharing accommodation were over. It wasn't that living with her was anything but usually perfectly fine. For several years they had shared a place on and off, interrupted by his return to his family home in Norwich, her stint in Fulham and visits to her homeland of Poland.

Marzena had expected as much when Tom said he probably needed the second bedroom for when his mother visited. She admired how he was good to his mother. He ticked every box for a husband in her eyes, except that she had absolutely no physical attraction for her friend, nor did she like his chosen line of work. Her friendship with him was strong enough for her to switch from working at a pub in Paddington not far from his old place of work to one near Camden, principally so that she could continue to see him easily and regularly. Any husband would have to deal with Tom for the rest of their days, whether he liked it (or indeed him) or not.

Entirely consistent with tackling the easier tasks firsts, he decided to turn his attention to Mr Casper's matter. But first he needed to clear his desk a little and work his way quickly through his current to-do list.

All of Thursday and Friday was devoted to paperwork and speaking to clients on the phone and updating them on his progress with their matters. He also needed to wait for John Brownlan to return the questionnaire.

Mrs Balzear wanted to know if the whereabouts of her late sister's safe-deposit box could be established. As she only had one bank account and it wasn't located at the bank, he reminded her she needed to go through Marjorie's paperwork and bring it all into the office and see if that could shed some light. It was all very important because she was sure her great grandmother's wedding ring was in that box.

Ted Roundtree wanted a report sent to him on four companies he was considering investing in. He knew they were profitable and wanted to know if they were ethical. He'd made a mistake in the past on that score and he didn't want to do that again. Ted didn't trust his financial planner who was clearly working on a commission. Tom wanted to know what he considered unethical. He submitted a massive list of categories in his questionnaire form, with many specific examples. Tom gave all companies a clean rap sheet, except one that only failed Ted's test because it had shares in a company that had previously been involved in the importation of palm oil. The orangutan was just one of dozens of vulnerable animals specifically mentioned in Mr Roundtree's lists. Their habitat protection was paramount, the company was ruled out and the report emailed on Friday morning.

Mrs Gaynor's suspicion that her elderly husband, Gerald, was having an affair was unfounded. Tom had posted a letter to her private box that said she should call him to 'discuss further'.

Gerald's disappearances on Tuesday afternoons, he carefully explained to her when she rang, was to a clinic specialising in assisting gentlemen of his age with impotency issues.

From everything she had told him together with everything that Tom had found out, it pointed to anything but an affair and it was more likely embarrassment on his part as the reason for both his secrecy and his lack of interest in her in that particular way.

"Are you happy for me to wrap things up with this matter and forward my account?" he asked her. She seemed thrown a bit and didn't answer. He decided to get off the phone before she could ask him to look into what may cause the condition. "I'm not a doctor," was something he said to clients at least every few months, on average.

Late Friday afternoon Cathy told Tom that Mr Casper had phoned in with his girlfriend's address. She lived not all that far from Casper in Kensal Green. The curiosity factor was there for Tom with this case and he was interested to see if he could somehow meet this Cat lady, this *Ms De Chambeau.*

CHAPTER SIX

Twice, Tom had occasion in the last year to be in Kensal Green or nearby Kensal Rise. It seemed to him to be an area of London increasingly described by some as trendy, if not cool and hip.

It was a trip to the Kensal Green Cemetery first and very unexpectedly on account of the untimely death of an elderly client who had engaged him three months prior to look into the shady dealings of his business partner. The whole investigation was wound up by his widow shortly after the man died and, as Tom had taken a liking to him, he recalled the whole saga had been very sad.

The man had lost a considerable amount of his fortune in the course of a very short time and perhaps the stress had hastened his demise.

Tom attended the funeral and was later invited by the man's daughter on an outing, if not an outright date.

As they walked together to the grave site, Tom remarked on what a beautiful, grand old cemetery it was. It had been established well before 1850 and was the final resting place of many inspiring and influential people. She had said something then that he had recalled whenever cemeteries had come up in conversation (which fortunately hadn't been often). "He's very lucky to have got in here, you know."

Tom's first thought was that her father's luck had run out.

"There's only very limited grave space," she added, leaning in to his ear and speaking ever so softly, even though there was no one next to them. "It was very important to all of us that his final resting place was here."

At the wake he discovered that the man's daughter was only twenty-one and studying English history at Cambridge. When he observed quite rightly that the cemetery seemed "adorned" in history, she rattled off the names of various people buried there. "All very famous in their own way," she said.

"I had no idea," Tom had replied as he sipped on his tea while standing near the table of biscuits. He didn't let on that he had no idea who some of them were but the history of notable persons was not his strength. He nodded in agreement with her every word, nevertheless.

When she called a week later and invited him to morning tea at a café in Kensal Rise, he was surprised. Later that afternoon, when he was under the sheets with her, he asked what the difference was between Kensal Rise and Kensal Green as he couldn't tell the difference. She climbed on top of him and told him it depended on who you spoke to.

Earlier, she had mentioned that the street in which they had tea was once named "the hippest" in Europe. Tom said that he could think of at least two laneways in Norwich that were far better and besides, he never got a chance to throw his twopence worth into the decision.

She never answered when he asked had she been to Norwich, "… where I spent my first twenty-three years."

For at least a week he felt hip himself, if not cool, in some odd way, and then things cooled and there was no need to revisit Kensal Green or Kensal Rise or whatever it was called anymore.

Today he would revisit the area and choose to mix pleasure and business. A Saturday usually meant only the former, but he was eager to make a start for Mr Casper and keen to lay eyes on Cat.

Her website seemed full of information, with a statement confirming thirty-plus years of experience. She had gone to some effort to define the term 'clairvoyant' as deriving from the French, with *clair* meaning 'clear' and *voyance* 'vision'. This was her specialty, her focus, but she also offered spiritual healing, tarot readings, relationship advice, compatibility readings, psychic consultations, site visits, spells and casting out demonic entities.

Contacting the dead was also available, upon request.

Tom sat in the same café in Kensal Rise that he had been to before and scrolled down her web page on his small tablet. He chuckled to himself thinking at least she didn't have to go far, given that the cemetery was only a short distance from her residence.

He noted, however, that theft was not on her list, although at £80 per half hour, that was debatable.

Perhaps he could ring for a consultation. It occurred to him as he considered a second cup of coffee, he could use some psychic help with a few of his other cases. She might come in handy. The police sometimes brought in a psychic if they were desperate. But he wasn't going to pay those prices. And it was too risky. What if she *was* as good as Mr Casper said she was and told him he was a private investigator engaged by her boyfriend? It would be a very good test of her abilities. But surely there was a better way.

It was clear from the website that she didn't work from home. He left the car near the café and walked past her home. He noticed there was no sign in front or anything else to suggest her line of business. Her website said she could come to you and that she had a place of 'ambience and tranquillity' in Notting Hill for those who preferred to come to her.

His brief was simple. All he had to do was find out, more likely just confirm, beyond any shadow of a doubt, that she was stealing from a blind man. Seemed easy enough, he thought. The difficulty was establishing what he suspected was true, without letting on that he existed.

Breaking into homes for clients was not only illegal, but unethical in his eyes, so that was out. It was tempting all the same and he could justify it in the circumstances, almost issuing himself a warrant, granted by way of special moral permission and expedience. But again, it was too risky and probably too hard.

He decided to grab something to eat, repark the car closer to her flat, and have an early lunch while he thought about it. But finding a space proved too difficult and now that he had noted where she lived and got his bearings, he figured it wasn't worth the effort. If he wanted to follow her, it wasn't going to be possible to sit in his car and wait. Not in that street.

She had a good photo on her website, so he knew what she looked like. He decided to go home and call her. And it was on the drive home that he thought about Mr Casper's rules and that booking in for a session with her wasn't going to break any of them. He was willing to pay just for the experience and see what type of person she was.

He suspected she was a fraud.

"I was wondering if I could see you tomorrow. I was impressed with your website, which I'm on now, actually," he said.

"I don't work on Sundays. Sometimes rarely, but not tomorrow. I can, however, fit you in late this afternoon," she said. "Provided it's not a house call. That *you* come to me."

"That would be fine. What time? And where are you based, exactly?"

She said she could squeeze him in as her last appointment for the day. It would be at 5 pm for half an hour and gave him the address of her 'rooms' in Notting Hill. "There's one car space out the front, reserved for my premises, if you're driving," she told him.

He thought to himself sarcastically that she should know whether he was driving or not.

"Thank you kindly," he said. "I'll see you then."

On the phone she had seemed in a rush but polite. She hadn't asked what he was seeking, and just as well, because he wasn't quite prepared for that question. When he got there, he figured he would just request a general reading about his future, if that was perfectly alright.

There was no time for an elaborate disguise and it didn't seem necessary, but sometimes a mild distraction of sorts was called for, in case their paths ever crossed again. He didn't want to be immediately or easily recognised. He had a wardrobe of clothes for such one-off occasions, clothes he would not normally wear. Cathy once said to him that he should consider wearing those clothes full-time and ditch his regular attire. He thought she was joking.

He covered most of his blond hair with a smart-looking bespoke cap and put on thick framed glasses that were just clear glass. He had never worn a ring so he put on what would look like a gold wedding band. He had paid a small fortune for shoes with inserts that made him almost three inches taller. As a short man, he liked that aspect of dressing up. He couldn't justify it out of vanity normally yet considered it was entirely appropriate if your job required it.

"If you fall over and break your bloody neck, you can't sue me," the bootmaker had joked, half serious, when Tom collected the shoes about two years ago.

On the way to Cat's he practised in his head some of the things he might say because he wanted to sound sincere.

And when he had to go up a set of steep steps at the front of Cat's premises in those built-up shoes, he knew he needed to proceed with caution, in more ways than one.

As he entered the front door, he was expecting a certain atmosphere, befitting his anticipation and from what he had gathered from her website. One filled with colour, perhaps candles and trinkets from exotic locations. Incense sticks burning and possibly miniatures of dragons and serpents. Things hanging. Everything and anything ethereal. But there was none of that.

Instead, there were four walls and a ceiling, all painted white, from which could be seen a long, narrow hallway. A single chair was placed to the left of the front door. There was no table and no reception. Minimalistic was an understatement.

He sat in the chair. After a minute he wondered if he was in the right place. He was only going on the street number she had given him. He sat in absolute silence and solitude. Would she even know he was there, that he had turned up? Well, if she was any damn good, he said to himself, she no doubt would.

By quarter past five he started to think he was definitely in the wrong place and he thought about leaving. Then she appeared. The photo on the website must have been old because her hair was brilliant white and long. It was wavy in a natural flowing style extending well over her shoulders and, in total contrast with the premises, she was dressed like a hippy from the seventies, with every colour in the rainbow and more.

She smiled at him and said, "Please, come down."

She walked down the hallway and stopped and then turned at an opening covered by the faintest of light-green, see-through cloth. "Please," she said again and held out her arm for him to enter through the cloth.

Inside was just as spare as the waiting area. No art, no paintings. There was a small rectangular timber table and a bookcase with a series of small drawers with nothing on it at all but some cards. The table was partially covered in a crimson felt cloth. There was no crystal ball.

He sat on the chair that had its back to the entry and she sat on the chair opposite, intimately close, divided only by the table. The chairs were like something bought from a cheap office furniture outlet. They made a noise with the slightest move. Perhaps she had just moved in, he considered, and hadn't yet had time for any sort of fit out.

"You were expecting a crystal ball?" she said with a smile as she settled and looked at her customer.

"No, not really," he said.

"I've never had one. They collect too much dust," she said, with an even bigger grin, pushing her hair confidently to one side, as if it was time to get down to business.

"Thank you for seeing me," he said. He had forgotten to clean the glasses and there was a smudge that was annoying him. He rejected the sudden urge to take them off.

"Thank you for consulting me," she said. She paused as if she was going to say something. Then she leaned in even closer and looked deeply into his eyes.

He held her gaze through the useless glasses. When she kept staring, he felt slightly uncomfortable. Like it was a test.

"Hmmm," she said.

"Is something wrong?" he said.

"Possibly," she replied. She sat back in her chair. She looked at him as if she knew he was being a naughty little boy, like a fond aunty might look at her favourite nephew. She lifted the tip of her tongue to the left corner of her top lip before retracting it and tilted her head ever so slightly, carefully measuring his every reaction.

There was a certain charm if not sexiness about her, he could not help but notice. He could see that, even if Mr Casper could perhaps only feel it.

"You're here for a very specific purpose and it's not …" Slowly blinking her eyes, holding his gaze, she appeared to be concentrating intensely on him for a moment, thinking. "I just can't work that out. Help me. Why don't we start by *you* helping me," she said.

It was a nice way for him to begin.

"I've had a fortunate life so far. Would you like to know my name?" He was ready to give a false one.

"No. That's not necessary," she said. "Tell me more about *why* you think you have had a fortunate life. Why you are here." She placed her hands under her chin. Was she flirting with him? He was a little thrown.

"I don't know. Lucky, I suppose. I was interested to know what you see in my future. I've never been to a fortune teller before."

"I can tell," she said, as if she was really wanting to say much, much more but holding back. "Would you like to record what I say, what I tell you?"

"Why would I want to do that?"

"Some people like to. I allow it. You can then go back and analyse it more deeply."

"I think I'm fine not to. I have a good memory."

"Yes. You do have a good memory. You are good at a few things, some a little … how should I say? What am I feeling?" She looked deeply into his eyes again with an even more serious look of intense concentration. "Some a little … *controversial*, that's what I was looking for, than average. Let me hold your left hand please." She placed her hand face up on the cloth.

He extended his hand face down across the table, keeping her gaze. She turned it over slowly and gently and looked at his palm. She ran her fingers lightly over the palm and up and down the lines on his skin. It felt sensual. She extended her fingers in between his and touched the ring. She closed her eyes. "I don't see a woman or a man with that ring. Odd. But I don't. That ring means something else. Am I right?"

"In a way, yes."

She opened her eyes. They contained a different look now, like she had seen something when they were closed. They widened. "There is a man, however. He is much older. I see him as much older. Not your father." She bent her head down a little. And took a deep breath. She looked up and then down and stared at his chest. "He's in your heart, as much as your father. He's ... like a father."

"Go on," he said. He felt like she was indeed good, just as Mr Casper had said.

"He has helped you a lot."

"Yes."

"He doesn't have children. You're his son, in his eyes. The son he never had."

Tom fell under her spell. He leaned in.

"Arrghh!" she exclaimed and flipped her head back.

"What is it?" he said, surprised, as he watched her demeanour change.

She composed herself. "I don't know yet. Let me have your other hand."

He gave it freely. She turned it over. "You will continue in good health for some considerable time yet. Your family loves you. I can tell your mother is very important to you. She will need one day for you to be even stronger than what you are now. I see you have a sister. Her name begins with an R. Is it Rachael or Rebecca?"

"Rebecca." He was in shock. His heart was pumping.

"She loves you very much. Make sure you're always there for her, too."

"I will. I will."

"I see that in your past, you did not live in London. That you prefer where you grew up."

"That's true."

"That you have constant misgivings about your job. Sometimes you lie ... you lie in bed wondering if that's what you should be doing. It has something to do with crime. Are you a police officer?"

"No."

"I haven't felt this powerful, this strong in a long time," she said. "But it's draining on me." She closed her eyes once more. "There is a man who needs your help. I can feel it. I can't see him, but I can feel it. He has lost someone very close to him. He's grieving. You want to help him."

"Who?"

"You will know who."

"When?"

"When you leave here today. But there is a girl, as well. She … she is somehow connected to this man. She is young, perhaps a child."

"Will we find her?" he said, without thinking.

She looked at him but did not speak. "It is too hard for me to tell. I don't know, yet. I'm running out of energy. Oh …" she seemed to turn a lighter shade, like the blood had drained from her face. She had stopped looking at him. "This has *never* happened to me before. I'm sorry, we're going to have to wrap it up."

"We are?"

She sighed and nodded her head, looked at the floor for a moment and returned to his face. "I'm afraid so. I don't feel well."

He thought she looked awful, like something had suddenly over-powered her. She started to sigh heavily, like she was concentrating again. He dared not speak.

"There is one more thing," she said, after a few more deep breaths.

"Yes?"

"The older man who has helped you. It's time for you to help him now."

"How? How can I help him?"

She stood up, all of a sudden. "I'm sorry," she said. "I have to close up. How are you paying?"

"Um, um, is cash okay?" He got up and reached into his pocket for his wallet.

"Of course. I have a debit machine as well," and she pulled it out of the tiny drawer in the book case, blowing a wisp of hair out of her eyes. "Forty will be fine, given I ended it early." He handed her the cash.

"Thank you," he said.

"You're welcome. Good luck, young man," she said, as she led him out of the room and down the hallway. "You're going to need it," she added from the landing at the top of the stairs as she watched him descend.

It seemed like it was all over in a flash and he forgot to watch his step with his ridiculous shoes, almost tripping on the second last step. He felt like he was in some sort of daze as he got in the car, reversed and headed off.

Cat returned down the hallway, went to the bathroom and was violently ill.

CHAPTER SEVEN

For the first few hours after Tom got home, he sat in front of the television mindlessly watching motor sport. The cars sped around and around the track. Never once did it occur to him that he had absolutely no interest in what was taking place on the screen. The drive home had been as if his car had been set on auto pilot. Something akin to a driverless car. Like, it had a mind of its own and was delivering him to his door, whether he liked it or not.

When his stomach growled, he realised he hadn't had dinner but he didn't feel hungry; he felt numb. That somehow, his brain was clicking over in some other universe outside of his body, as if it was processing what had gone down that afternoon, like a computer processing updates, but not ready to operate.

Then there were the questions slowly surfacing. *Why did she say that? What did she mean? Why, all of a sudden, was I basically asked to leave?* Mr Casper was far removed from his thoughts. He didn't seem to matter. *Who did matter?*

He reached for his phone but couldn't find it. He realised he must have left it in the car and when he found it there, he immediately dialled Alister's number from his driveway. It was cold and he shivered. The street lamp, almost directly above, shined its eerie light into a faint mist.

But again, there was no answer, in fact nothing at all. Not even a ring tone. He was annoyed now. He went back in the house and got his jacket, locked up and returned to the car. He looked at his watch and noticed it was much later than he thought. Just where *did* that time go? It was the last thing he felt like doing, driving out to Alister's semi-detached terrace in Hammersmith. But now he was worried.

The traffic was light for a Saturday evening and he pulled into the driveway in front of Alister's blue roller door in what seemed like no time. He knew Alister always parked his Mercedes inside the locked garage, directly underneath the first floor. A small path led to the door and he made his way straight there, noticing the curtains at the front had not been pulled over the window. He peered in but there was only darkness in the small entry space.

The front door received a good smack with his knuckles, as a sensor light came on and startled him. For a second he thought Alister had switched it on. He waited. And waited. And when Alister still didn't appear after knocking harder, he walked around the side of the building. The one window on that side had blinds covering it. A gentle tap on the glass produced no result.

He wondered if he'd gone to his local for a late dinner, as he often did. But before giving up, he decided to check the back door.

Alister's jet black cat was in the rear garden. She meowed and leapt out at him, flashing her eyes in his direction before skittling off over the back fence. It wasn't inconceivable that he was asleep on the top floor so he stood outside the door and looked up. Then he stepped back a little and called out, "Alister!"

Having concluded it was all a waste of time, he decided to leave without even knocking on the back door. But before he stepped away, he grabbed the round handle on the door and gave it a twist. It turned. It turned completely around and he let himself in.

No lights were on, yet he thought he heard voices as he moved slowly through the darkness. In the lounge room he found Alister sitting in the recliner, mouth open, head tilted back. The voices were coming from the television. "Alister?" he said softly. "Alister …"

No response. Nothing.

"Oh, Alister," he said and touched his cheek and then his neck. "What have you gone and done?"

Cold.

Next Friday would have been his eightieth birthday.

He knew he shouldn't grab the remote and switch the television off before the police got there, but there was nothing suspicious.

Silence was far more important.

He sat in the dark with this man who had meant so much to him, been so good to him, until they arrived.

SHUTTERS AND SHUDDERS

CHAPTER EIGHT

The mentor had once told his trainee he must learn to be more resilient. *Toughen up*. To *carry on* in the face of adversity, *for there really isn't any other choice.*

See loss as opportunity. Look at it that way. A fresh start.

And *don't worry about it.*

Hope. You may see hope, my boy, arrive after its journey to you. It can dock at your port with empty bags ready to be filled with the things you want it to take away from you. But your eyes can play tricks on you, behind and in front.

Maybe it's where you're not looking. Where you don't want to look.

Tom knew that his voice could only ever be imagined now. And sometimes, it was better to master things alone.

Tom stood on the trail alone. He then moved further along. It was 5 pm.

He felt he might be in or near the spot John had described to him, but he couldn't be sure. He walked further along and then off the edge and down to the River Exe.

It all seemed beautiful, idyllic … it *was*, idyllic.

Perhaps the walk was part of the Samaritans Way South West, he figured, a longer 'way marked' walk of 103 miles that crossed Exmoor, including through the village of Exford.

The ground was dry and the water flowed pure. It didn't seem to be here that it happened. There were other shorter walks. It didn't make sense, he agreed.

He wasn't there to search, and he realised it didn't really matter if he wasn't in the exact area Anna had disappeared, or on the right walk or trail. Every inch, for several square miles, had been carefully inspected many times already, sometimes by men and women crawling on their knees for clues.

Tom was sure John had dropped to his knees many times since, and now each day was a living, breathing nightmare for him.

He checked into the same B&B near Exford that the Brownlans had stayed at. John had nodded when he told him he was going to do that. He didn't say anything, just nodded. Like he was drugged to be agreeable.

It was important for him to travel to Exmoor and go over some of the steps they had taken that day, as best he could, he told him, to get a sense of what they experienced and how they went about things. It wasn't with the expectation that it would shed any light on the disappearance. That he was ever going to be able to stand in the very spot from which she had vanished, unless John was with him and showed him. He knew John wasn't up to going back there again.

Tom told his hosts who he was and how John had engaged him directly to look into the case.

"What an awful tragedy, Mr Greer," Margaret said.

And "Is there anything you think we can help with?" Robert added.

The couple sat with him in the B&B's large living space as their daughter placed a pot of tea on the table. "It all seems like yesterday," Margaret said. "Yet so long ago. She would be 11, maybe 12."

"Yes, it's very sad. But no, I don't mean to interview anyone, really. It was just something I felt I needed to do," Tom replied. "Just come here, to the area where it happened and walk around just a little bit."

"How are they doing? We heard that, well, that they're no longer together. It must have been extremely hard for them," Margaret asked, but Tom could tell her husband was just as interested to know if there was any news at all.

"Yes, that's right. I understand it put an enormous strain on their relationship. Unimaginable, really."

Their daughter poured the tea, starting with his cup.

"Thank you," he said, looking up with a smile.

"And she moved back to Australia?" Robert asked. "Is that right?"

"Yes. I believe so." He knew it was true, and wasn't surprised that Robert knew, given not all the press had kept that private.

"That poor man," Margaret said.

After the tea had been poured, their daughter left the large pot on the table and went into the kitchen.

"Did you meet the little one, Anna?" Tom asked, even though he already knew the answer.

"No. They weren't due to check in until after their walk," Robert said. "And when they got back late that night, of course, it had already occurred."

"Have you been to these parts before, Mr Greer?" Margaret asked.

"Yes. A couple of times. Only briefly. I've a friend whose family has a holiday cottage not far away. It's hard to reconcile such a beautiful part of the country with this whole thing. It beggars belief, in more ways than one."

"Oh, yes. That's what we feel," Robert said, looking at his wife. He was, perhaps, in his early fifties, with kind eyes, she, maybe ten years older. They both seemed perfectly suited to running the little establishment and shooting the breeze with their many and varied guests. But this was a breeze that had blown an ill wind.

"It's lovely here." Tom looked in the direction of the windows and then around the walls. He sipped his tea. "Have you had the place long?" A grandfather clock sounded its hourly chime.

"We've owned Kesterland House for just under five years. Thank you, it *is* lovely. We like it very much," replied Margaret. "There are some lovely walks even around here. Starting from just out there, in fact. Not all signposted, mind you, like in some other parts of Exmoor. But rewarding. Actually, we've some travellers from Canada who are booked in next week. They stay with us annually and they always start out the front."

"That's wonderful," Tom said. "Your gardens are certainly beautiful." He could see them through the windows from where he sat. "Are you both gardeners?"

"Yes. And our daughter, Marie," said Robert.

"Do you mind if I take some photos, perhaps tomorrow morning, before I leave? It's just a hobby. But my eye has caught some things already. I could send some to you."

"Of course, we'd love you to do that," Margaret said. "We want all our guests to feel at home and enjoy their stay. Even though in the present circumstances, it must be hard for you, I think."

"Photography takes my mind off things when I need it to. I've disciplined myself to pack my camera even when travelling for work. It's a welcome distraction when I want to look at beauty. Or, allow myself to see it. There's so much of it around here."

Everyone smiled.

Margaret took a sip of her tea. "There must be so much you see in your occupation that isn't very beautiful, Mr Greer. I don't envy you. We're so lucky. People come here to be on vacation. They want to relax and have a good time." She got up. "You'll have to excuse me, though. I just need to check a few things in the kitchen. Will you be here for dinner?"

"I was thinking of going into town. But, would breakfast tomorrow be alright?"

"Yes. Yes, of course," she said. "It's served at 8."

"Brilliant."

Robert poured them both another cup, almost draining the pot.

"I can't say that I'm not envious of you and Margaret. Your lifestyle here must bring you a great deal of joy."

"The change has been good for us. We were both school teachers for many years and it's been a very nice thing for us both. Not that we didn't enjoy teaching. When Margaret was looking to retire, much earlier than me, I decided I may as well have a change myself. I'd had enough of it really. Where do you come from, Tom?"

"I was raised in Norwich. But I've been working in London now for several years."

"And do you like London? I've never spent much time there. We travel there very rarely these days."

"Yes and no. Yes, because it's a good place to be young and working. No, because I miss Norfolk, especially Norwich. I like that Norwich is quaint by comparison to the bigger cities. I like its art scene, the people. Where did you teach?"

"Devon. I was at a school in Plymouth for fifteen odd years and then I met Margaret when I transferred to Exeter."

"And your daughter? Did she make the move with you?"

"Not at first. She finished boarding school and then moved here for a little while. Now she is studying in Bath. She's on a break, sort of studying at the same time. We like that she comes and stays with us. We can pay her, so it works out well. Kind of takes some of the daily tasks off Margaret, so she gets not only to catch up with her but gets a wee bit of respite as well."

After they had finished their tea, and during a moment's pause in the conversation, Tom thought of one final question. "Did you form any impression of Anna's mother, Samantha, if I may ask? I know she would have been in a state, of course."

When Robert didn't respond at first, Tom realised he had put him on the spot a little unexpectedly. "I understand it might be inappropriate of me to ask to talk about one of your guests," he added, hoping he would nevertheless do so.

Robert shook his head. "Not really. I could see … it was very stressful for her. So, we didn't … talk a lot. When they checked out, I remember noticing her hands shaking. We heard them arguing in their room. Some shouting. But that was completely understandable – with the stress they were under."

"And him?"

"Courteous. Not overly. More so than her, I suppose."

Upon thanking Robert for the tea and his time, Tom went to his room. He looked more closely at the archived press reportage of the incident on the internet.

Cathy had said many times since he had accepted the case that she was 'intimately' aware of it and was surprised he hadn't heard of it before. Most of the headlines contained some variation of the word 'baffled' in describing the reaction of the police and various groups of people who conducted the search. 'Police baffled at girl's disappearance.' And 'Local force stumped by possible abduction.'

Mabel O'Gorman, a local resident, said she had "never heard of anything like it in my sixty years in Somerset." Her husband Tony had "not had a wink's sleep in three days, searching far and wide for the young girl."

"It was like she was snatched without a trace. We're finding it hard to come to grips with, to be honest," Inspector Reed told a reporter from the BBC five days after the search had begun. "A lot of people have become very upset in the last week."

Then appeared the series of headlines and analysis after that week, putting even further pressure on the police. 'Inspector justifies his men despite failings.' And 'Police and community doing their best but no results.'

John was reported in several press outlets as saying, "I can't leave. I haven't been able to sleep. I will be staying even if the police call it off." One reporter said that Mrs Brownlan was refusing to talk to reporters. "Mr Brownlan appealed to the press yesterday to respect his and his wife's privacy during 'this horrendous time for our family and loved ones'." Tom shook his head and muttered something under his breath about having good luck with that one.

Eventually the headlines started to say things such as, 'Parents devastated by failed search.' And then, 'Authorities reluctantly call off search' and 'Police to focus elsewhere for missing 9 year old.'

It turned into one of the coldest of cold cases in almost record time and he already knew from speaking to Inspector Reed on the phone that both parents had been informed that despite thousands of hours of combined investigation, there were currently no leads. And that Mr and Mrs Brownlan were not, and never had been, under any form of suspicion, contrary to what one news outlet had falsely suggested.

The devastation seemed compounded by the fact that it had been a last-minute decision to take a short walk; just a taste to see if they might like the experience of a longer walk, perhaps coming back one day and doing the entire 51-mile journey of the Coleridge Way or another beautiful Exmoor walk. "No one expects to lose their daughter," John had said to Tom, "on a simple afternoon stroll. No one."

Tom had not spoken with Samantha Brownlan. It was something he needed to raise with John when he got back. That, yes, he understood she didn't know he had been engaged to look into the case. But it was necessary, he felt, to talk with her, despite what John felt about her knowing and that they were now estranged. Otherwise, it would be an incomplete effort.

But enough of all this sadness, he thought. He picked up his wallet and the keys and headed out the door of his room, downstairs and out of the guesthouse. He saw Robert watering the front garden. "It's not that far to walk, is it, to one of the locals?" Tom asked him.

"No. Not at all. Mostly downhill all the way. The walk uphill after dinner and a few pints might be a different story. It's a lovely evening for a walk."

"Thanks Robert. I'll see you a bit later."

Later that evening, after ox tongue and root vegetables, washed down with two Devon ales, he found it was not difficult to navigate his way up the road, then across a track and through a gate, back to his accommodation.

CHAPTER NINE

The early afternoon sun filtered through the small yard at the rear of Mr Casper's flat. Bob seemed to be enjoying the moment. He got up and greeted Tom, opening the side gate and stepping into the outdoor space.

"Good afternoon, Bob. How are you doing?" Tom asked.

A wag of the tail indicated he was just fine, as usual.

"He should be feeling very good indeed. Shouldn't you, Bob? You had far more than I usually allow for your breakfast this morning. That means you're going to have to walk it off this afternoon, you know," Mr Casper added. "Good afternoon, Mr Greer. Please, take a seat. Bob, allow our guest some room, please."

Bob took a corner position in the sun, possibly his favourite, and stretched out with his belly and paws flat on the pavers.

"Thank you," Tom said, as he sat down. "It was a very nice morning. Kind of crisp, though. I hope the weather stays that way. I haven't seen the forecast."

"I try not to hear the forecast. It doesn't matter. The forecast doesn't change the weather. It'll do what it wants to do. I usually take an umbrella wherever I go these days anyway. I have never minded getting wet though. Just not too wet. Isn't that right, Bob?"

Bob's tail went up and down once.

"Now, you're sure we're not going to get a surprise visit? I haven't made an exit plan. Perhaps the side gate," Tom said, looking at Mr Casper. "Or I could climb over that back fence."

"You mean Cat? Oh no, not at all. She never visits me unannounced. It's always arranged beforehand. Not necessarily well beforehand, mind you. I'm seeing her tonight. Looking forward to it. We'll have dinner. I'm cooking pasta with a Tuscan sauce. One of her favourites, this time. She's working."

"You have the day off?"

"Not the whole day. I'm not going in to the university today. I don't have to be there until Wednesday. But I do have a student later this afternoon."

"Have any other things gone missing since we last spoke?" Tom asked.

Bob raised his head as if he was waiting for his master to tell Tom all about it.

"Well, yes. It's been fairly regular. The bottle of French Cognac I told you about that she gave me – it's gone. That particularly annoyed me, as it was half full. Or half empty. And another towel. I have plenty of towels, but I have three favourites. Two of the three are now gone. Quite annoying."

If it was high annoyance, Tom was struggling to see it. It seemed to be more mild frustration. If anything, Tom could see more of a curiosity on his face about what he was experiencing.

Bob looked at them, still with his head raised, the sunshine mottling over his shiny fur and the pavers warming his belly.

"It would seem odd that she would give you the bottle, only to steal it back."

"Precisely. But I don't see any other explanation."

"And you still don't want to mention it to her?"

"No."

"Has she made any comment about it? The bottle, not being around, I mean?"

"No. She said she would not make any comment about bottles of anything after our little tiff. She probably thinks I've drunk it."

"You know there's one way to make it stop. A little drastic, and perhaps you may have to come up with some explanation …"

"What's that?"

"Inside cameras. It's not common, but it's becoming more common. And less expensive. People are increasingly doing it for security. It can even be linked to your mobile phone. I suppose that wouldn't help, but I think you would find your problem would stop."

"I don't think I would feel comfortable with that. Knowing there were cameras in my house."

"I know some people who have them installed and not have them on. The fact that they're there sometimes works just as well. I mean … you could say to her that a chap came to visit you, and recommended it. That would be the truth, wouldn't it? That you got a good deal and not even mention the issue again. That it seemed a good idea, for your safety, given you live alone."

"I don't live alone. Do I, Bob?"

Bob got up and walked slowly over to his bowl of water, as if he were thinking as he did it and needed a drink to properly consider all this, over a slurp, and a stretch of the legs. After returning to his spot, Mr Casper asked if Tom would like a cup of tea.

"No thank you. I need to be back in the office shortly and you have your student arriving."

"Oh, he won't be here for a while. To be perfectly honest, just at this point, I'm more interested in knowing whether, as I suspect, she *is* doing it, rather than stopping it. The problem with stopping it is that it has no economy to it."

"Economy? How do you mean?" Tom asked.

"I want it to stop *after* I know for certain whether she's doing it. If it stops before, I'll never know."

"Would you be content if I set her a trap, as it were? You mentioned you didn't care how I find out."

"What sort of a trap?"

"Does something go missing after each visit?"

"No. Not usually. Occasionally. It also depends when I notice it missing. Sometimes I don't notice for some time."

"If she's coming over for dinner tonight, why couldn't we set a trap before I leave?"

"We could."

"Perhaps not such a subtle trap. What about the third towel? Leaving it out, visible somewhere. Do you have any other suggestions?"

"I'm a bit reluctant to be too obvious. I have a cheap bottle of brandy. I'd rather something go that I can easily replace."

"Let's leave out a bottle of brandy and one of your favourite towels."

"Follow me, then," Mr Casper said, as he got up.

Bob followed as they moved inside to the kitchen. Tom took a peek around and noticed the ceilings were quite high and a couple of small cameras would be absolutely ideal. They would hardly even impact the homeliness of the dwelling. He was sure Bob would agree, if he could speak.

The whole place was rather minimalistic with plenty of room to move. Not as minimalistic as Cat's rooms, but they were extreme. There was no framed art or anything displayed on the walls.

In one corner of the room next to the kitchen, a living-cum-lounge room of sorts, stood two sculptures about three feet high. One was of a woman and the other, a man. The figures were naked and exhibited a smooth, metallic form in a deep-olive bronze colour. They faced each other, each having one arm stretched out at eye level, palm up, almost touching.

Mr Casper held the bottle in his hand.

"Those figures – the sculptures. They're very beautiful," Tom said.

"Indeed they are."

Tom stepped closer.

"Run your hands over them," Mr Casper said.

"Exquisite," he said.

"They were a gift from a student. My first PhD student. She studied sculpture before commerce. It's very hard to earn a living in the arts. I would have paid handsomely for those. Where should we leave this bottle?"

"Do you have a linen cupboard?" Tom asked, as he turned around.

"Of course."

"Let's put it in there, with the towel just near it."

"Alright. This way."

When they reached the closet built into the hallway wall, Mr Casper opened the doors. It was very neat and tidy. Almost everything was white, including all the towels. He grabbed one of the towels and moved it towards the front of the shelf. He then placed the bottle of brandy right next to it.

"What makes the towel one of your favourites? Aren't they all the same?"

"It's more absorbent. I don't like how a new towel sometimes just pushes the water over and around your body. It takes a bit of use and quite a few washes for a towel to come into its own."

Tom nodded and looked down at Bob.

"Right. What about if we make it just a tad more subtle," Tom said. "Let's not put the bottle right at the front. Let's make it look like you're hiding it." He moved the bottle to the back of the closet. Not happy with where he put it, he moved it again. "There," he said and stepped back. "It's at the very back in the right-hand corner about two inches from the wall. You can see the neck of the bottle above the sheets there."

"Very good," Mr Casper said.

Tom then closed the doors and pulled them open again. He did it again.

"Why are you doing that?" asked Mr Casper.

"I'm listening to see if they make any sound, whether you would be able to hear them being opened and closed. But they don't really. Very little, anyway. I forgot to ask, do you have a cleaner who comes in?"

"Sometimes. When I go on vacation. About every six months. She's not our culprit. I've known her and her mother for ten years. Indonesian. Lovely people."

"Does she clean when you are here? Or does she have a key?"

"Always when I'm here. No key."

"Okay. Well, that's set. Is Cat still visiting you three or four evenings every week?"

"Yes. Usually three."

"Okay. Well, I'll call you soon. Unless there's something else you can think of today, I should be going."

"Thank you, Mr Greer. I'll walk you out."

When he got to the front door, Tom bent down and gave Bob a pat. "Talk soon. Bye Bob. Take care," he said.

When he got back to the office, he found Cathy wanting an update. "How's he doing? Is she still stealing from him?"

"It would seem so. I think we'll find out soon. For a very smart fellow he's a tad frustrating. I would have thought it's not rocket science, or microeconomics, or whatever he's into, to have set a trap for her himself by now. Sometimes I think he's enjoying this whole thing. That he'll be disappointed when it's over."

"Did you tell him you paid her a visit?"

"No. When's my next appointment?"

"I haven't booked any today. There's a packed schedule tomorrow. This afternoon you have Mr Brownlan, at his place."

"What time, again?"

"4."

After a very late lunch, he took his second drive for the day and pulled into John Brownlan's semi-circular double driveway. Getting out of the office usually lifted his mood. But this was not an appointment he was particularly looking forward to. He braced himself as he pressed the remote on his key to lock the car and made his way over the coloured pebbles and knocked on the front door.

A very beautiful front space it was and certainly from the outside, the house itself was nothing short of stunning. It also seemed to be a very big place, yet perhaps now a lonely one for the sole occupant.

"Good afternoon, John. I hope I'm not too late. Some road works held me up."

"It's fine. Come in," he said.

Tom followed him past the front rooms and down the hallway.

The sun had a hint of warmth outside but the house felt cold. "Take a seat," John said, when they reached a large room with a tiled floor. They both sat down opposite each other in single chairs.

The chairs seemed to Tom to be a little out of place, like they had been moved there in preparation for his visit.

He noticed that John was dressed casually but smartly, consistent with the other occasions he'd seen him. His beard seemed doubly thick.

It seemed appropriate to get right down to business.

"I mentioned I went to Exmoor," Tom began.

When there was no yes or a nod, not even a blink of an eye, he continued.

"Robert and Margaret, both quite nice people, pass their thoughts and regards onto you."

John crossed his legs, looked at the wall momentarily and raised an eyebrow.

"I think I got to the area you mentioned. I wasn't quite certain. The weather was good. It's been a bit dry of late, according to Margaret."

John sniffed.

"I went to the pub. I asked a few questions. Nice folk. Very nice people, over there. I think I only came across one set of tourists. Though Margaret said they were about to be inundated with Canadians and—"

"Is that right?"

"What?"

John shook his head.

Tom didn't know if it was some sort of look of incredulity he was giving him or just a complete absence of patience.

"Was it worth it?" John said, after a moment.

"What?"

"The trip!"

"Well, yes ... In a way. In the sense that I had to see it for myself – that area. To put it into perspective. It was so uncanny. That ... she was there one minute, thirty yards away, and not the next. Inspector Reed said they interviewed dozens and dozens of people. I couldn't see that many houses. And they seemed a long way away, those that were there. Per square mile, it has a relatively low density. Probably has more wild deer, than people."

Tom could see John was losing interest. And his demeanour was shaking his confidence a little, given he really had very little to report. But he pressed on. "The police are not suspicious of the good folk there.

Instead, they think it could have been some random who was there, somehow."

"What, lurking in the fucking bushes, behind some beech tree, waiting all day for a little child to come along, then snatch her and run away, metres from her father?"

"I agree it sounds implausible."

"No screams. No sound of footsteps running away. No ... village idiot!"

"The thing is John, I would like to talk to Samantha." This was the real purpose of his visit. "I know you said you didn't really want her to know you've hired me. That, it wasn't necessary."

"She can't tell you anything that I can't tell you. That I haven't already told you."

"I know, but—"

"And *I'm* your client! Not her."

"Yes. I know, but, it's just that, for the sake of completeness at this stage, I would like to hear it from her direct. Sometimes just one little thing makes all the difference. Tiny details, miniscule things, sometimes make a massive difference." He held John's gaze. "Right. That's all. What harm would it do?"

"I haven't spoken to her for months."

"All I need is a phone number. You wouldn't have to talk to her. She can't stop me investigating. Is that what you're concerned about?"

"I don't think she would try to stop you. I just feel she was the one who walked away. Leaving not only me ... but our daughter. She doesn't even deserve to know."

"I understand, John. I do. I wouldn't recommend it if I didn't think it prudent. You're paying me for my thoughts as much as my actions. You may as well get *something*. Allow *something* to be gained. Think of it as something you need to do for Anna." He hadn't wanted to play that card; however, he could tell by the look on John's face that it had registered.

"How many times do you want to talk to her?"

"Just the once, really. Only once." He said this with conviction to nudge John along, even though he had no intention of keeping this promise if it was going to get in the way of advancing the investigation.

John ran his hand over the whiskers on his chin. "I'll email her and tell her first. That she can expect a call."

"That's fine. A perfectly good idea."

"I'll get you the number." He got up and returned a moment later with a piece of paper. "I don't have her mobile number. I heard she changed it but she hasn't given it to me and I haven't asked for it. That's the landline."

"Thank you, John. I'll leave it a few days."

John did not sit back down. Tom got up.

"The police have assured me there were no ex-prisoners, child sex offenders, or the like who lived in or moved to the area that they knew of. That doesn't mean that's absolutely the case. It can be a bit tricky to track these people down and keep an eye on their every movement. But it's very likely to be right. In one of the pubs, I did mention I was a detective looking into the disappearance. I didn't say I was a private one or mention you. People are eager to help in these cases. The fellow behind the bar had worked there at the time. He was working the day it happened and remembers it well. He remembered there had been very few tourists for weeks and it was very quiet. There was no one that stood out to anyone, as far as he knew. He seemed to know a lot of people."

"The police have told me similar things, Tom. I'm aware of all that."

"Goodbye, John. Take care." He held out his hand to shake. For a moment he didn't think John was going to extend his hand. But finally he did, and then he showed Tom to the door.

CHAPTER TEN

There were some jobs Tom knew he was never going to be right for.

Alister had told him that upon arrival to the office each day, he should be prepared for the unexpected.

You don't know who is going to walk through the door. Don't consider ditching the job, because, my boy, I can tell you, how quickly you'll grow tired of any job that has a strong degree of consistency or routine. Most jobs have rules. Don't get me wrong, he would add. *Rules are there for good reason. In our line of work, there are some rules, but they're less defined and quite a few are there to be broken. Not all of them mind you, but so long as you get a result, you are at liberty to lie sometimes and break a rule. Lots of people will turn a blind eye when you do.*

A full schedule of office appointments usually meant four. Two in the morning and two in the afternoon. This particular Tuesday, there were three first-time clients and one who had been to see Tom several times in the last six weeks. Erica Tomlinson, 46, had taken the last spot at 4 pm and he didn't have good news for her. But on the scale of bad news, he felt she would cope.

Bad news, if that's what you could call it, sometimes meant there had been no developments, absolutely no advancements, on a case. But for curious Erica, that would not be the case today.

Erica suspected her husband, Max, was having an affair with a man. She believed he had been very careful not to leave any clues – either online or on his phone. She had done that investigation herself.

But her woman's intuition, as she put it, was telling her something was wrong. She just needed it confirmed.

Tom had followed him at lunchtimes, and on a few evenings, to some gay bars and nightclubs. The hardest part had been drinking dry ginger ales all night, pretending each was a whisky and dry. He never spoke to Max and always stayed a good distance away from him. He'd struck up a few conversations with some other men and apart from the fact there were no women, he didn't really mind the work. It was more interesting than just waiting and watching from his parked car.

Tom had some nice photo enlargements that he had placed in an envelope ready to give Erica. He was particularly pleased that his expensive telephoto lens had already paid for itself many times over. In his favourite photo, you could see Steven, Max's lover, as he moved in to kiss Max. What made it all the more impressive was it was under a street lamp, late at night, in front of Steven's house. The mist in the background was beautifully captured and the depth of field was perfect. They were saying goodbye after a night out.

It would seem that Erica was also now going to be saying goodbye. Tom was so pleased with the photo that he felt like entering it into a competition. But he knew he couldn't do that.

Cathy had told him about the first two appointments in some detail, but not the third due at 2.30 pm. She had merely written in his diary 'Arlie Harmonsen' with '38' next to it.

For Tom's liking, his second appointment was a little too close to home. He knew Darius Abnan from the Middle Eastern food outlet a few blocks away. He had already spoken to him several times at lunch breaks. Darius was sure suppliers were ripping him off and he wanted him to investigate some wholesalers who had some sort of vendetta against his family. He was somewhat obsessed about it and despite apologies for raising it with Tom the last several times he was eating at his establishment, he had continued to do so. Finally, Tom had told him to call Cathy and make an appointment. If it wasn't for Darius's brilliant harissa lamb, Tom would have told him he didn't work for 'friends' or people he associated with.

Tom had decided he just needed a brief chat with Craig, his first appointment, before he had to deal with Darius. Craig had failed to be promoted from police constable far too many times in his eyes and thought something wasn't quite right. A sergeant who Tom knew through his dealings with the police agreed and had recommended Tom.

Tom took Craig into his office at 10.30 am.

Cathy was surprised when he was led back out the door at 10.45 am.

After Craig had left, Cathy said, "That was quick. What happened?"

"I decided I wasn't going to take the case. That I'd considered the matter carefully and he was best to keep the pressure on from his end. It's way too tricky for me to be looking into the police. He understood."

"I put a lot of work into that brief. Damn! Are we sending him a bill?"

"No."

Darius, unfortunately, didn't have the best command of English. His restaurant was called The Persian Bronze Pearl. He could say that clearly, but very little else. Tom had informed him of Alister's passing, given they had been regulars at the restaurant which was more like an outlet than a restaurant, although at night it did seem to take on a different atmosphere.

"While you work for me, I no cost you. You no pay, is on house when you eat. Deal?" Darius said, shortly into the consult.

"Thanks Darius. However, it's my invariable policy *never* to accept freebies from clients."

That was also not entirely true. It was more a general rule. He broke it occasionally, but never at the outset. If he did break it, it would only be part the way through a matter or, if it was appropriate, at its end. It was essential not to confuse things by accepting something for free at the beginning, when he knew he would have to send a bill at some stage.

There was a fine bottle of single malt whisky in the top drawer of his desk that had been delivered to him just last week by an owner of a small, independent shop who had asked him to check out the older boyfriend of his young daughter. It was a bonus, an act of gratitude, *after* the job had been done to the client's satisfaction.

"You charge me your normal prices at your restaurant, and I'll charge you mine." Best there be no little misunderstandings, particularly given the language barrier.

After an hour of hearing all about the brother of someone who sounded dodgy, but was just trying to make a living, and his wife, who was just as bad in Darius's eyes, and the 'filthy' mother of some other fellow who supplied the bread and about how he was thinking of bringing a gun to work and keeping it in the kitchen in case things got worse, Tom thought seriously about taking the shot glass off his bookcase and pulling the whisky bottle out from the drawer. He wasn't certain Darius drank, yet after listening to his paranoia, he was never more certain why *he* did.

He decided he would avoid The Persian Bronze Pearl for a while, at least until he'd done something on the case, whatever it was.

At lunchtime, Tom walked to the nearest pub. A steak pie and mash with a couple of pints might make him sleepy but, so be it, he thought. He should be able to leave work today no later than 4.30 pm, shortly after giving the photos to Erica.

Cathy had a saying for these type of final appointments: 'Photos, bye, bill'.

"He's so good looking," she said when Tom put the photo of Steven and Max in Cathy's hands as he was waiting for the 2.30 pm appointment to turn up.

The two pints had put him in a bit of a jolly mood. "Don't you think the photo is just brilliant? One of my best?" he asked her. He had forgotten to ask her anything about the client booked in at 2.30 pm, still proud of the photo he was ready to give Erica at 4.

"Just gorgeous," she said, still staring at it.

"The photo, you mean?"

"No. Max."

"Give it here!" he said, snatching it from her and stomped into his office.

Five minutes later, when he saw Arlie Harmonsen sitting in the waiting room, the first thing he noticed was the first thing she seemed to want him to notice. How was it possible to not look at them? It wasn't. And when she stood up to greet him, she placed her cleavage just under his chin. She might have been a little taller than him in bare feet, but with the heels she was wearing, he stood much lower and just the right height for him to notice. He was in shock and awe.

Cathy and Barbara giggled as they watched him take her into his office.

"Where's his camera when we need it?" Cathy said to Barbara.

"Did you tell him about her?" Barbara asked when Tom's door closed.

"No. He would have agreed to at least one appointment, anyway. Clearly! I hope he's not going to get upset with me, though, and that he keeps his sense of humour."

"Arlie, is it?" Tom said, after he'd offered her a seat in front of his desk. He avoided looking directly at her, sat down opposite her and dragged a notepad across the desk while scratching his eye.

"Yes. It's not my real name, though."

"I see. What is your real name?"

"You mean my stage name or my other name?"

"How many names do you have?"

"Let me see. I started with Arlie. Then … I'm thinking, I've had four. My professional name is Arlie Harmonsen. But my online name is 'Mistress Arlie'."

"Your online name?"

"Yes."

"Right. What is on your birth certificate?"

"That's a good question. I haven't seen it for a while. I must try and find it."

"What were you born as?"

"A girl."

"Sorry, Arlie." He cleared his throat. "I meant … *when* you were born, what name were you given?"

"Monica."

"Surname?"

"Monica Brabinsky."

"Right. How can I help you? I'm sorry, I've been a bit busy of late. I haven't had a chance to obtain any information from Cathy, my assistant, with whom you made the appointment."

"Oh, Tom ... can I call you Tom?"

"Absolutely."

"In my line of work, I've been very successful. I own my own home. I have a lovely new Audi. I also have a holiday villa in Tuscany. But, just of late, some opportunities that *should* have come my way, have *not* come my way. In fact, they're not coming at all."

"I see. What is your line of work?" He had a feeling he knew the answer.

"High-end erotica."

"Not ..." he paused. "High-end ... you mean—"

"Porn?" she said.

Tom raised his eyebrows a little and nodded.

"I don't call it that. Some might. Porn is something I did in my twenties. It has no art to it. Sure, it was fun and at times, lucrative. They wanted me to work with the lady boys for a while. I tried it, but it didn't do anything for me. But erotica is a different category altogether."

"It is?"

"Of course! I'm not interested in porn anymore. Erotica is an art form. It's more sophisticated. More subtle." She uncrossed her legs momentarily as Tom held her gaze, then she crossed her legs the other way and repositioned herself a little on the seat. He realised the couch would have been far better for this consult, but he was not thinking clearly when he brought her in.

"That's interesting," he said, even though he felt that description didn't seem quite right.

"It is!" she said nodding with enthusiasm, like he had made some startling revelation and she was very pleased to hear it. "I've always said that."

The beers were wearing off, however, he was by no means sleepy. Her hair reminded him of some glamorous movie star's from the 1950s.

Her face looked remarkably wrinkle free. Her eyebrows were dark, but the whites of her eyes were brilliant. She held a rather large bag in her hands, a very expensive, designer-looking bag. She wore no rings and had a series of gold bracelets around one wrist.

"You seem a very smart man," she said. "How old are you?"

"I'm almost thirty." He wasn't fond of giving too much precise detail to any client.

"In the prime of your life. I thought I was, until I started losing some work to my competitors. Some of them are real bitches, Tom. I don't mind telling you. Do you mind me telling you?"

"No. Not at all."

"The stories I could tell you. It would make not only the hairs on your head curl. Though, I can see, it's already curly. You have such lovely hair. Has anyone ever told you that?"

"My mum, a long time ago."

"Ha! That's funny," she said.

"So, Arlie, you've come to me; you think I can help somehow?"

"Well, I'm hoping so. When I missed out on the part I've been waiting for *all* my life, to someone who is *far* less well known, far less competent – to me, anyway – I knew it was time to get a professional. Someone who could go behind the scenes and see what's really going on, if you know what I mean."

"I think so. What part do you mean?"

"In a movie. Look, years ago, movies were dying. It's all become about the five-minute grab here, or the twenty-minute cam girl there. Flash this, flash that ... now give me your credit card. That's a huge part of the industry. It's not really even an *industry* anymore. It's really ... just a mess. It's rubbish really. There are so many hundreds of thousands of girls all trying to make a quid. Even old tarts who should stay in their flats and never come out at night. I mean, there are actually *professional amateurs*! Think about that, Tom!"

"Seems like an oxymoron!"

"That's what I always say! Too many morons."

"And ... you were saying?"

"There are a few visionaries in the industry. And they can see things others can't. They're not blind! Far from it. One, in particular, has helped me a great deal. He produced all my DVDs up until two years ago and now handles all my downloads, and my site! But I don't just work with Toddy."

"No?"

"I work with Allan and Billy and a heap of others. There's a feeling that high-end erotica in a movie form might make a comeback in a big way. I think it will. People are busting their balls, literally, to be the first to make the next classic. People pay good money for classics. They keep them, like they keep anything else they collect."

"I see."

"I haven't got any work in the area for three bloody months, Tom! And when I missed out on the part … to that *wench*, I'm saying enough is enough. I think you would too!"

"A particular movie?"

"Yes. They're producing it as we speak. It's going to be called *Careful Who You Thrust* and I should have been the star! I want you to find out why I keep getting rejected."

"That sounds like a challenge. I mean, it's not …" *The old rejection problem* came into his mind.

"I've a few ideas, Tommy. Do you ever get called Tommy?"

"Well, I … not for—"

"I could get you on the set! No problem. I'm on speaking terms with all the crew. They're lucky I talk to them at all! Especially that bitch, Miss Gina Dongdoer. Oh, that's not her real name."

"Really?"

"No. It's Sharlene, hmmm, Sharlene … I can't think of it right now."

"I have to think about this a bit, Arlie. Can I?"

"Yes. I knew you would. Look, I've brought one of my previous movies for you." She reached into her bag and placed a DVD on the desk. "It's one of my best, though it's a few years old. I think you'll see what I mean; that I shouldn't have been overlooked. I'll ask you a few questions about it, after you've watched it, and see if you agree. I'm sure you will."

"Thanks for that," he said, trying not to look at it, smiling … thinking … wondering how he was going to get out of this one.

"When do you think you'll get back to me? After you've thought about it a bit, I mean. Cathy has my details. She seemed to think this might be right up your alley. Something you could really get into."

"She did, did she? Right, well. Yes, I expect I'll be speaking to her further about it all, this afternoon in fact. A real good chat about it. Let me see. What … about … if I get back to you in a week? Would that be okay?"

"Oh, shit, for sure! I thought you were going to say a month!"

"No, no. I *am* busy, but I'll let you know if I'm taking the case within a week. Tell me, Arlie, just out of interest and if you don't mind. How much would that movie retail for?"

"When it was first released it was 50 quid. In America it got as high as $45. For you, Tommy, it's a freebie."

CHAPTER ELEVEN

At some point in time, Tom knew he would stop thinking about Alister every day. He felt Alister had been right about the things he had told him about the job and he missed him a lot. If there had been a grave, he could have visited it and talked to him. However, burial was not Alister's style and at his cremation his brother had said that one day he would like to scatter the ashes into the River Ness. There was no urgency of course, he had assured Tom. Just one weekend that he had free and could fly to Scotland.

Tom was keeping his weekends free as much as possible, following his mentor's advice to ensure he had down time. *Watch a movie, lie on the couch, chill. But don't forget to spend time doing your research for your cases, all the same.*

He arrived home and tossed the DVD Arlie had given him on the couch. He shook his head when he thought how watching movies *was* doing research in this case. He hadn't thought they could ever be combined.

Tom's friend, Marzena, arrived for dinner and they sat on the couch eating pizza and drinking beer. He had forgotten to remove the DVD and it had slipped into the couch. She picked it up.

"It's come to this, has it?" she said, with a big grin, turning it over and examining the back of the case. "Charming."

"No. It's not what you think."

"Oh, really?"

"No! Give it here."

"It's a bit old, isn't it? It says here, date of production, 2004. *The Adventures of—* "

He snatched it out of her hand and got up. "It's work related. A client gave it to me."

"I'm sure that's what you tell all the girls."

He opened a drawer in the little TV setting, threw it in there and closed the drawer with his foot, before sitting back on the couch.

"Are you still seeing what's his name?" he asked.

"Brad? No. He's moved on. So have I."

"Have you?"

"Most definitely. He wasn't really my type. A bit too straight-one-eighty. Nice guy, though."

"You meet too many nice guys. Then end up deciding you don't like them."

"True," she said indifferently as she picked up another slice of pizza.

Their catch-ups were always similar – mild, mutual insults acknowledged as having some semblance of validity. They had grown to be very close friends, and each took the time and effort to maintain contact. There would always be genuine interest in each other's lives, almost every time they sat together. She knew him well enough to ask how his mother was doing. Likewise, he would always think to ask how her parents in Poland were. It was hardly a friendship based on things in common. Separate lives and different interests didn't preclude a bond. His friend, Paddo, once remarked they may as well be a couple, what with the amount of time they spent together. "You do everything except …" But that wasn't what the relationship was about.

They hadn't seen each other since Alister's passing. She had never met him; however, she did know what Tom thought of him.

"One day, you might be able to do the same thing for some young upstart like yourself. I'm sure you'd have some great advice." Her English had come a long way even though her Polish accent remained strong.

Mid-week catch-ups were never late affairs. By 9.30, Marzena had said goodbye. Tom went straight to bed. As he hit the pillow, he sorted out his workload priorities. Some cases were more important than others and some brought a smile – a welcome distraction of sorts.

He didn't want to ring John again but nor did he want to leave ringing his ex-wife much longer. Sometimes, clients would badger him, constantly wanting updates. Not John.

Richard had called a few times and was always polite. "Be patient with him. He's damaged goods," he reminded him.

That was all very well, but this was an exceedingly difficult case and there were times when he wasn't at all sure that John cared whether he was working on it or not.

"That's his depression showing, that's all," Richard said. "Please, Tom, stick with it, and bear with him, if you can."

It meant going into the office near on midnight, if he wanted to reach her around 9 am Sydney time. Motivation was required and the right setting. His empty office was going to have to do. Biting the bullet, while biting his tongue, seemed to be the name of the game.

"Good morning, is that Sam? Samantha Brownlan?"

There was a slight delay. "Yes." And then another pause.

"Good morning. It's Tom Greer, from London, calling." He winced as he thought that was somehow a tad not right. He didn't want to sound upbeat. Just the right tone of something that felt appropriate … professional. It didn't always come easy to him, especially at this hour.

"Hello?" Another pause. Tom thought about the evil of international phone calls with people you have never met. For a second, he hated landlines, the interruptions, the lack of rapport.

"I …" She began to say something as he spoke and they both stopped again.

"Did you …" he said, as she went to say something again. "I'm sorry," he said.

When there was silence, yet again, he asked if she was still there. She said she was. Time to get on a roll, and get it over with.

"I believe you've heard from John Brownlan that he has engaged me. I'm a private investigator in Camden in London. Engaged by John to look into the tragic events of a couple of years ago involving your daughter, Anna. I thought out of courtesy that I should speak with you personally. Perhaps in the first instance, instead of by email. I hope that I'm not calling at an inconvenient time?"

"No. It's fine."

"I'm happy to arrange a face-to-face, real-time connection on a computer or cell phone, if that suits you better. Then we can see each other. I also would like to extend my sincere sympathy … for what must be, and must continue to be, a very dreadful situation for you and your family."

"Thank you. How can I help you?"

Even with the distance and without being able to see her face, he guessed she had just said that so he'd get to the point. Fair enough. This was not at all easy for her. She was told to expect a call and was probably dreading it.

"I wanted to know … please forgive me, I know it must be very difficult. I do understand."

"Yes. It is," she said.

"I wanted to know what you think happened." He almost relayed the basics of what John had told him, but stopped. Sometimes a very straightforward question produced a very clear and illuminating answer. It seemed entirely consistent with her vibe, that she wanted him to reveal his purpose with the most minimal delay.

"What happened?"

"Yes. With your daughter. That day." There was another pause, this time longer than the others. He waited.

"I don't know. I wasn't there."

"You weren't there?"

"Well, no. I was a hundred yards away. I wasn't there. So, I can't say, can I?"

While he digested that, he understood what she was getting at, but he hardly expected it to be delivered so coldly, so precisely factual.

"No one seemed to be there? Is that right?"

"My husband was. He was closer than I was." Was there a tone of bitterness, if not blame there as well?

"I mean *around the area.* The trail, the track you were taking."

"Not that I saw."

"So, you have no feelings about what happened? What could have happened?" He knew he had perhaps made a mistake with how he put that first question, but he cared just a little less than at the start of the conversation.

"My daughter is gone, Mr Greer. I have plenty of feelings. I can only assume that she was taken somehow and that someone knows what happened. I can't tell you anything more than what I was told by my husband. That ... he had taken his eyes off her. That she was close by. And what happened after that. What *I* witnessed."

Of all the things she could have said, the words "he had taken his eyes off her" struck him with the most force, as she had possibly intended.

"When you say, 'after that', you mean, the search?"

"Yes."

"Were you happy that everything that could have been done with the search was done?"

"Happy? I wouldn't say I was happy. I understood what we were told during it and then, why it was ultimately called off. It seemed a waste of time to continue. John didn't get it, that it couldn't go on forever. I think people did their best, if that's what you mean. I'm not blaming the people who were involved every day for almost two weeks of their lives."

"Do you mind if I ask ... you and John, are you on speaking terms?"

"We email."

"Do you believe his account of what happened?" He needed to know the answer to that and while it was particularly direct, they *were* separated after all, and he might not get another opportunity. "I'm sorry to put you through this. I truly am."

There was a pause. He thought he may have stepped over the line. Stepping over the line, across a phone line, across thousands of miles, now seemed easier than doing it any other way.

"Yes. John is, he's ... not, not someone who lies."

He thought she might elaborate about some other trait, so he waited. Just when he thought she wasn't going to, she added, "He has his issues. Telling lies isn't one of them."

"I also wanted to ask you whether there was anything you specifically wanted me to investigate. To look into." He thought that made sense, that it was only right.

"*He's* the one that has engaged you!"

"Of course. I just mean … from *your* point of view."

"If you can find my daughter, Mr Greer, I would be forever grateful. However, there's nothing that I can suggest to you now. I discussed *a lot* of things with the police in the twelve months, all in the first year after it happened. Their focus was on abduction. What were they left with? It wasn't falling into the stream. It wasn't drowning. Until, it all went absolutely nowhere. And I mean, *nowhere*. No leads, no suspects. No one saw anything or anyone. I'm sure you've perhaps looked into the *actual* facts … Maybe you should if you haven't. I mean no disrespect. I don't. But what can you possibly do that the police can't?"

He had heard this before.

"At this point, I don't honestly know. I've told John the same thing. I don't continue to work for clients if I feel the chances of me being able to offer some meaningful help is slim or non-existent."

She fell silent again. There didn't seem a lot of point to press further.

"Would you like me to email progress reports?" he asked.

"You do whatever you think is appropriate. Do *not* however send *me* your invoices."

"Thank you for your time, Mrs Brownlan."

"That's fine. Goodbye."

CHAPTER TWELVE

Sooner than Tom anticipated, thoughts of another trip to Exmoor entered his mind. A mini escape of sorts seemed doable, this time mixing a little work with leisure and hopefully pleasure. When he woke at 6 am on Saturday, he decided he would take this opportunity and need not mention the details to anyone. He figured he would send a message to Cathy at a reasonable hour that morning saying he wouldn't be in on Monday. He could tell her why later. There were no appointments and everything else could wait.

As usual, there was no one else to please but himself. He would decide later whether or not he would charge John for a few hours of work. It depended to what extent it was useful work. And he figured if he got off to a very early start he could be at Dulverton on the southern edge of Exmoor well before dark, as long as he kept his stops to a minimum. His fondness for food might stand in the way of that.

After three eggs, bacon, mushrooms and toast, he was heading in the direction of Somerset in his car.

Ever since his first visit to Exmoor National Park, when his friend Paddo had invited him to stay in his parents' holiday cottage, the whole region had always been in the back of his consciousness, exacting some sort of a pull on him to return. The allure was not something he could put his finger on. But it was an intangible grip that took hold as soon as he entered an invisible gateway and he knew he was firmly inside its territorial control.

Nor was there any one feature or particular activity he could do whilst there causing him to set it all apart. The discourse in his mind on the subject of its mysterious power over him seemed private, almost indescribable. Yet it was real. It wasn't about hiking the Two Moors Way or the Coleridge Way or the South West Coast Path, for he hadn't done any of those, although one day he promised himself he would. It wasn't the offer of horse riding along its many bridleways. He was a little scared of horses, if the truth be known. It wasn't exploring the coastline around the towns of Lynton or Lynmouth and gazing out at the stunning Bristol Channel or taking photographs of Great Hangman, the highest sea cliff in all of England, or waiting for the light to be just right, before taking artistic snaps of the shadows in the impressive Valley of Rocks.

As he headed for Exmoor, he thought about John's case. It wasn't lost on him that Anna had been to the Valley of Rocks on the morning of that fateful day. Much of the walking in Exmoor was described as 'heavenly' and rightly so, but it also wasn't lost on him that the Valley of Rocks had a rock formation known as the Devil's Cheesewring.

But a visit to it wasn't on his agenda. Nor did he plan to go fishing or hunting or foraging, despite all these activities being on offer, particularly at this time of the year. Autumn in Exmoor was the favourite season for a good proportion of the locals.

Photographs *were* on his mind, though, just not anywhere near that Cheesewring. And this time he had packed not only two cameras and two of his favourite lenses, but also an old adapted telescope that he could mount on one SLR. It was the first weekend of the annual stargazing festival and if he was lucky enough and made good time, he could even catch the introductory talk on astrophotography in Dulverton put on by the Royal Photographic Society.

He knew a little bit about night-sky photography from his university days in Norwich, but opportunities to actually partake in the craft were rare. The universe was aligning itself for Sunday night, he hoped, according to the weather reports. Dark skies promised lighter times, perhaps, away from the pollution of the city and the clouds in his mind.

The golden leaves and the clear streams and the blue ocean and the red deer would all have to give way to the ink of the night sky. It seemed to make sense to him as his little visit would coincide with the officially named 'Exmoor Dark Skies Festival', which also recognised Exmoor's status as Europe's first International Dark Sky Reserve.

He made it not only in good time but also in time enough to get a bite to eat in town before thinking about heading to the hall where the talk was arranged.

A fishing tackle store, which also sold hunting equipment was open. Not that it was likely he'd go hunting. Live and let live was more his style. But to each their own. The population of the place was less than 1500 and tourism, which included hunting, was important to its very existence. It was also the headquarters of the Exmoor National Park Authority, he duly noted.

Before heading to the hall, he decided to sit back in his car and do a little bit of research about the town, nearby attractions and where to stay overnight.

A few miles north west of the town, the River Barle ran underneath the Tarr Steps, a form of clapper bridge, thought to date as far back as 1000 BC by some folk and by others at least to 1400 AD. Either way, he thought it sounded very bloody old and was worth a look. Heavy stone slabs, weighing up to two tons each, sat nearly forty inches above the normal water level.

Staying at one of the places out of town was an option. Like Exford, the Dulverton area was a good base for day trips to explore Exmoor. It was small but far bigger than Exford. He thought about heading in the direction of the ancient monument and checking it out in the twilight, but there really wasn't time. He settled on a B&B nearer the town. Probably best to check into a place before he went to the talk; sound advice he gave himself. And there was no one else in the car to suggest otherwise. He put his phone back in his pocket and took the short drive there and checked in.

It's busy, the lady at reception noted, what with the festival and all, and he was lucky to get their last room.

The talk was already underway when he got there. He paid the young man at the door the entrance fee and looked for a spot to sit. It seemed the two back rows had a few vacant seats and he made his way there, politely excusing himself as he shuffled past peoples' knees. He wondered as he sat down whether he might be the only one in the hall who held a university degree in photography, apart from the lady presenter. It didn't matter if the talk was aimed at beginners, as he suspected. It was more about just being with like-minded people who enjoyed some of the same things as him, and getting out of London and into the national park.

"The darker the location, the better you will be," the lady said.

He looked at the one-page leaflet that the man at the door had given him. The lady's name was Elinor Hobson, from York, and he thought he may have heard of her, vaguely. Sitting next to him on his left was a girl of perhaps his own age, maybe a little older; the seat on his right was vacant; and then an older gentleman with a long white beard was next to it. He turned and said hello softly to both, but only the man nodded and smiled.

"I'm assuming everyone knows all about the f-stops on a lens, together with shutter settings for the camera. The other core basic is, of course, the ISO camera setting, which is a handy thing for taking photos in darker conditions. A high ISO sometimes helps and you may wish to experiment with settings at the higher end. The general rule is the higher the ISO, the less light is needed. But as with everything, there's a compromise. I'll get to that later. But for now, we'll go through some of the basics of how we can all take fabulous photos of the night sky with just a camera and tripod."

The talk was set for one and a half hours and Tom had missed the first ten minutes. It wasn't until she got to the topic of editing the images that he really took serious interest. He was happy that she didn't dumb it down, although he understood she was catering for people who had not studied the subject in some detail.

Bringing the photographs to life from their original images and what was the latest in commercial software to do this was covered in the last twenty minutes.

Everyone seemed in awe of her series of before and after image manipulations, and she apologised a little unnecessarily, in his view, for getting a bit technical with detailed descriptions of processing to reduce image noise. She spoke of 'stacking the images' and was really very clear on how to go about it. "So, don't put your camera away when the sun goes down. Get out there and capture some star trails or follow the rules I mentioned if you wish to avoid them. It's all up to you in this universe! Thank you all very much. If you have any other questions, I'll be staying for a cup of tea. Thank you."

A round of enthusiastic applause followed.

The man with the white beard got up immediately as if he might want to be the first to get a cup of tea or to make his way over to the speaker. As other people got up, Tom noticed the hall was perhaps half full and there were more vacant seats in the front that he hadn't noticed. It all had an intimate feel about it.

A biscuit and a cup of tea before heading back to the B&B sounded just fine.

"Well, that was very interesting. Did you enjoy that? I did," Tom said, turning slightly to the girl sitting next to him.

She bent down and picked up her handbag she had placed on the floor in front of her. "Yeah, I thought it was good," she said as she opened her bag and removed her phone. She then opened its case and pressed a few buttons.

Tom noticed most of the crowd was slowly making their way to the table with the cups and saucers. It was mostly an older crowd and perhaps mainly locals. He was sure some may have come from Minehead or even further.

It was apparent there was no rush for refreshments. Life's pace in these parts was slower, welcomingly slower. He sat there for a moment and then took his own phone out and switched it from silent mode. "Are you having a cup of tea?" he said to the girl, once more trying to strike up a conversation.

She looked up, a little distracted. "I'm sorry?" she said.

"A cup of tea?"

"Yes, I think I will. I was hoping I could ask her a question before she leaves."

"Good. She's very knowledgeable."

He got up and so did she. He made his way to the right and she could have gone either way, but she followed him.

Lots of little groups of people clustered together had started chatting, like they knew each other. He could see that the man with the white beard had indeed made himself first in line for a private tuition and was well into explaining something to Elinor, that he no doubt found very interesting. She was nodding her head.

A little bottleneck in the tea queue had developed. As they took their spot in the line, he turned back towards the girl and said, "Tom's my name, by the way."

"Audrey," she said.

Soon they both had a white cup and saucer in their hands with a biscuit on the rim.

A small congregation of people were waiting to pick Elinor's brain. They both moved aside. "You may have a little bit of a wait," he said.

"Yes, poor woman. She can't even get a cup of tea."

"Maybe someone should ask her if she would like one. She did say she was staying for one."

"I'll do that. Good idea," she said.

Tom watched her go over and interrupt. At first, Elinor looked as if she was confused. But then she nodded and said something and Audrey went to the table and placed her own cup and saucer down, poured a black tea and returned to give it to Elinor.

"Thank you, my dear," he saw Elinor say.

Audrey collected her own cup and saucer, grabbed another biscuit and returned.

"That was a polite thing to do," Tom said.

"I don't think she was going to get one otherwise. I'm not going to line up. She's going to be lucky not to be here all night."

"I might be able to help with your question," Tom said.

"Really?" she said.

"I can try. What is it?"

"I didn't catch what she meant by the '600 rule'. I didn't want to put my hand up."

"Well, it's an oldie but a goody, as they say. It's all about avoiding the stars moving across the photograph, given the Earth's rotation. Even though they look stationary, even a fraction of a second makes a difference to the image. To prevent it showing, you take 600 and then divide it by the focal length of the lens you're using. So, if you are using the standard 50mm lens say, on a full frame camera, 600 divided by 50 is 12 seconds exposure. 100mm lens would be 6 seconds, and so on. That way the trail of the stars won't be noticeable."

"That's all it is?"

"Yep."

"I'll definitely give that a try!"

"It's fun, actually." He took a sip of his tea. She took another bite of her biscuit. "Are you a local?" he said.

"I was. Not anymore."

"No?"

"I used to live in Dulverton. My parents still do."

"Just visiting?"

"Yes."

"Me too," he replied.

"Where are you from?"

"I'm working in London."

"So am I."

Tom was eager to keep this pleasant interlude going before it was time to leave. But before he could speak again, she said, "Excuse me," then, "Hello, Mrs Daley!" and took a couple of steps away from him.

Audrey greeted an elderly lady and a man.

"Oh, hello, dear! My, haven't you got taller. Haven't seen you for years. Not since you were at school. How's your mother doing?"

"She's fine. She wanted to come tonight but Dad talked her out of it."

"Is he still a stick in the mud?" The lady laughed.

"Oh, for sure! He drives us all crazy. My mother, especially."

"I was just saying to Harold the other day," she said, as she placed her hand on Audrey's arm. "We must drop around and see them. I've never returned that doily I borrowed from her last winter, for Becky's christening. Tell her I will be over to see her soon, lovey."

"Are you still into your nature photography? And growing your orchids?" Audrey asked.

"Oh, my word I am, dear. And now I'm going to give this night stuff a go, I think."

"She'll have to drive herself," her husband said. "I'm usually in bed by dark, these days," They all had a good chuckle.

"You should do that! Lovely to see you both."

Audrey turned back to Tom. "Sorry about that. They're old friends of my parents." She took the last sip of her tea. "It reminds me, actually. I have to get back. What's the time?" she looked at her watch. "I'd best be going. Nice to meet you."

"Nice to meet you," he said, as he watched her return the empty cup and saucer to the table before grabbing one more biscuit on her way out the side door.

CHAPTER THIRTEEN

A sound sleep did not result in an early rise and there was no need anyway. All he had to do today, at some stage, was find accommodation for the night, as he had set his mind to vary things up and travel further into Exmoor and stay somewhere different. It was a nice feeling.

When he got out of bed, he didn't know where he would next lay his head. The abandonment of certainty would allow the unleashing of freedom. The first decision would be what to have for breakfast. It had been a little while since he'd had a full English breakfast cooked for him. He knew that would be on offer in the dining room or he could request it.

"I'll have the full breakfast, if that's alright, thanks. Oh, and with the extra mushrooms, please."

"Very good," the lady owner said. "Please help yourself to the cereals and toast as well. I'll be back with the coffee shortly."

"Thank you."

He had brought a flyer for the Tarr Steps to the table. A wide selection of flyers and the like were on display in the hallway but this was one he found particularly interesting. The ancient stone clapper bridge was described as Exmoor's most famous landmark. *A big call* he thought, thinking about the other attractions. It was easily accessible with a short drive from town. The twelve-mile return hike along the River Barle was tempting but too time consuming, given he was just on a weekend visit.

He smiled when he read that according to local folklore, the heavy stone stepping slabs had been placed across the river by the devil to allow him to sunbathe on them. Seemed a lot of effort to go to, when he could have easily settled for a lie down on the grassy bank.

A couple sitting opposite him and already enjoying their morning meal saw him smile at the brochure.

"The Tarr Bridge?" the man said. "We went there yesterday. It's well worth the trip."

"Steps. The Tarr Steps," his female companion corrected him.

"I'll probably take a look this morning," Tom said. "I've always been a fan of the devil's architecture. Assuming I have the right devil, that is. I've been told there's more than one. Maybe I'm getting confused with demons."

The man laughed. "Yes, it's all part of the history apparently. It's been washed away by floods in parts a few times. I'm not certain he factored that in when laying it so low to the surface of the water."

"That'd be God sending the floods, I assume. Just to annoy him," Tom said. "He sent a pretty big one some time back, I believe."

"I think the flood waters more annoyed the men who had to restore the thing and retrieve the slabs in the stream, then put them back. Bloody heavy two-ton pieces of rock! What a job that would have been."

"That'd be the devil's style. Leaving the hard work to someone else! I would have thought he could've found a better place to sunbathe. I mean, I know he likes heat. And cheese, apparently, what with that cheesewring out at the Valley of Rocks."

"Where are you from?" the lady said. "Are you staying a few nights?"

"Norwich originally. London now. Just the one."

The couple told him they had been travelling for a few weeks and were heading to Dartmoor National Park next. They chatted some more until Tom's breakfast arrived. He hardly ever volunteered that he was a private investigator in such chats and always tried to keep it a bit vague as to what he did for a living. The conversation would always go in a different direction once people knew and he often hoped they didn't ask.

By 10 am he was walking across the Tarr Steps which seemed in fine condition for their age. He took the walk from the car park, which took him down to the bank of the river and then on to the bridge itself. It was much narrower than he had pictured and a bit longer. The largest slab seemed about five-feet wide. Probably a dozen or so people crossed the bridge about the time he did. He felt invigorated from the little walk and seeing the clean, flowing water and standing on ancient stone.

Back on the road, he decided he would head to Minehead next. It skirted Exmoor and was often described as its northern gateway.

He had never been to Minehead and he figured it might be a good place to stay because of its proximity to Dunkery Beacon. Exford offered good proximity too, but he'd already been there when he stayed in the same guesthouse that John and his wife had stayed.

Located on Dunkery Hill, the Beacon was the highest point in all of Exmoor and promised outstanding views on a clear day, from north to south and east to west. It *was* a clear day. And he had a clear head for a Sunday morning.

During the roughly forty-minute drive, he decided he would have lunch in town and then take the short drive south west and walk up to the Beacon. Only a few clouds were about and if the weather held out, which seemed to be quite likely, he would go back into town, check into a place to stay, then drive back in the evening and walk up the hill again, with his telescope mounted to his camera. It all seemed like a plan and he felt excited now that he'd formulated one.

A corned beef, tomato and relish sandwich ticked off lunch and as he washed it down with some flavoured mineral water, he researched places to stay. *May as well book in now*, he thought, as he found an attractive proposition at a very reasonable rate that offered 'boutique style' accommodation with both a separate bar and restaurant. Of course, he might not be able to take full advantage of the bar and restaurant given his plan to drive that night, but he booked in anyway. He could have an early dinner, preceded by a few ales and possibly an afternoon nap.

The drive to the Beacon took just over twenty minutes and by 2.30 pm, he was in the car park and ready to take the steady climb up the hill. It was an easy ascent, but by the time he'd reached the top, he was glad he'd had a light lunch, by his standards. He had walked slowly, not at London pace, and it hadn't seemed to take long at all. At 1,705 feet, it was the second highest point in southern England. The purple heather would have been as spectacular as the panoramic views of the moors and the coast, but it was well past its seasonal peak.

He'd read that the views of the hills could extend more than eighty miles. He didn't doubt it as he peered across the expanse and snapped a few photos. A plaque on the summit commemorated the handing over of the land for the benefit of the nation to the National Trust for Places of Historical Interest or Natural Beauty from private ownership. He saw a wild Exmoor pony in the distance, but knew his telephoto lens was not quite good enough to capture it properly. He hadn't expected to see such a sight so soon. A wildlife photographer he knew he was not.

It all seemed a bonus to him, for it was all supposed to be about the stars.

A couple of teenagers took turns to climb the cairn at the summit and after a few more snaps, Tom turned and took the path back down.

On the way back, he struck up a conversation with a fellow who said he had hiked all the way from Minehead. The seven-mile walk had taken him just under three hours. Tom offered him a lift back, but he said his wife was picking him up from the car park. When Tom told him that he planned to come back that evening, the man mentioned that the National Park Authority had planned two nights of a guided walk to the summit starting at 9.45 pm. And that he planned to join in the one on the following evening. He knew one of the local rangers who was doing the second night's walk.

"Wow. I didn't know that! Do you have to book?" he asked the man as they arrived at the car park.

"No. You meet here and just turn up," he said.

"Thanks for the info. I just might do that," Tom said.

When he got back to his accommodation, he went to the bar and had a pint of ale. Then he had a shower and fell asleep on his bed.

He awoke from a dream about an hour later and he thought he'd been dreaming about the missing girl, Anna. He wasn't sure, as it was all a bit of a blur.

As he got up and splashed water on his face, he looked into the mirror and felt a pang of guilt that he wasn't doing anything on the case. He could go and visit the office of the National Park Authority on Monday before he left and see what information they could give him on the search, and perhaps anything else the rangers might know that could in some way be helpful. But all that seemed not overly useful. He already knew from the research he'd done that the rangers were as baffled as the police. Even with their local knowledge of the terrain, what happened to the young girl was a complete mystery.

Unlike most of his successes with finding missing people, there had already been a massive and long search undertaken, involving hundreds of people. The police didn't always treat a missing person case as a crime. In this case, it seemed it couldn't have been anything but, yet there were still no clues, not a single piece of clothing, a shoe or tracks. It was absurd.

He knew he would be heading back into the park that night with Anna on his mind, unable to shake the frustration.

The same strategy would prevail. A light dinner to carry him up the hill, then come back to the accommodation at his leisure.

The car's headlights preceded him into the car park and shone through a small group of half a dozen or so people standing at the gate near the pathway. He turned and parked. He got out and bundled up his tripod, camera and telescope, and threw a lens bag over his shoulder, then hurried towards the group who had started to walk off, following the ranger.

He caught up to them and after strolling along for a minute or two, he heard a voice nearby say, "Hello, again."

He looked up and saw that it was Audrey, from the night before. "Oh, hello!" he said and smiled. "Nice to see you again!"

"Looks like you have some gear there. Some serious equipment." She only had a camera hanging from her shoulder.

"Oh, not really. It's just an old camera with an old telescope. I've had it for years. Probably needs a bloody good clean. It looks fancy, but it's not."

"I've only had my camera for a week. I haven't even taken a single photo yet."

"Really?" he said, while thinking what an added bonus it was that he would have company.

She was much more rugged up than she had been the night before. The air had a definite chill in it and autumn was starting to bite. Her boots looked new and as he looked down at his own shoes, he thought they looked like they should have been thrown away a year ago.

After a minute of silence, she stopped walking. He stopped too and waited as she undid her shoe laces. "These boots are new," she said. "I just need to loosen them a bit."

When they resumed the walk, they found themselves at the rear of the small group. The ranger was saying something to the people at the front.

"I didn't even know about this walk until a fellow told me today. He'd hiked from Minehead and is doing the walk tomorrow night. I've driven here from Minehead. I found it amazing he had walked that far. Did you drive from Dulverton?" he asked.

"Yes. I didn't know about it until this morning, either."

"I was planning on coming up here by myself. But I'll be interested to hear what the ranger has to say."

"Me too," she said. She stopped again. "I think I've a pebble or something in my shoe. Sorry." She pulled the boot off her left foot and turned it upside down. A rock fell out. She shook her head. "How would that get in there?" She pulled her boot back on, bouncing on her other leg for a moment, and then bent down to retie her lace.

The breeze had picked up as they had ascended the track. Tom noticed her hair flicking around her cheeks. She wore trousers much like a ranger might wear. Khaki perhaps, although it was hard to tell in the dark.

"Sounds like the ranger is saying something. You don't have to wait for me," she said.

"It's fine," he said. He was far more interested in what she had to say. "I came up earlier today. Have you seen it? In the day I mean," he said as they continued further up the track.

"When I was a kid. I don't remember much about it, other than falling off a pile of rocks at the top and skinning my knee. I must have been about nine."

"With your parents?"

"Yes."

"It's such a gorgeous part of the world. You must have enjoyed growing up here, in Exmoor."

"I went away to boarding school for a few years. What did you say your name was? Sorry."

"Tom. Tom Greer. Audrey, isn't it?"

"Yes."

The group at the front stopped. The ranger was pointing at something in the distance. A group of red deer could be seen and he was explaining that deer had roamed the wilder parts of the area since ancient times.

The journey to the summit was not that much further and just as they caught up to the group, the ranger mentioned to keep a look out for more.

"I saw a wild pony today!" Tom said to Audrey.

"I had a tame one when I was a kid," she said. "Ronnie was his name. We kept him at my uncle's farm."

"Every girl needs a pony," Tom said.

"They need some space," she said.

"They do," he said, pretending he knew about ponies.

At the summit, the ranger spoke about the geology of the hill, how it had been visited since the Bronze Age, and how it contained a number of burial mounds. His knowledge was extensive. He talked about King Henry II and how this had once been a part of the Royal Forest of Exmoor. But for Tom, the ranger was simply a distraction now. He'd prefer to continue his conversation with Audrey.

At some point it became clear the photographers were developing itchy fingers. The ranger said, "I'm sure everyone is keen to test their shutter bug skills so I'll leave you to do that. I'll be walking back in about half an hour. Enjoy!"

As Tom had been to Australia and the outback, he'd seen the night sky as bright, but never so much in the northern hemisphere. He noticed Audrey didn't have a tripod. "Here, please use mine," he said.

"But what will you use?"

"Let's set yours up first and then we can set my camera up. The universal mounts come in handy," he said, as he screwed her camera on and set it up pointing to the heavens. "A great time to test out the 600 rule," he said. "It's a lovely camera you have here. Full frame, too!"

Half an hour passed quickly. They experimented with the ISO settings and different exposure times, and Tom explained lots of things about the features of her camera that she'd no idea it had. They picked up the tripod and took it to different spots around the summit. Her camera was the same brand as his and he fitted one of his lenses on it, all the time chatting about photography and what constellations they might be seeing.

When the ranger started giving indications it might be time to head back down, Audrey pointed out that Tom hadn't even taken any photos with his camera.

"Well, I guess we don't have to go back with the others," he said, "but I suppose we should." He then unscrewed her camera and set his up with the telescope. "I can snap a few quickly, even with the bulb setting and wing it."

"You look like a pro. Is this what you do in London? You're very fast and good at it."

"No. I mean, not for a living. Just a hobby. I studied photography at university in Norwich."

"Oh, you did? Well, maybe you *should* be a professional photographer. What do you do? In London?"

"I'm a private investigator." He didn't look at her. He bent down and adjusted the setting on the camera. "There. That should do it. I'll take just a few more."

She put her camera back in its case. "I didn't ... that must be interesting," she said.

"Sometimes," he said. "Not always." He straightened up and looked at her. "I think you said last night you were working in London. What do you do?"

"I'm a pre-school teacher."

"That must be very rewarding."

"Not financially so much. But I love working with children."

After a few more photos, he started to pack up his gear. "We best be heading back, I suppose," he said.

She looked around. "Just when we have all this to ourselves."

He looked down at the track. "Maybe not for long. I think there's another group getting ready to head up. Maybe that's why the ranger headed back. Shall *we* head back?"

"I suppose so."

On the way down, she thanked him for being so generous with his time and said she felt awful that he didn't get to take many photos on his camera.

"It was more fun helping you take them on your new camera. I like fun. I was only thinking of myself!"

She laughed.

The trip back went all too fast for Tom's liking and when they got to the car park, the ranger took another group up. Again they found themselves alone. "You've driven from Dulverton?" he said, already knowing that she had.

"Yes. I have my parent's car. I'm just parked over there."

"I'm staying in Minehead. I'm going in the opposite direction." He paused. She waited. She kicked at some gravel, glanced down and then up at him again. "You know, it's not far," he said. "Only twenty minutes. Would you like to follow me back? For … What about a cup of coffee? The place where I'm staying has a bar. I'm sure it would be open. I know you're driving. It probably … doesn't make much sense at this hour…" He knew it didn't.

"I'd like to but I don't think I can. I'd get back too late. My parents are worry warts. Even if I call them and let them know, they won't sleep until I get back."

He shook his head. "When are you heading back? Back to London?"

"Tomorrow."

"Are you driving?"

"No. I'm getting the bus."

"I'm heading back tomorrow. What about … *what if* I saved you the bus trip? I could use the company on the drive."

"I've already booked the bus."

"Oh," he said. "Well, what if you cancelled it?"

"Well, I could. I suppose."

"I could pick you up at 10. Or any time you want, really. What do you say?"

He could tell she was at least tempted to say okay. He never expected to make any such suggestion, standing there in the dark in the car park, but he was making it all the same. And he wanted very much for her to just say yes.

Their eyes had adjusted to the light and he could see that her eyes were brown and her skin fair. Her hair was long and wavy and a natural light brown. They were almost identical in height.

"Alright," she said.

"Great! I'll need your address."

She paused. For a moment he thought she'd changed her mind. She looked like she was thinking again. But then she gave it to him and he took his phone out and entered it.

"What time would you like to leave?"

"Well, would 9 be too early?" she asked. "I actually have to be back. I've got a few things to do."

"No. No, that's perfect. I'll see you then. Let me walk you to your car."

When she got in, she wound down the window. "See you tomorrow," she said.

CHAPTER FOURTEEN

Any thoughts that he did have about visiting the National Park Authority were now dashed, but it didn't stop him from thinking about Anna on his drive to Audrey's house the next morning. As he passed by the building where the Authority's offices were located, he felt somehow he'd let John down.

If the weekend had been a little different, he knew he could have attempted to be the first one in there on a Monday morning, politely asking for any information they could tell him, being very upfront that he'd been engaged privately to assist with the case of missing Anna Brownlan, and offering his own assistance, as limited as it might be. He justified his change of plans by telling himself there was a strong likelihood they couldn't tell him much anyway and that he was entitled to take his mind off work, which after all, was the main point of the trip.

Missing persons were not the responsibility of any National Park Authority. He knew that. The Exmoor National Park Authority, like other similar authorities, had been established to focus on the conservation and enhancement of the natural beauty, wildlife and cultural heritage of the area and promotion of opportunities for understanding and enjoying the national park.

He knew in a matter of minutes he would be driving out of Exmoor, having got nowhere for John. And that didn't sit easy.

He looked at the row of houses along the street until he found the number she had given him. As he wouldn't be staying long, he pulled up behind the little car parked in the driveway. A nicely manicured front lawn with a garden seat made for a lovely homely setting. It looked like a small house, at least smaller than the houses either side, perhaps two or three bedrooms, with one bedroom upstairs with a single window.

He went to knock on the door but just as he lifted his hand and made a fist to do so, a man opened it. An elderly man. "Oh, good morning," Tom said.

The man didn't respond at first but looked Tom up and down.

Maybe it's not such a good morning, Tom thought.

He was about to ask if he had the right place, that he was here to pick up Audrey, when the man said, "You must be Tom."

"Yes, that's right." He would have added, *and you must be Mr...* but he didn't know her surname. "I had an arrangement to pick up Audrey. At 9."

"So we've been told," the man said. He didn't smile, continued to hold the door and they both stood in a moment of silence. Audrey then appeared and did smile. The biggest smile he'd seen so far from her.

"Please come in, Tom. My parents would like to meet you before we leave, if that's okay."

The man shook his head as if that wasn't quite true and only just made the effort to step aside so Tom could enter.

He was led through the carpeted entrance way and into the kitchen. The smell of bacon, and perhaps some other cooked food, filled the air of the house. He expected to see breakfast makings, but it was spotless and when he saw an elderly lady with a tea towel in one hand putting away what looked like the last of some dishes with her other, he was certain it was her mother.

Her parents were much older than he had expected. Almost 70, if not older, he gathered.

"Mum, Dad, this is Tom," Audrey said.

Tom shook hands with her father.

Her mother put the tea towel down, turned and faced him but kept a distance. "Hello, young man."

"Lovely to meet you," he said and smiled. "It's a bit more chilly this morning," he said. "I think we've already had the best of the good weather for a while."

"Oh, it's not *too* bad," Audrey's mother said.

A moment of silence ensued and Tom looked at Audrey.

"Would you like a cup of tea, or anything? Before we go," Audrey asked.

"I'm fine, I think. But thank you. I haven't long had breakfast. Would you like one?"

Again, there was a moment's silence. Then Audrey shook her head. Her mother opened her mouth as if to say something but closed it again.

"I'll get my bag," Audrey said. "I'll just be a minute." She hurried upstairs.

"Our daughter tells us that you're a private investigator, Mr Greer," Audrey's father said.

Tom was surprised he knew his surname. No doubt, Audrey had remembered it.

"Yes. That's right."

"What sort of things do you investigate?"

"Oh, ah … lots of things, really."

"Like what?"

"Well, fraudulent dealings, um, infidelity, some crime – not a lot – I mean, of crime that is, a bit of white collar, estate matters … missing persons. Anything really, I suppose, that concerns people which they might need some assistance with."

"What do mean by *infidelity*?" Audrey's mother said, with a frown, now resting her back against the kitchen bench with her arms folded.

Tom paused, wondering if this was an indication of quite a few more questions to come. "People – ladies mainly – who suspect that their other half might be cheating on them and want them checked out. Having an affair."

She looked at her husband, raised her eyebrows and widened her eyes.

Tom felt it best not to elaborate and instead, wait for the next question.

"That sounds a bit seedy. A bit *grubby*," she said, almost like he might be a grub.

"Well, it definitely can be. Very unpleasant stuff at times. But it pays well," he added, with a smile.

Audrey reappeared with a suitcase. "Should we go?" she said. "I'm ready."

"Sure," Tom said immediately.

Audrey took her bag and placed it near the front door. When she got back to the kitchen she said, "Let's go," and went over to her mother. "Bye, Mum. I'm going to miss you! I'll email every week. Just don't worry if it's not *exactly* every seven days. I don't want you to worry. Please don't. It'll depend a little bit where I am at the time."

Tom looked on as she gave her mother a big hug.

"Please luv, look after yourself. And please stay safe. Don't be taking any silly risks. No strangers! Promise me, now."

"Bye, Dad," she said, turning to her father, giving him just as big of a hug, and kissing him on the cheek. "Now, don't forget to take your pills. And your appointment with Dr Larsen, next Monday."

"Have a good break. Come back safe," he said.

"I'll make sure he doesn't forget," her mother said.

"I *am* going to worry, you know that," her father said.

"Well, don't!" Audrey said. "Worry can shorten your life." She turned to Tom with a smile. "Ready?"

"Yes."

Audrey went into the lounge room and grabbed her handbag and then made it to the door first and opened it. Her parents seemed to be reluctant to go in that direction and when they got there, Tom picked up the suitcase. It seemed a lot heavier than what it looked.

"Thank you, Tom. You're a gentleman," she said with a smile, as she looked at her mother to make sure it registered with her.

He felt her parents were by no means convinced.

"Lovely to meet you, sir," Tom said, swapping the bag to his left hand and holding out his right to shake her father's hand once more. It was a handshake with no reciprocal compliment. "And ... lovely to meet you," he said, with a nod in her mother's direction.

They all went out the front. Tom popped the back of the car and placed the bag in it. He opened the door for her and left it ajar.

"Bye," Audrey said, again, as she got in.

Tom gave a smile and nod to her parents and got in.

Her mother said something and Audrey went to roll down the window. Tom pressed a button and it descended.

"What did you say? I couldn't hear," Audrey called out.

"I said, have you got everything?"

"I think so," she replied, rifling through her handbag for a moment before placing it on the floor in front of her.

He reversed slowly and she waved again, and both parents slowly raised their hands, with rather depressed looks on their faces. Tom could see Audrey was smiling in stark contrast. He gave a pip of the horn just as he was about to head down the street, though he knew it was a tad out of step with everything.

"Thank you for this," Audrey said as he took the first corner.

"It's my pleasure. Thank you for coming back with me."

"I woke up this morning thinking I'm really glad I'm not getting the bus."

"So am I. I mean, I'm glad you're not getting the bus too. Did you come by bus?"

"Yes. The overnight."

"How long was your stay?"

"A week, just under."

"Do you visit your parents often?"

"I try to."

"Was that the house that you lived in? That you grew up in?"

"Yes."

"I like Dulverton," he said. "And that's a nice street."

"Yes. It is."

She sighed. Tom took that as a sign she felt comfortable with him and relief that she was now on her way to her other home.

"Big morning?" he said.

"Sort of. I told you my parents worry. They're doubly worried now."

"Why? Not because of me, I hope."

She laughed. "A little. They had a minor fit when I told them I wasn't catching the bus. Maybe not so minor."

"And going home with a man you'd just met!"

"Yep. And they were already worried."

"About what?"

"I'm going overseas on Wednesday. That's why I spent a little bit longer with them this time."

"Right. I was wondering why your mother said something about not taking silly risks and no strangers. You've already broken two rules with me, before you've even gone," he said, then laughed.

She smiled. "Well, you're not a stranger anymore, are you?" she said. "And I think it's more risky on the bus."

"Doesn't mean I'm not strange," he said as he picked up speed. He turned and smiled at her again. "Where are you off to?"

"I'm starting in China, but then I'm going to Burma, Thailand, Cambodia and eventually, Vietnam."

"Wow," he said. "That's brilliant! How long are you going for?"

"About three months."

"Are you spending your time equally between the countries?"

"I'm spending the least amount in Burma. There's a school that I'm volunteering at, for a week. I don't expect to be doing much sightseeing there. I'm spending the most amount of time in Thailand."

"I've heard it's very beautiful there. And the people too," he said.

She mentioned that it was her first time to Asia and her first time travelling by herself. And that, as an only child, her parents were going to miss her.

Tom mentioned he had been to Australia and had enjoyed a road trip there with his friends. "Seems a long time ago, for me, now," he said.

He made her laugh with a few stories about it. She said she hoped to get there one day.

He said it had been on his agenda to get back for a holiday every year since he had been there, more than five years ago. "But every year

I've found some excuse not to go. Work, really. Now that I run my own business, it's much harder to take a decent amount of time off. It's tricky to get one day off."

"You came for a long weekend. That's something. Why Exmoor? Was it just the festival? Do you know people in Somerset?"

"I've a friend who has a holiday cottage but I ... he wasn't there. I could have asked to borrow it, I suppose. But it's actually his mother's. He hopes to be a ranger in the park, one day. Maybe live there then. I just like the area a lot."

"That would be a pretty cool life," she said.

"He thinks so, too."

Questions about their work really didn't arise until they were about an hour from London. They stopped for a bite to eat and to stretch their legs. "Where am I dropping you?" he asked, as they sat in a small café, annexed to the petrol station they had filled up at.

"I live in Gospel Oak. It's in North London."

"Oh, I know it well. I'm not far from there at all. I live and work in Camden. That's bloody convenient, that you're so close!"

"Thanks again so much for this," she said. They both ordered the same thing. A hamburger with a side of fries, without salad.

"Did my mum give you the third degree? Ask you about your job?" she said, when they got back in the car.

"Oh, she asked a few questions."

"Sorry about that," she said.

"No, its fine. It's natural. I would do the same."

"Do you enjoy what you do?" she asked.

"I have to say yes. The first year was hard. It took a while. But I'm a bit more experienced now. I roll with the punches a bit better."

"You do?"

"Yeah. I don't take it as much to heart. I had a very good, experienced trainer. Sort of a mentor, if you like. He taught me a lot: how to handle the more tricky times and cases."

"It's so wonderful to have a person like that. Is he a lot older than you?"

"He passed away a little while back."

"Oh, I'm sorry."

"It's fine. Thanks. He was a very good man. I miss him a lot, actually."

"I imagine at times it might be hard not to, in your job … that is … not to get upset. The police must go through the same or similar. I don't know how they do it."

"It's just like any job. It has its ups and downs. How long have you been teaching?"

"About four years," she replied.

She mentioned there were a lot of good schools in the borough and she was able to walk to her work.

"I can too," he said. "It's kind of good, isn't it? Except, I don't always walk, I have to admit. I can be a bit lazy."

Time seemed to fly and the traffic wasn't heavy until they got closer to London. It was getting on towards the later part of the afternoon when he was close to pulling up in front of her flat. "You know, I don't know your surname," he said. "And I don't have your number."

"Easily fixed," she said and picked up her handbag. He saw a break in the traffic and pulled in close to the curb, momentarily double parking. She reached into her handbag. "My surname is Brockwell. I'll write my number down." She tore off a little page from the coil of a small pad.

"Thanks," he said.

"No … thank you."

"What time are you leaving on Wednesday?"

"The flight is not until 10 pm."

"If I shouted you dinner tomorrow, do you think … you could fit it in, before you go?"

"I think so," she said. "That'd be good."

"Okay. That's great! I'll get your bag." He got out of the car. He hadn't left much room for cars to pass and a lady grumbled at him as she had to wait for him to close his door. He lifted his hand with an apologetic smile.

"Goodbye then," he said, as she appeared at the back of the car. "I'll do some research on where we might go for dinner. Can I be here at say 7?"

"You can," she said, and gave him a kiss on the cheek. "Thanks again."

CHAPTER FIFTEEN

"You seem to be in a very chipper mood for so early in the week," Cathy said, arriving at work and seeing him smiling at his desk early Tuesday morning.

"I am!"

"Did you get out of town?" she asked.

"I did! I forgot to tell you where. I went to Exmoor."

"Did you find that girl … Anna?"

"No, I didn't."

"What did you do?"

"I went for some walks. Did some stargazing. Took some photos. Stayed in some cool places. Met some really nice people. What did you do? How was your weekend?"

"I got drunk on Friday night at a pub. Went to a girlfriend's birthday on Saturday. Slept."

"Oh, good."

"Do you want to know what happened yesterday?" she asked.

"Not really. But I suppose you'd better fill me in."

"I don't think you're going to want to know. I didn't want to interrupt your *long* weekend and call you about it."

"Know what? Spit it out. What are you going to tell me?" It didn't take long for a little bit of that sinking feeling to emerge that he normally associated with sitting behind his desk early in the week.

"Don Creighton," she said, pausing to see his reaction.

"Yeah. What about that nutcase?"

"His warehouse burned down yesterday afternoon."

"What?"

"Yeah. He rang about 4 and told us. Said he wanted to speak to you, urgently."

"Why?"

"I said you were out. He said, it wouldn't have happened, if you'd done your job."

"What! What a bloody ... screw him! How did it burn down?"

"Quickly, apparently."

"Did you send that letter?" he asked, standing up now.

"What letter?"

"Cathy! I told you to send him a letter with an invoice! Telling him he should get a bloody security firm, not a damn PI! *Don't* tell me you didn't send it!"

"I don't remember you asking me. I don't think you did."

"Christ! Where's his number?"

She ducked out of the office and returned with the number on a sticky note.

Tom was sitting upright behind his desk, shaking his head. "Blaming me, is he! Well, I didn't light the bloody fire."

She thought it best to leave.

Now leaning back in his chair, he had gathered himself, and returned the call. "Don. How are you? I'm sorry I was unavailable yesterday."

"A bad day to be out of your office. Or, was it?" Creighton said.

"Yes, Cathy mentioned ... you called. Otherwise—"

"Yes, I did. Several times!"

"So, they're sure it was arson?"

"Definitely! It didn't burn down by itself. It wasn't spontaneous combustion! I told you!"

"There's no way ... no way I could have ... The common sense thing to have done, Don, was to get a security patrol. Blind Freddy could have seen that—"

"I came to you with my suspicions, Greer! Why couldn't you see? See what I was talking about!"

"Ah, *no* you didn't! You came to me to say you had suspicions then sent me out there with no information. No names. No enemies. No reason for someone to burn your joint down. Excuse me for feeling that it's all a little *odd* now it's happened! And you're getting up me for it, instead of looking for the arsonist!"

"What ya mean, odd?"

"Odd, as in *strange,* Don. Odd, as in something's *not quite right* about the whole thing, *from the beginning*!"

"Something's not quite right with you, Greer!" And he hung up.

Tom was pleased the call had ended and he hoped it was the last he'd hear from Creighton, but he suspected not. If anyone was going to sour his mood, it was going to be him.

The afternoon went better and he sent Creighton a bill and confirmed in writing "… what was clearly mentioned in the first consultation that you would be better served by a security firm, in the circumstances, and may wish to engage one without delay."

After he'd got Creighton out of the way and out of his head as best he could manage, he called Mr Casper.

"The brandy and the towel are still there," he informed Tom. "Cat's been over twice," he added.

"Right. Well, perhaps we need to think of something or someone else," Tom replied.

"Something else has gone missing, though," Mr Casper said. "It's actually been cut off."

"What do you mean?"

"The remote control on my recliner."

"A chair, you mean?"

"Yes. The chair in my lounge room. It's got … well, it had … a control that's been removed. I can't use it."

"Well, that's outrageous! When did that happen?"

"Yesterday."

"Was Cat there yesterday?"

"No. The last time I was with her was on Sunday evening."

"And you first noticed it when, did you say?"

"Yesterday afternoon. When I got back from the college."

"Right. When would be a good time to come over and see you? I'd like to see it for myself."

"I'm home tomorrow morning. My week is otherwise a bit full."

"How about ten-ish?"

"Good. That would be very good of you, Mr Greer."

"See you Wednesday morning, Mr Casper."

CHAPTER SIXTEEN

In the back of his mind, all during the conversation at dinner, he knew lurked the obvious. A sort of pain mixed with excitement. The pain had started to surface already and he knew it wouldn't properly kick in until after the flight – Wednesday 10 pm. The excitement was what he actually felt – a feeling that was new, and somehow had a chance of lasting.

Timing. Everything was always about timing. Just when things had started, she was going to leave.

She didn't have to give him a chance. He didn't ask.

But every minute was better than the last, and when Audrey said, after dinner, that it would *not* be the last time they would see each other, he knew he would see her again. That he … *they*, had that chance.

In three months, she reassured him. But he was ready to see her tomorrow and the next day, and the day after that.

The three months apart would be *her* time. But for now – right now – it was *their* time.

As they walked slowly up the stairs nothing was spoken. It didn't seem necessary. Tom knew. They both knew. And when he saw her naked, he was so amazed, so grateful, that they would have this opportunity. They held each other. He kissed her breast. Her skin was so pure, so smooth. He moved slowly, up and down her neck.

He could feel his heart beating faster. And for the first time, he knew the meaning of making love.

There was no time to waste on sleep afterwards and he held her, and she held him, again.

Her left breast rested in the cup of his hand. Underneath the letter 'A' was tattooed.

It was tiny. She knew that he had noticed it.

Then, she spoke of things he never expected to hear. Not from her...

It's near my heart but below it. Away from eyes ... unless you know it's there. Or, you look carefully. You can see it, if you look carefully. No one has seen it ... The letter A. It's ... for her. For the girl. The girl, who went missing. For I couldn't ... and no one could. No one could find her. We looked for weeks. It was my school holidays and ... Yes. I was a volunteer, searching. Trying to help. There were dogs. Bloodhounds. I can hear them to this day. Someone said cadaver dogs. I absolutely hated that word. And infrared heat-seeking equipment and helicopters. And ... nothing. I cried. I just couldn't move on. Not, for a long while. I became ... obsessed. Needed to do something. Something, to help me move on. But not forget. So, I got the letter A. I didn't want my parents to know ...

She fell quiet when she saw the look in his eyes.

And he told her.

FILTERS AND FOCAL POINTS

CHAPTER SEVENTEEN

"I've seen some odd things, but this is certainly up there," Tom said, staring at it.

The large, dark grey, single recliner chair was clearly otherwise in pristine condition.

"It's nothing short of vandalism, really. Why would anyone want to do that to a perfectly good … I'm clearly missing something. Help me out here, Mr Casper."

"Yes, well, I'm very disappointed, to say the least. I reached down for the remote. You can see there's a little pocket there." He bent down and slipped three fingers into the space while Bob sniffed at it. "That's where it lived. I always put the remote back in there, religiously, every time I used it. The store that I purchased it from said that was the best place for it. I never left it hanging to the side or on the seat or the side cushion. It was in perfect order."

Tom picked up the black cord and could see where it had been neatly cut. "Someone would have had to cut the power supply." He walked around the back of the chair and noticed a cord that went under a rug to the wall. He picked up the transformer. "Someone has unplugged this," he said.

"I know," Mr Casper said. "It's got a back-up battery supply, but I can't even use that."

Tom went down on one knee and slipped open the back of the unit. "Looks like it takes two nine-volt batteries," he said.

"The batteries should be in the transformer. There's a space for them there. They only kick in when the power's cut. I've never had to use it, but it's part of the reason I bought it."

"There are no batteries in here," Tom said, shaking his head.

"What? That's odd. I put them in there when I got the recliner. They're missing too?"

Tom stood up. "How long have you had the chair?"

"A couple of years, I think. It's still under warranty."

"It's not a warranty issue, obviously. More of an insurance issue. Police, really. It's criminal. That's what it bloody is!"

"I've already called a repairer. He said he'd never heard of such a thing. He's coming over to have a look tomorrow. It's unlikely that he can just replace the remote."

"I don't imagine it's going be a cheap repair," Tom said. "I mean, this has kind of escalated a bit, hasn't it? It's gone from trivial things to much more serious things. It's downright nasty! And you say Cat was here on the Sunday evening, and you noticed it on the Monday?"

"Yes, that's right. I was at work in the morning. I came home and sat in the chair in the afternoon. I like to listen to a program on the BBC on Monday afternoons, if I can. It comes on at 3. I got home a little after lunch. I sat down and reached for the remote, to recline. Sometimes I use it to recline a lot and then tip me forward, if my arthritis is playing up. I was feeling rather good that day and just wanted to lie back. Bob comes in and keeps me company and we both listen. I said, 'Bob, where's the remote?' He came over and I think he was as shocked as I was. We really couldn't work it out."

"Is it possible that she cut the remote off on the Sunday, in the evening, and you didn't become aware of it until later?"

"Well, I thought about that. And it is. But she would have had to have been very sneaky about it."

"Like, when she went to the bathroom? Or something? Or you?"

"Yes, I suppose."

"And quick. But, one problem with that – correct me if I'm missing something, Mr Casper. If she wants to be very careful and secretive about all of this – and the question in any event, is why would she be doing it, what's the bloody motive – would she not run the risk that you'd used the chair before she came over and then, soon after she had left? Like, it would be bleeding obvious then that she'd done it."

"Yes. It doesn't seem to make sense, does it? I'm going to have a cup of tea. Can I make you one, Mr Greer? Do you have to get back to your office?"

"Well, I do. But it can wait. That would be nice, thank you."

Bob headed to the kitchen first and they both followed him in. Tom watched Mr Casper lift the kettle, go to the sink, fill the kettle, set it to boil, reach for the pot, place it on the table, open the jar on the bench containing tea leaves, bring the jar to the table, place three large scoops of black tea in the pot without spilling a leaf, take the cosy off a little hook, place it near the pot, all keeping his head fairly still. He had a faint hint of that familiar smile back on his face.

"It's all very strange," Mr Casper said. "Very strange."

"I can think of stronger words. It would be driving me nuts. You're a very patient man," Tom observed.

"Well, there's no point in getting all hot under the collar about it. I would like to know, though."

Mr Casper poured the water into the pot, placed the cosy around it and sat down. "Please, take a seat, Mr Greer. Would you like some cake? I've some fresh butter cake. It's just store bought, I'm afraid."

"Only if you're having some."

"We can all have a slice. But Bob, you can have but a sliver. I think he's putting on weight, but don't say it too loudly, if you agree."

Tom looked at Bob and Bob looked at Tom. "It's hard to say. He looks good." Bob gave a wag of his tail.

After a few moments, within which Mr Casper explained the importance of letting tea draw before pouring it, he got up, picked up the teapot and shuffled slightly to his left. Using the side of his shoe, he pushed Bob's bowl across the floor a fraction. He bent down and poured a little of the tea into the bowl. He returned the pot to the table and then opened the fridge, got the bottle of milk and poured a good amount into the bowl. "He doesn't like it too strong. And it's not good for him, if it is. Too much caffeine. I'm limiting him to only a couple of mild cups a week. I used to give him a bit more, but I couldn't put up with his gas. It's the lactose. Some dogs can't handle a drop. The vet suggested a type of herbal tea however he turned his nose up to it. I didn't blame him, really. It was awful."

He placed a cake tin on the table and sat down. Bob came over to his bowl and lapped up some tea.

"The police should be informed about this," Tom said.

"I don't want to do that. Not just yet."

"You're going to raise it with her, surely? And, wouldn't that lead to the other things? Other questions?" Tom asked.

"I'm not going to raise the other things. That's a little bit in the past. But I will show her the chair."

"When is she over next?"

"This evening."

"You know, I'm not convinced it's Cat," Tom said, as Mr Casper poured the tea into his own cup. "It doesn't fit. I'd like to know what she says when you show her. But surely, you must have your doubts that it *is* her. I mean, do you *really* think she would do something like that? It's sick."

"Please, Mr Greer, pour yourself a cup."

He did so and took a sip.

"Cake?" Mr Casper said.

"Thanks," Tom said.

"Cut a tiny slice off for Bob, if you would be so good. Wafer thin."

Tom did as he was asked and held it in his hand. "Where should I put it?"

"Just drop it in the bowl." He got up and did that and sat back down.

"You said that students visit you. Any recently?"

"No. Oh, one the other day. Well before this happened."

"Do you have a lot of students?"

"Not really."

"How many would you have had, say, in the last year?"

"You mean students that I have tutored here?"

"Yes."

"Four."

"And the year before?"

"Let me see." Tom waited while he watched Mr Casper have a think. "Heather, then there was Rick. Neva, she was a prodigy. Three. I had three last year."

Tom took a couple of bites of cake. "Would you be able to get me a list of those students? The seven that have been in your home, in the last two years," he said, with his mouth half full.

"I suppose I could. I would be stepping over the line, what with privacy."

"I'm not going to be telling anyone," he reassured him. "You might want to phone it through to Cathy. Or I can pick it up."

"There's not that many. I could tell you now."

"Good idea," Tom said. He got out a little notepad and pen from his pocket.

"Ready?" Mr Casper said.

"Yes. Fire away."

"Okay. Well, I'm currently seeing Arko. Arko Robinson. He's 26, I think. His thesis is due in a week. I've also been seeing Monty McBride. He's a nice fellow and I think one day will become a professor. Highly intelligent and very, very diligent. Then there are the two girls, but they were much earlier in the year. And both were one-off visits, really. Sort of just picking my brain, I think. About possible options. That would be Marissa Clark and Catriona Kelly."

"Right. Now, these are the only students who have been here, right?"

"Yes."

"You said there were three last year."

"Yes. Heather Thompson, Rick Bonnington and Neva Slough. All PhD students. Oh, actually not Rick. He was just doing his masters."

"I see. That's the lot of them?"

"I think so."

"And when you have a student, on average, how long would they stay?"

"Sometimes an hour. Sometimes less. Depends."

"On what?"

"Sometimes they read their work to me. Other times we just chat."

"Right. And of that group you just mentioned, were there ... is there anyone who stands out?"

"In what way? Monty is brilliant. Probably the best student I've ever had. Also, Neva is clever."

"No, not in that way, necessarily. I mean, like, more difficult."

"Oh, well that would be Rick."

"Why do say that?"

"He thinks he knows much more than what he does. He likes to argue. Especially about his marks, even feedback, when he gets it."

"Is that right? Where would I find Rick then?"

"On the campus, somewhere. I'm sure he's still there. He called me the other day, in fact. Asking for something."

"What?"

"Where I thought might be a good place to do his doctorate. I said he was putting the cart before the horse, as it were. That he needed to finish his masters."

"He hasn't finished?"

"No. He needs to bring his marks up. I actually had to fail him once."

"How many times did he come here?"

"Probably three times."

"Anyone else? I mean, that stands out in a negative way?"

"Arko, the current chap, is a bit slow. More lazy than slow. He says some very strange things."

"Like what?"

"He once said that Bob smelt bad. He asked me did I get the carpet cleaned regularly."

Tom looked at Bob. "That's a bit rude."

"Bob would agree with you there, I think, Mr Greer."

"Nothing else comes to mind? About any of them?"

"Not really. They're just young kids, doing their best. I can't place any of them doing it. I mean, it wouldn't be possible anyway. They can't get in."

"Do you mind if I have a look at your locks?" Tom asked. "I've seen them, but I haven't looked at them closely or recently."

"No, not at all."

Tom took a final sip of his tea and went to the front and back doors. Then the windows in the bedroom.

When he returned, Bob was standing next to Mr Casper having his head scratched. "You've only got a single lock on the back door. The front door is dead latched. That back door lock is not the best."

"Do you think I should change the locks?"

"Yes, I do. I should have suggested it earlier."

"Well, I'm not going to get to it for a week or so. I want that chair fixed first."

CHAPTER EIGHTEEN

"John. JOHN!"

Knock again Richard was told.

"Alex. I've knocked twice! I know he's in there."

"Let's go around the back."

"Wait. I hear him. He's coming to the door."

He pulled the door open. "Sorry. I'm sorry. Didn't hear you."

"We were worried, John. Why didn't you turn up? Why didn't you show? We've been waiting at the restaurant for an hour!"

"I fell asleep. What time is it?"

"It's 7. We were supposed to meet at 6," Alex said.

John ran his hands through his hair. His bare feet looked cold. His eyes shot.

"Dinner! Don't you remember?"

"What do you want me to say? WHAT?" John said.

"Nothing," Richard said. "Nothing ... at all."

"I'd invite you in. But ..."

"Whatever... It's fine. Ring next time. Just RING, would you! A simple courtesy."

Tom had forgotten to ask Mr Casper what time that evening he was expecting Cat to arrive. Now he would have to make a guess. It wasn't that he doubted him, but he needed to see for himself that she was actually visiting him.

Even his ex-boss Jason had told him never to get so involved in a case that you forget to check out your own client. Everything had checked out thus far. Stephen Roderick Casper was a well-respected member of the faculty. He had published a number of papers. He gave entertaining lectures. He was popular among the students. Someone had it in for him, though, there was no doubt about that. Cat didn't seem to be the type to have it in for anyone.

Tom figured the easiest thing to do was position himself somewhere in the street where he could still see Mr Casper's place but be of sufficient distance away that it would be unlikely he would be noticed. That way, he could just watch her arrive or leave and be done with it. If he took the earlier option and he was successful, that would be ideal, however if that didn't work, he would have to come back. He didn't fancy doing that.

Parking in that street was always a bit of a problem so, at 7 pm, he stood further up the street and on the other side in dark clothes wearing a dark cap, leaning against a fence, looking at his phone. He knew he couldn't stay too long and loiter, but if some nosy person asked, he was ready to say he was waiting for a taxi.

Of course, there was never any guarantee he would not be noticed. He had been sprung more than a few times before and once had the police called on him out of suspicion of being a peeping Tom, he was fond of telling clients. But he was very pleased with himself this time, when fifteen minutes later he watched a car pull up, then turn and park in Mr Casper's small driveway. Cat got out and entered through the front door without even a glance in his direction.

He wondered whether Mr Casper would show her the chair with the missing remote, like he said he would, and exactly how she would react.

At 9 am the next morning, curiosity had got the better of him. He called Mr Casper's mobile. "Did you show her?" he asked, straight to the point.

"Oh, yes. Later in the evening, though. I didn't want it to dominate discussion. There were far better things to talk about."

"Right. Well what did she say?"

"She couldn't understand it at all. Said it was … what was the word she used? Sinister. That's what she said. Like a bad spirit had entered the place."

"Ghosts don't exist, Mr Casper. And if they do, they don't steal bottles of booze and cut remotes off expensive recliners. And steal towels! They don't have any use for any of those things, anymore." Tom was almost relieved that she had responded in such a way. It fitted.

"Of course. That's unquestionably true. Listen, I was just heading out the door with Bob, Mr Greer. I have an early lecture."

"My apologies. I just needed to know, so that I can plan my next steps. We can safely exclude her, then, yes?"

"Oh yes."

"You're happy for me to stay on the case? You don't want to just call the police? That might be better."

"I don't want to bother them. I'm happy to pay you. Keep going. Unless it's all too much bother."

"It's no bother. But, you're sure?"

"Yes. Oh, and Cat agreed with you."

"About what?"

"That I should change the locks."

"Good."

"I have a man coming the day after tomorrow."

"Very good, Mr Casper. I'll be in touch."

"Thank you, Mr Greer. Have a lovely day. Goodbye."

It occurred to Tom when he got off the phone that he should look into at least two of the students Mr Casper had mentioned, but that the whole strange episode may very well wind down soon, once the locks had been changed.

He didn't expect it would take him long to track down Arko and this Rick fellow. The others could be ruled out. Rick in particular seemed to have a possible motive, if Mr Casper had failed him. How he would have got a key to Mr Casper's flat was another thing altogether; however, once he was inside it may have been possible for him to have found a spare key, got another one made and put it back. But many people didn't leave their spare key in plain sight. He didn't think to check if Mr Casper had one hanging somewhere obvious, like his mother did.

Or, if Rick was clever, which apparently he wasn't, a copy of the original key could be made, even while he was with Mr Casper. That took some knowhow and skill, and working quickly and quietly, but some of the process could be achieved even partially with a clay mould or even a quality photograph of the key, using a scale like a ruler.

Once, just after he had completed the investigation course, Tom had taken a good photocopy of his own key and provided it to a locksmith he knew who successfully produced a key that worked. It really depended on the key. And whether it had been marked 'Do Not Copy', although that was no guarantee it couldn't or wouldn't be. But it all seemed a bit far-fetched.

In a way, he felt it was a shame that Cat had been ruled out, given she certainly had the access and time, just no motive.

By lunchtime, with Cathy's help on the computer and the software he subscribed to, Tom knew they lived in student accommodation and who some of their friends were. He'd gathered Arko was a tad boring, as well as slow and lazy, and Rick was a big fan of himself. Rick was tall, skinny, English and had a rather large nose. That would help him stand out. He decided not to even bother with Arko and to focus his attention on Rick.

He didn't want to devote too much time to this case anymore and have to send a large bill to Mr Casper. He didn't think Mr Casper was short of a quid and felt he would pay him whatever he asked. It just didn't feel right to take money for this case, but he felt he would have to charge something and that Mr Casper would insist. The recliner may very well have been Mr Casper's most expensive purchase in the last several years, apart from the occasional holiday. Perhaps his holidays were not that expensive either, as sightseeing would not generally be on the list of things to do.

He decided he would have some fun and take photos of Rick from some distance away, and again test out his telephoto lens. So, he did that the next day when Rick was strolling through an open space near his student digs. His gait was long and gangly.

He tried to work out if Rick looked like a crook. Some evil, nasty type, who held a grudge against a blind man. A professor, no less, who in Rick's eyes, just couldn't see how brilliant he was, and had failed him. It wasn't quite what he thought as he snapped away, pretending to be focusing and lining up some shot of the architecture. But he decided there seemed to be something unlikeable about him in any event.

No need to print any photos just yet, he figured, and if and when he did, there would be no point in taking them to Mr Casper.

Tom had successfully kept himself entertained enough to get through the week, knowing Audrey had gone. But because it had just begun, it still left a hollow in his stomach and he knew there would be another hump next week and many bumps in the road ahead, waiting for her to return.

His thoughts of Audrey and what she had told him made him think of John. He was about to pick up the phone and call him, when Cathy told him that John's friend Richard was on the phone. Right. The timing seemed appropriate.

"Can we meet?" Richard asked.

They met in a café that afternoon. When he got there, he noticed that Richard was sitting with another fellow. "This is my husband, Alex," Richard said. Alex and Richard got up and shook Tom's hand. Tom sat and they all ordered coffee.

"Thanks for seeing us, Tom," Richard said, as soon as the young waitress left after taking the order.

"No problem. How is John doing?" Tom asked.

"Not so good. Has he been in contact with you?" asked Richard. "At all?"

"Not for a while. I was meaning to call him. It's on my agenda. Is he unwell?"

Richard scratched his chin. "We think so. He didn't meet up for dinner with us the other night. We had to go and check on him, but he didn't want to see us. Look, Tom. We want to be honest with you. Part of the reason we suggested he come and see you was ..." He glanced at Alex. A man of about Richard's age and very well dressed, Alex wore a nice sports coat that matched the colour of his eyes. Richard continued. "Because, for want of a better way to put it – to buy some time. To ... I don't know, give some more purpose to his life. He's ... we've both been very worried he has given up."

"Given up on finding Anna?"

"More than that," Alex said.

"How long have you been friends?" He felt these men would be very good friends for anyone to have. There was no question of their genuine concern; that they were doing their very best in difficult circumstances.

"Many years. I've known John for a very long time. We've also known each other on a business level. And so has Alex. And John's been a very good friend to us. Both he and Samantha. I think I speak for both of us."

"Is he still seeing his psychiatrist?" Tom asked. "He's been very upfront about that part. The whole trauma. Upfront, but not elaborative, more ... informative."

"We don't know. He's not telling us much anymore," Alex said.

"Hmmm," Tom said.

"We're not telling you this to add more pressure on you. We don't want you to think that, Tom. It's just that we thought you should know," Richard said.

"And also, that he's not a well man," added Alex. "You might have gathered it anyway."

"Well, yes. I figured as much. It's horrendous, given what he's had to endure. Are you saying that he is ... suicidal? Is that ..."

"We think it's a possibility," Richard said, looking at Alex, who nodded. "Look, he's continuing to cut himself off. Not only from us. Do you have *any* news to report? Anything at all? No matter how ridiculously trivial. We don't expect you to give him false hope."

"Anything that might—" Alex said.

"Keep him going, you mean?" Tom said.

They both stared at Tom, and when there was no response but a blink of their eyes, he felt it was evident that's what they were seeking.

"Does he ever even ring you?" asked Alex.

"No. I ring him. I haven't told him yet, but I've spoken with Sam. But, there's not a lot to say about that. She's ..." He thought about the right diplomatic word to describe his experience with her.

"Aloof?" Richard said.

"Was she always like that?" Tom asked.

"No. Maybe a touch. The tragedy has changed them. Changed them both. A lot. Don't you think?" Alex said, turning to his husband for confirmation.

"Immensely. She was ... has always been a little bit more easy-going, actually. Especially with Anna. Events have hardened her. We didn't know the extent to which their marriage was already under strain. She's moved on. But, he can't," Richard said. "He needs to know more. Something. Anything."

Tom realised he needed to say something meaningful, even if it would not relieve their concerns or advance the case in any way. "Sometimes no news is good news, or at least not bad. There's been no body found. No clothes. There's no one on the police's radar that they suspect. At least that I know of. There's other things that don't add up, of course. The dogs failed to pick up a scent. That's very unusual. They thought they had in the beginning, but it appeared not. One of the dogs sat down not long into the search and wouldn't move. I've heard that dog is usually the leader of the pack. Jumps at every opportunity, as soon as he's off the truck. That there's not one clue this long after the event ... I've never come across anything like it. It's like, like she vanished off the face of the Earth. He knows all of this. From what I've gathered, it appears everyone feels the same. But, there's no body, no bones. I'm hitting dead ends, just like the police have."

The coffee arrived. "Look, at this point, Tom ... it's a dreadful thing to say," Richard said, with some apparent urgency in his voice. "But it would be better if they actually *found* a body. If something turned up that pointed to … at least he would know."

"It's the *not* knowing that's killing him," Alex added.

"Have you tried to get him back into the business?" Tom asked, even though he already knew the answer.

"Yes. Many times," Richard said. "He doesn't need the money. He needs the interaction."

"He can't see that?"

"He agreed, a long time ago. But he hasn't done anything about it."

"What is his work exactly? I know the basics. What sort of software did he specialise in?"

"He's a bit of a genius. He did a lot of work in the early days of camera and imaging programs, file sorting and image manipulation. He spent some time in Japan during the digital revolution, then America. Some work for NASA even," Richard said.

"Really? I didn't know that."

"He was always a leader. A quiet leader. With action, not really words. The other guys looked up to him," Alex said. "When it happened, he'd just signed several multi-million pound contracts in the medical imagery field. Working on cutting edge medical software. Not just with surgeons but universities. It's been a huge loss, for a lot of people. He just walked away from it."

"He enjoyed being a father too?"

"Oh, for sure! He and Sam decided to have a child fairly late," Richard added. "In fact, they sometimes said they didn't think they ever would. They went back to Australia. She wanted to be near her parents for the early years of Anna's life. They were ecstatic. For this to now happen blows my mind."

"Did Sam work much?"

"No," Alex said.

"When did they come back to the UK?"

"Anna was six, I think," Richard said. "Is that right?" he asked, turning to Alex.

"That's right," Alex said.

Tom put his cup down. "Normally, when I hit dead ends – that's my term for nowhere to go, practically – I send a polite letter and a final account. But, I'm not sure I should be doing that yet."

"We understand. And again, this is not about putting the burden on to you."

"Not at all," Alex added.

"If she was an adult, I would have more to work with. I could go back a long way. Search many things that a child simply doesn't have. She was so young. She went to a great school. There's nothing in her past that sheds any light. Nine-year-old girls just don't have the footprint. I mean, it's diabolical that they didn't even find any *actual* footprints. Just bizarre," Tom said.

"Well, look. If you feel you need to wrap things up, please, we know we can't stand in your way. Just give me a call before you do that. Perhaps a couple of days in advance. Just so that I can have a chat to him," Richard said. "But if you could hang in—"

"That's if he opens the door or answers the phone," Alex said, smiling, but shaking his head.

"For certain. I will," Tom said. "You have my word on that."

CHAPTER NINETEEN

It was the day before hump day the following week when he decided to follow Rick. Mainly to get out of the office and to kill some time, it was also about getting out from behind his desk, which was also becoming an increasing priority. It took his mind off Audrey.

A good idea, Cathy had observed, except don't forget *we*, meaning Barbara and her, couldn't do *all* the paperwork. It was a reminder she gave to him often.

In truth, there wasn't that much paperwork at that time. A lot of the time was spent on the phone and serving the never-ending supply of court documents and tracking down people who were dodging them. Cathy was now as good as Tom when it came to these tasks and more patient than he was using the computer to do so.

Following people using the Tube was a hit and miss affair at the best of times. He first had to wait for Rick to emerge from the Gordon Street location of the Department of Economics then follow him to Euston Square Station. Rick had entered the building at Gordon Street with a large yellow envelope and emerged without it. A worn leather bag hung from his shoulder. When he took the line to Baker Street he didn't know where he would end up, but when he ultimately took the Jubilee line to St John's Wood Station and headed out, he was jubilant. There could only be one reason for getting off here, Tom figured, especially given Mr Casper was at the college the entire day.

When he turned into Mr Casper's street, Tom knew it was essential that he not be noticed and spook him. Carrying his camera and large lens was out of the question. So, at these times he always carried a small camera that had a quality digital zoom and which he could fit into his pocket. Even then, he needed to be very careful. He only ever used his phone camera as a back-up.

Tom watched him enter the little path in front of Mr Casper's flat and then knock on his door.

He waited.

He wondered if Rick knew Mr Casper wasn't there and this was just a way of checking, before he entered, that someone else wasn't there? But Tom knew that Mr Casper had already changed the locks, so he was hardly expecting him to slip a key in and enter. Anything seemed possible, though.

He watched him knock again. After a few seconds, Rick suddenly turned around and Tom thought he'd been seen where he was standing, diagonally across the road. Tom looked down, pretending to have stopped to look at his phone. He waited a moment before glancing again. It seemed it was more like Rick was staring at nothing in particular, considering his next move, his back to the front door.

Rick then walked away and headed back in the direction of the station. Tom followed him from about forty feet away. It was too difficult to try and snap any photographs. It was all very disappointing and pointless in a way. Why would he try and visit Mr Casper on a day he was working? Wouldn't he have known that, particularly given he had gone to Gordon Street and presumably dropped that envelope off? It was all very frustrating.

Perhaps he was even less smart than Mr Casper thought. It was so disappointing, that he thought he needed a boost. It was too early for an ale, though he felt tempted. 'I'm not a maniac when it comes to alcohol,' he said to himself, so instead, he walked around to Lord's Cricket Shop. He browsed for a while and decided to buy Mr Casper a gift; a conversation piece – a special cricket ball in a glass case just like the one he had, fitted the bill. "Thank you," he said to the young man who gift wrapped it, very pleased with his decision, though wondering if one day it too would disappear.

He didn't get back into the office until well after lunch.

Wednesday morning arrived and he found himself in the most familiar of territory, back behind his desk. An email had come in overnight from Mr Creighton's solicitors. 'Our client considers he has no alternative but to put you on notice that he considers you to have been negligent and/or in breach of your retainer for having failed to carry out proper investigations prior to the recent arson attack on his premises.' It went on to say something about their client considering options available.

He knew that Creighton had the premises insured for a considerable sum. Why would he bother with a claim against him? Perhaps it was all to record in writing that he had been to see him "with suspicions" and had been worried, but that he had lit the fire himself and was disingenuously demonstrating his innocence and covering his tracks. He wouldn't put it past Creighton; it seemed plausible the more he thought about it.

Whilst hearing from Creighton again was not surprising, he hadn't expected a phone call from Mr Casper. "Put him through," he said to Cathy.

She was always keen to hear from Mr Casper and was amazed the setbacks in the case never seemed to really get to him much. "What scum would do that to such a lovely man?" she said to Barbara, as she pressed Tom's extension, still in disbelief that someone was treating him so badly.

"Oh, good morning, Mr Greer. I sincerely hope I haven't called you at an inappropriate time?"

"No. Not at all. How are you this morning?"

"I'm well. But I'm afraid there is rather bad news."

"Really? What is it now?"

"Well, I have had something else taken."

"You have? Hang on. You changed the locks, didn't you?"

"Oh, yes. A few days ago, now."

"What's gone missing this time?"

"Well, you know how I told you I like to listen to the BBC? I went to turn the radio on in the lounge room. I couldn't, on account that it's not there. It's been taken."

"You're kidding!"

"No. I wish I was. It was rather special to me. I got the chair fixed. But now, I can't listen to the radio."

"So, hang on a minute. When did this happen?"

"I heard my program on Monday afternoon, as usual. I worked at the college yesterday. I noticed when I got home last night, late yesterday afternoon, in fact, that it was gone. So, I assume it went yesterday, sometime."

"Did you work from the department in Gordon Street?"

"No. I was in meetings at different parts of the campus all day."

"What time did you get home?"

"About 5 pm."

"Was there any sign of forced entry? Was anything else taken?"

"No. I should say no signs of any break in at all. The place seemed exactly like I left it. I did a bit of a scout around, with Bob. It's just the radio. It was quite a lovely radio, I must say. I've had it many years. It's most disappointing."

"It's time to call the police. And get an alarm system installed. This is outrageous!"

"That's what Cat said."

"Are you? Going to call the police this time?"

"I have. I called them, but they said I need to go down to the station, or file a report or something. I got the impression they were quite busy."

"Did you explain your circumstances?"

"That I'm blind, you mean?"

"It's relevant. Yes."

"No."

Tom closed his eyes and ran his hand down his face in frustration. "Look … are you going to be home this afternoon? I'd like to come over."

"Yes."

"Can I see you around 4?"

"That would be lovely."

"Right. Well, I'll see you then."

As he was leaving, Cathy asked if she could also come.

"No," he said firmly. "I'm not planning on staying long, then, I'm going home. See you tomorrow." He opened the door to leave but suddenly stopped and turned. "Oh alright, come on," he said. "Hurry up! I'm bloody over this case! It's driving me absolutely bonkers!"

"I just need to get my bag. Bye Barbara," she said, and quickly went and got it. "We'll get that other stuff done in the morning."

When they got there the first thing Tom did was inspect the locks. "They're much better," he said. "Let me have a look at the keys, please."

"It's the same key for the front and back locks," Mr Casper said, handing his set to him. Tom noticed the key had inscribed on it 'Do not Duplicate'.

"And how many keys have you got?" Tom asked.

"I have one spare key."

"And you have that hidden? In a safe place?"

"Yes."

Cathy was bending down patting Bob. "What a good boy you are, aren't you?" she said. "Yes, you are."

"Don't flatter him too much," Mr Casper said. "It goes to his head."

They went into the lounge room. Tom could see a shiny new remote back on the recliner. "I never took any notice of the radio," Tom said. "Where was it exactly?"

"It sat here, just here, on this shelf." He turned not exactly in the direction of the shelf, towards the wall.

Tom could see there was a dust mark around where it used to be. "Was it just a radio? Or also a CD player? A stereo?"

"Just a radio. My stereo is over in the corner."

"Right," Tom said, glancing at it. There were a few CDs near it. All Classical music, neatly arranged in a tall holder.

"This ... arsehole! Whoever it is! Excuse my language, Mr Casper. This ... *individual* is not interested in doing this to obtain valuables. They're doing it for sport! Some sort of sick game that's entertaining them!"

"Hmmm," Mr Casper said. "It's very interesting, isn't it?" he said.

"It is," Cathy said, in agreement, wandering the lounge room. "You have such a lovely place here. I wish I lived in a place like this. Those ornamental statues. How lovely."

"Yes. Go and run your hands up and down them, my dear. They're absolute treasures," Mr Casper said.

Cathy did that and stood there for a moment admiring them. "You wouldn't want *them* stolen," she said, unable to take her eyes off them.

"Mr Casper," Tom said, "You say 'interesting', but, look, whoever is doing this is the only one who finds it bloody interesting! I assume it's a him. What did Cat say this time, besides calling the police?" He was finding it hard to control his exasperation.

"She said I might want to consider getting a specialist in."

"A specialist? What sort of *specialist*?"

"Like a person who casts demons out. Who cleanses houses from poltergeists and the like. It was out of *her* league, she said."

"Mr Casper. For fu … Sorry … for Pete's sake!" Tom took a deep breath. He looked at Cathy with his teeth clenched. "It's not THAT! It's real, not some … bloody ghost! It's some arsehole with a grudge or something against you. Who've you pissed off? I'm sorry to be blunt. I don't mean …"

"No. That's perfectly fine, Mr Greer. Don't apologise. I understand your frustration. Besides my ex-wife, bless her soul, no one that I know of. Bob, sometimes. That Rick fellow, perhaps."

"Look, I followed him to your flat yesterday."

"You did?"

"Yes!" Tom said with even more frustration. "And he just knocked on the door and left!"

"Oh, that explains it," Mr Casper said.

"What? Explains what?"

"He turned up expecting to see me at the department. I wasn't there. He left a message saying he wanted to see me. He must have assumed I was home."

"What did he want to see you for?"

"I don't know yet. It's usually something annoyingly trivial."

Tom rubbed his eyes and shook his head. He was tired. Tired of missing things and tired of missing people and getting nowhere fast.

And, missing Audrey.

When he hadn't heard him speak for a moment, Mr Casper said, "Can I get you both a cup of tea?"

"Ah, no. No, thank you," he answered before Cathy even had a chance to respond. The last thing he wanted was another cup of tea. "I have to get back." His mind felt like jelly. "Now, can I suggest that you *actually call the police again* and demand they come out? Tell them everything! I will see what I can do. But it's best coming from you in the first instance."

"Yes. I should have a chance to do that tomorrow," he said.

"Can I just have a look out the back?" Tom said. "Before we go? Where we sat the other time."

"Of course. By all means."

Mr Casper's invariably jolly demeanour was starting to annoy him. He felt awful for thinking it.

When they got out to the rear outdoor area he noticed some things that he hadn't noticed before, including a little table and pot plant and another pot that held two umbrellas. There was also a door mat. The back section was entirely flat and paved. A fence made of square, brownish-orange bricks lined the edges. You could peer over it easily and it had gaps you could see through. Tom sighed. "I can't understand this whole situation," he said. "Do you see your neighbours much?" he asked. "I mean, do you know them?"

Cathy peered over the back fence, taking time to make her own assessment of the surrounds.

"I know that Mrs Kent lives on that side," Mr Casper said, as he put his arm out to his right. "There's a whole block of flats at the back. I wouldn't know anyone there. And on this side," he said, stepping out a little and turning to his left, "Mr Peobles lives there. Hugh."

"How well do you know him?"

"Hugh?"

"Yes."

"I wouldn't say very well. He keeps to himself. Occasionally, he says good morning when he sees me leave and he's watering his front garden. Nice enough fellow."

"I might have a chat to him. You wouldn't mind? Does he know? Have you told him?" Tom said, firing the questions off now in quick succession, his dreaded weakness when it came to patience starting to emerge in the face of all this calmness.

"No. Only Cat."

"I might knock on his door."

"Alright."

Tom took a look at the block of flats behind. "You know, it's not very private here, in your backyard. Two or three of those flats can see right down into here."

Cathy took a few steps and peered over the fence towards Mr Peobles's place.

"There's not much to see," Mr Casper said. "They can look all they want."

Cathy stepped away from the fence and walked over to the pot plant. "That's a lovely plant," she said.

Tom turned around and did his best to avoid saying what went through his mind about such an observation at this juncture: *I don't give a flaming shit about that plant!*

"By the way, Mr Casper," Cathy said. "Where do you keep your spare key?"

"Why, right under that pot plant," Mr Casper said.

Cathy tilted the pot a little and slipped out the key. "This is the new key?" she said, twirling it in her fingers.

"Yes," Mr Casper said.

"How long have you been doing that?" Tom said.

"Ever since I've been here," he replied. "A good ten years, I suppose."

"Why there?" he asked.

"Besides my sight, I have a very bad weakness. I'm sometimes frightfully forgetful. I can't tell you how many times I have walked out the door and forgotten my keys. Cat sometimes calls me an absent-minded professor."

"Has it ever occurred to you, someone may have *seen* you put it there?" Tom asked.

"Well, no. I don't suppose it has."

"Here, give me that key!" Tom said to Cathy. She handed it to him. "It's not quite as bad as leaving it under that mat, I suppose. But ... let's think about this for a moment. This could explain it! You don't want any more stuff going missing. Tonight, when it's dark, come back out here, and if you *have* to have a key outside, put it in the soil around the plant, just below the surface. Or, somewhere else that's not obvious!"

"Do it for him now," Cathy said.

"No. Someone could be looking at us. Believe me. I know! Look, just position it relative to the little trunk on this plant for the time being. I think it's better than somewhere out the front. Ideally, you should not be doing this at all."

"I will follow your advice, Mr Greer. It's no bother. No bother at all."

CHAPTER TWENTY

"What did you think of the movie?"

He knew that would be Arlie Harmonsen's first question and he had to be prepared.

The way he chose to be 'prepared', having done nothing at all about her case, was to talk to Cathy and ask for her advice. After all, he told her, it was *all* her *damn fault* for not properly 'screening' her in the first place, only to watch him struggle. Oh yes, he said, it's all very amusing to you and Barbara. "What the hell am I supposed to tell a porn star who is not getting any work?"

Cathy did give him some advice, and he eventually took it twenty minutes before Arlie arrived for her appointment, but not before he had objected. "You can't tell someone *that* these days, no matter what industry they're in!"

"I'm sorry, Tom," Cathy had said. "Barbara and I didn't realise it was going to stress you out. I should have knocked her back. Where's your sense of humour gone? But, if you tell her *that*, and she probably needs to hear it, I guarantee you won't have to worry about her again, as she won't be back to see you."

"Very well made, I must say, Arlie," he answered her first question, keeping it vague and remaining calm. He hoped she wouldn't ask him anything specific about her movie, given that he had fast-forwarded through it, stopped at the credits and relied on the blurb on the back of the case for the storyline. Though he suspected there really wasn't one.

"What about the glamour shots at the end? The stills."

Fortunately, he had seen those, as they were interspersed between the credits.

"Quite an impressive use of soft-focus filters. Also, the mist and diffusion techniques used by the director of photography, Aaron, um, I can't remember his full name ..."

"Barbaro," she said. "He's such a professional."

"Yes, him. Quite stunning," he said. "Gave it that lush, velvety look."

"Well, where do we go from here?" she asked, raising her eyebrows and flapping the longest, most perfect eyelashes he'd ever seen.

Again, she was dressed well, classy even. She obviously spent a lot of money on clothes and kept in shape. Or shapes, evidently, he thought, as he eyes tried to avoid them.

"Arlie, I *have* given it some thought, as I said I would. And I'm sorry for the delay."

"Yes," she said, enthusiastically. "I knew you would."

"I suppose I have a combination of good news and bad news," he said.

"You do? Already?"

"Sort of," he said.

"What is it?" she asked.

He could almost see the reflection of his face in her glossy lips which remained parted, pending further information.

"The thing is ..." He realised he needed to be delicate but informative. "The thing is, I did a little bit of research. I also tracked Aaron down and complimented him on his skills. He's a craftsman, and doesn't just work in the adult entertainment industry. I think you respect him."

"He's one of the best. A gentleman."

"Yes. I agree," he said, pleased how his fibs had worked and how this had all started.

"And he's a hard worker," she said, before he could go on. "It's not easy to hang around a set all day. Sometimes there's quite lengthy delays, you know. Some days, some of the men can't keep it up, if you know what I mean. Then we have to wait until the blue pill kicks in. It's a lot harder for them. And then, when you're paying sound managers and lighting people and what not, by the hour, it adds to the pressure. Aaron is a very patient man. But sometimes it's hard for him."

"I'm sure it is … I mean, can be, with those long days," he said. "Anyway, I didn't tell him I was a … that, well, you know, that you'd come to see me. I said I was *interested* in photography, right, which is actually quite true. It's a hobby of mine. So, I said I was thinking of getting into the industry as a glamour photographer. I tried to be charming, sound genuine, if you get my drift."

"Most definitely," she said.

"Anyway, in the course of, I don't know, perhaps a fifteen-minute chat, he said something very interesting."

"About me?" she asked.

"No. Not really. Just … generally. He said that the average age for the high-end professional was coming down. The ones that are getting the movie deals, that is. Like you said, *he said*, the industry is not what it used to be, because, as you know, any Joe Blow can set up a website and an online following. And mostly they're younger, looking for easy, quick money."

"*Tell* me about it," she said.

"And perhaps anywhere between 21 and 25, maybe, is what it takes now." He waited. "You mentioned you were 38." He paused again and waited to see if the penny was going to drop, or if he had completely misfired, inappropriately.

"They … those girls don't have the experience," she said.

"Yes, but somewhat ironically, perhaps that's an advantage. Perhaps, that's what the … is it the customer? The men, audience, are looking for these days, whether that's right or wrong, I don't know."

"Hmmm," she said.

"Too much experience can, it would seem, strangely work against people in that industry. At least that's what I've found out. I suppose what I'm saying is that there would be no doubt that you have huge respect within the industry. But, unlike what *you* suspect, it's not personal that you're missing out on the roles that are going to younger professionals. It makes sense, don't you think?"

"Well ..." she said. The penny was dislodged but hadn't fallen. "You said something about good and bad news."

"I think that it's mostly good news. It might be bad, depending upon what you think, I suppose. Good, in the sense that it really doesn't appear to have anything at all to do with you personally. I mean, tennis players and cricketers can't compete at the top level forever. In fact, many have retired around the 38-year-old mark. Any bat and ball sport is similar. Think of it that way."

"You really think so?" she asked.

"Well, maybe it's time, an opportunity, to do something else altogether."

"Tom," she said. "What would you do, I mean seriously, if you were me? It's been my life. I don't know if I could do anything else."

"It's a good question. I suppose, if it were me, I'd take a holiday and think about it. Take a year, if need be. Don't think too hard. I'm sure, with your talents, something will come along. But, if you're asking me, I'd ultimately pull up stumps, I think."

"Pull up stumps?"

"Oh, sorry. It's a cricket term. Like, pulling the stumps out of the ground at the end of the day's play. It's a metaphor for retiring. To be contrasted with taking your bat and going home. Another cricket analogy. That sort of means leaving because ... because you didn't get your own way and went off in a huff at the end of the game. That's not—"

"Very dignified?" she said.

"You are much better than that."

"Thank you, Tom. I feel better. I feel better for, I don't know, having seen you. I suppose it's my turn to do some thinking. Oh, I feel like a bit of a fool."

"No. You shouldn't. Not at all."

"No?"

"No. You've made a lot of people happy. You've given a lot of yourself in a very challenging industry. Maybe it's time to take the time to make yourself happy. Think of it like, sorry to mention the cricket analogy again, that you've had a good innings, but you can now walk away with your bat raised and move on to even better things, new opportunities. You're a legend! And legendary status usually only comes with retirement."

CHAPTER TWENTY-ONE

It was time to get serious and try a few things.

Tom went over to see his friend Jack who had a photographic studio and arranged for him to print several 8 x 10s of the photos he had taken of Rick. Even though Rick could not be completely ruled out, and was hardly Mr Casper's favourite student, it seemed unlikely he was their man. Nevertheless, Tom felt Rick could now be of some use, without him ever knowing. "If you can use the highest gloss paper you've got, I'd really appreciate it," he told Jack. "And don't fuss too much about them. Just print them."

Jack was quite the perfectionist and he knew Tom was similar.

"What? And I thought you said you only ever use matte?" Jack responded.

"These aren't for me. This time I want high gloss. The highest grade. When can you have them ready?"

"This afternoon."

"Brilliant. I'll be back around 4."

When Tom returned to pick them up, he used gloves to put them in a brown paper bag that had a piece of cardboard in it to keep them straight. Then he took a drive to St John's Wood and found a park a few streets away from Mr Casper's place. He had no intention of calling in on him and headed in the direction of the flats at the back of his place.

The rain that had been forecast was fortunately very light and misty. He tucked the photos under his arm as he walked with an umbrella and when he got to the top of the stairs he placed the umbrella up against the side of the wall and knocked on the door of flat 6B. No answer. He then moved to the door a bit further along, 6C, and a man answered.

"Good afternoon, sir," Tom said.

"Hello," the man replied. He was of Indian appearance and wearing a stylish turban.

"Sorry to disturb you. But I'm trying to track down a fellow. He's a cousin of mine. He's missing. I'm a little worried about him. He's been seen in this street. I have a photo. I was wondering if I could show it to you, just take the briefest moment of your time, to see if you have seen him? I'm worried about his health." Tom carefully pulled out one of the photos and handed it to the man, without waiting for a response.

He took it.

The photo was not at all a great one, certainly by Tom's standards. It did, however, show a nice profile of Rick, particularly of his large nose. It wasn't even very sharp.

The man had glasses on but took them off to look closely at the photo.

"Have you seen him around at all? Perhaps last week?" Tom asked, trying to look desperate.

"No," he said. He handed the photo back and Tom carefully placed it back in the bag.

"Well, thank you, sir. Most appreciated. Sorry to bother you. Have a nice day."

The man gave a quick smile and quietly closed the door.

Tom went downstairs and tried to see if any of the other flats had a back view out of their windows into Mr Casper's back door area. It was possible, but unlikely, he decided.

It took a minute or so to get back around to the front of Mr Casper's place and knock on Mrs Kent's door. He was pleased with himself that he'd remembered her name. It was apparent his memory exercises were working, as he recalled Mr Casper had only mentioned her name briefly during his last visit. He had no intention of using it. But she wasn't home either. He crossed over in front of Mr Casper's front yard space and knocked on the door of Mr Peobles's flat. Hugh Peobles, he thought Mr Casper had said.

From experience, Tom knew that if he kept his visits quick, most people wouldn't have time to think, and some would willingly accept the photo he put in their hand, as long as both the photo and he looked harmless. The fact that he had an umbrella and spoke politely, might perhaps signal he was harmless, genuinely walking the street seeking information. But just in case Mr Peobles didn't want to take the photo, he planned to deliberately hand it to him print side up but upside down, so that he couldn't just look at it and say, no. He would manipulate him to turn it around.

It took him a little while to answer the door and Mr Peobles took the photo, turned it the right way up and examined it.

"Nope. Never seen him," he said, still holding the photo. He was a short, pudgy man perhaps similar in age to Mr Casper.

"Right, well. That's disappointing. I'm running out of luck. I *really* need to find him. Medication, you know … He's currently off it," Tom said.

"Can't help ya, I'm afraid. You say he's been seen around here?"

"A few times, actually, yes. But it's all unconfirmed. I can't be certain; that's why I'm checking."

"Does he live somewhere near here?"

"He did," Tom said. "But he's been institutionalised a few times. In and out, if you know what I mean."

"Hang on a minute," Mr Peobles said. Tom thought he was going to say something about having seen him. That *would* be interesting. "Here," he said, handing the photo back.

As Tom carefully placed the photo back in the brown paper bag, ensuring it went in as the last of the four photos on the bottom, Mr Peobles pushed past him and Tom had to move out of his way.

He shuffled in his slippers down his front path, picked up an old watering can that was lying on the edge of the garden, returned with it back up the path and placed it to the side of his front door. "Who did you say you were, again?" Mr Peobles asked.

"I'm his cousin. Have you lived in this area long?" Tom asked.

"More than thirty-odd years," he said. "You been knockin' on doors all around here, have ya?"

"A few. I've just started. Probably a waste of time, but I'm desperate to find him. He's a sick man."

"No use callin' on the old fella next door. He's blind, he is. He ain't gonna be able to say he's seen him." He let out a small chuckle. "He ain't seen a bloody thing, not for a while, poor bastard."

"Is that right?" Tom said.

"Yeah. His dog might have, though. His dog is a man of few words, very few," he said, with a cheeky grin.

"Well, I'll try not to bother him," Tom said, looking a little more closely at him. He had a round face, bald head, and rather disgusting teeth. He might work, he figured, but it wouldn't be in the hospitality industry. Not anywhere the public might be. "You know, that blind man … that must be bloody hard. He must live with someone. They might have seen my cousin." He stared at Mr Casper's place, pretending to be thinking over a possible visit. "My cousin wanders the streets when he's off his medication."

"Na. He lives alone. He thinks he's quite clever, he does. And he is, I suppose. Have to be. Blind as a bat. Anyway, I can't help ya. Good luck."

"Thank you, sir. Thank you for your time."

When he got back to his office, he put the gloves back on and took the photos carefully out of the bag and placed them on his desk. "Beautiful," he said.

"Praising yourself again, are you?" Cathy said, arriving at his desk.

"Ah, no. Not the photos. They're crappy. The fingerprints. Just awesome. Look at that thumb print. And I've only managed to touch the edges! I'm glad I got them bordered."

"Whose are they?"

"The Indian from the flats at the back of Casper's and Hugh Peobles next door. I can't wait to give these to Stan. Stan the Man."

"Stanley? The same Stanley who works in forensics down at the Met? The one you said I might like. Who tried to come on to me when we were all at the pub a few months back?"

"Yep." Tom was still admiring the prints.

"He's a creep."

"It's not relevant, Cathy. Just at the moment." He held one of the prints up and studied it. "He does very good work. I've already called him. And he said he would go down and take some prints inside Mr Casper's flat."

"He's not coming here, is he?"

"He'll be here in five minutes."

"Right. Well, I'm leaving!"

"Fine. It's late anyway. I'll see you tomorrow."

"If he's doing you a favour, don't organise drinks with him and invite me and not tell me you've invited him. Tom, I'm telling you! Don't do that. I have a boyfriend, now."

"Cathy! I wouldn't do that!"

"Well, don't. Bye," she said.

"Cathy, just before you go." He placed the print down on his desk. "Have you seen my camera? The new one. The little one."

"You've already showed it to me, Tom. More than once. It's very nice. Can I go now?"

"No, no. I mean, I can't find it."

"No. Did you take it today?"

"Well, I thought I did."

"Sorry. Haven't seen it. See you in the morning."

Stanley was late and after he collected the photos, they went and had an ale around the corner. He mentioned to Tom that he should be able to go with one of the constables on duty in the morning and give Mr Casper's place a good dusting over. And just how was Cathy doing these days?

CHAPTER TWENTY-TWO

A few days later there was another knock on Mr Peobles's door.

This time, it wasn't Tom doing the knocking. He sat quietly in Mr Casper's kitchen, waiting. As he thought about what was about to take place next door, he smiled. He couldn't help but notice that Mr Casper hadn't spoken much at all since they had sat down. Not since he had told him. His usual half smile was absent.

"Open the door, sir, please," came the request. "Sir! Open the door!"

Hugh Peobles took his time but, eventually, there was the sound of the three locks being slowly unlatched. "Hugh Peobles?"

With one hand on the door, he said, "Yes. How can I help you?"

"I'm PC Williams and my colleague here is PC Thompson. We have a warrant to inspect your premises." They showed it to him.

"What for?"

"We have reason to believe, to suspect, you may be in possession of stolen goods."

"That's bull."

"We need to come in, sir." They took a step forward.

"Jesus!" he said, as they went past him.

Tom patted Bob and looked at Mr Casper. He then got up and peered out the window. "I think they've gone in now," he said. "You're sure he has never been inside here? Never?"

"I don't think I've ever invited him in. I mean, I suppose I could have. Invited him, that is, but he's never come in. I didn't think we had that much in common."

"I don't think you have *anything* in common with him," Tom said, his heart beating just a little bit harder.

"When did you say they got the order for the warrant?" Mr Casper asked.

"This morning. It was all kind of fast tracked – once they found there was a match on the prints on the transformer. They also got one on the shiny pot out the front too and on the doors of your cupboard. He's had your key, you know that?" Tom said.

Mr Casper nodded.

"I think they would have got the warrant even quicker, but he wasn't in their database. There was a bit of explaining to do – how they had his print. I was worried it wasn't going to be enough. But luckily—"

Mr Casper's phone rang, before Tom could finish.

"Yes," he said. "I can do that. Of course. Now? No bother at all. Alright, goodbye."

"Who was that?" Tom asked.

"It was PC Thompson. He asked if I would come over to Hugh's flat."

"Let's go!" Tom said.

"Come on, Bob. Or do you want to stay? Mr Greer can come with me."

"Mr Casper. He's waited a long time for this."

"You're right. Let's all go."

When they got over to the flat they walked straight in the open door, then down the hallway where they found Mr Peobles and the two constables in the kitchen. Mr Peobles was sitting. The constables were standing.

"Hello, Stephen," Mr Peobles said to Mr Casper.

"Good afternoon, Hugh."

"Is this your radio, Mr Casper?" asked PC Williams. "It's just here on the table."

Mr Casper went over and put his arm out, his hand shaking.

"Just a little bit to your right," PC Thompson said.

He ran his hands over the outside, caressing it. He knew exactly where the two nobs were and he turned one and it clicked. "It's not plugged in," PC Williams said. "We can plug it in."

"No, no. That's not necessary," Mr Casper said. "Not necessary."

He stepped back from the table. In the silence, everyone but Mr Peobles looked at Mr Casper's face.

"Is it yours?" Tom asked.

He nodded. "Yes. Yes, it is." His lip quivered, ever so slightly.

Bob barked one sharp bark and everyone jumped.

"I think I'd like to go now," Mr Casper said. "May we?"

"Yes, sir. That's best," PC Thompson said, moving quickly around the side of the table.

"I'll walk back with him," Tom said. "You scum bag," he added, as he turned to Mr Peobles.

"Fuck you," came the reply, but rather feebly, softly.

Tom shook his head. "Let's get out of this hole." He took Mr Casper's arm.

"I'm fine. Lead the way, Bob."

They walked slowly back to Mr Casper's flat in silence. Mr Casper's hands shook as he placed the key in the front door. Tom followed him slowly down the hallway. Mr Casper opened the cupboard, grabbed a bottle of brandy and took it to the kitchen and placed it on the table. "Brandy, Mr Greer?"

"Yes. Thank you."

"I'm sorry, Bob. I know you want some too. I'll make you a cup of tea later."

They were on their second glass when the constables knocked on Mr Casper's front door. "We won't come in, sir. We just thought we'd let you know that we've had to take the radio down to the station for a little while, before we can return it to you," PC Williams said.

"Of course, I understand," Mr Casper said. "That's no bother."

"Our colleagues have collected quite a haul. Some thirty-seven wallets, numerous stolen IDs, licences, credit cards. We've taken his computer away. There's no sign of the remote to your chair, but he admitted to accessing your place by the key you leave outside. He's a very sick man, I'm afraid."

"I asked him why he would do that to you?" PC Thompson said.

"What did he say?" Mr Casper asked.

"Just because he could. Because, he found it *amusing*. He said he wasn't interested in your possessions. He actually felt sorry for you. But a man has to amuse himself somehow. That's what the bastard said. He said he was planning on putting your radio back next week, presumably just to screw with you."

Tom stood listening. Appalled. "What an arsehole ... where is he now?"

"We've got him. Don't worry."

"We suspect that when we look at his computer, we're going to see a trove of fraud. Who knows what else?" PC Williams said.

"In a way, it's a good thing we got him when we did," PC Thompson added. "He's been a very good London pick pocket for decades, it would seem, and got away with it. Very good indeed. You don't see the likes of him as much these days. A master of his trade, and he's done quite well for himself. He accepts he's been caught, finally. He's the type who can evade you forever. Take something from you in the street, and you wouldn't even know you'd seen him. He slipped up, didn't he? Living next to you and you never suspected a thing."

"I suppose I should have got to know him a little better," Mr Casper said.

"He's not worth knowing, Mr Casper," PC Thompson said.

"Oh, and by the way, Mr Greer," PC Williams said. "He said to give this back to you. We don't need to keep it now."

The constable reached into his pocket and pulled out a little camera.

CHAPTER TWENTY-THREE

The position in which Tom would find himself in the coming days and few weeks was not totally unfamiliar. He had been there before. Sometimes, after a case was resolved, there was more than just a sense of satisfaction. There was exhilaration. It was something he could share with the client and with Cathy and Barbara. And then move on to the next case.

But that wasn't what he felt. A sadness engulfed him when he thought about Mr Casper and what had happened. Once a matter concluded, particularly one that he cared more deeply about than he ever let himself acknowledge, there was always a strong possibility that his sense of purpose would cave in and his motivation evaporate. All his other cases would suffer as a result.

Cathy suggested they take Mr Casper out for dinner. She went over to his flat and took several more pot plants to keep the little plant he had outside his back door company. She made frequent calls to him to see how he was going and reported to Tom that he was doing just fine. She asked him about Bob and how he was doing. But the dinner never came about and as the weeks went by, each passing quicker than the last, Cathy's phone calls eventually became less frequent, and his name, less mentioned.

It wasn't helping Tom's mood that he hadn't heard from Audrey since her initial messages earlier on. He knew to expect otherwise was probably irrational, even fanciful. But it didn't stop him from thinking about her and keeping an eye on the calendar.

Gone were the days he could call up Alister and suggest dinner. Or get a call from him in the morning, when his desk was full of things he wanted to toss in the bin, suggesting lunch at the Persian place down the street, or better still, some new place nearby they hadn't tried.

Seeing friends when he was feeling like this wasn't fair on them.

It wasn't that he felt sorry for himself; he felt sorry for the world, hoping that Mr Casper's view of it, and the good people who occupied it, hadn't changed.

"Darius!" he said. "I don't think you're listening to me!" Tom took another mouthful of the minted lamb. "I've told you, numerous times." He swallowed. "There's nothing to it that I can see. I haven't found out a bloody thing suggesting they have it in for you!" He wanted to add, *Would you just let me finish my lunch!* But he exercised his discretion wisely.

"Pigs. Zay are pigs," Darius said softly, looking at the other customers to make sure no one was listening. He was sweating and it looked like his apron hadn't been washed for a month. Tom looked out the window at a man smoking a hookah. He'd rather join him than sit here with the hovering and badgering Darius.

"Look. That may well be the case. There are a lot of *pigs* in the world. Listen, can I have some more bread when you're ready? But look," he picked up his napkin and wiped his lips. "They're just like you. I mean, just ... they're businessmen, Darius! In it to get the money, enough to get by. Sure, you feel like they're ripping you off. And maybe they are. I know for certain you get charged more sometimes. But London is a big place, Darius. It's dog eat dog."

"His mother is a dog."

"You mean Akram? Akram's mother?"

"She bitch."

"Again. I don't necessarily disagree, right. But, find some other family to deal with! I know a baker. He will know someone who does what you want. Shop around. I do."

Tom knew he was going to be shopping around for a new place to get his Middle Eastern food. There was no escape from Darius's constant rage. Tom well knew the quality of the food supplied from the wholesalers Darius hated so much was in fact top notch. That's why he had so many customers. The flat bread was better than anywhere else. Why that was, it didn't matter. It was worth paying a little bit more. But Darius didn't want to pay and everything had to be a bargain.

At the end of the meal, Tom went to the till. "Look, I pay your bills as soon as I finish eating, don't I? I finished my report to you nearly three weeks ago. I'm not getting the same promptness, Darius. Keep *that* in mind when you next go to pay *your* dues. Thanks for lunch." There would be no 'See you next week', until that account was paid.

Tom knew he was getting bitter and to get better, it was time to get out of town. London would invariably take the blame when no one's throat was there to strangle. It had been too long. Too long since he had been back to Norwich. Too long since he had stayed overnight with his mother.

Rosemary had been accustomed to visits on short notice from her son and more often than not during times when he wasn't feeling in the best of spirits. Ideally, a visit when he was in good form would be preferable, she couldn't help but think, but she was always glad to see him and would take what she could. She also knew not to ask anything but a vague, general question about how work was going. Anything specific, anything detailed at all, was strictly off limits and she would be shut down if she breached the golden rule not to ask too much about work.

"I've come to see you and get away from it all, Mum. Please ..." was what she had learned to expect.

And this visit was no different, for the most part. So, she would talk as much about herself as she could manage, which she didn't normally do, but could do normally, if she had to, and fill him in on her life, and what his sister Rebecca was doing, while she was at it.

Rebecca also lived in Norwich with her boyfriend. He could visit her and get it first-hand. Although, this trip he would probably just spend time with Rosemary, he anticipated.

His mother had taken up mahjong. "I'm finding it quite addictive," she said, as they sat in the kitchen. Tom was eating cake, one that she had especially baked as soon as she knew he was coming for the weekend.

"This is really good," he said, picking up his second slice. "Who do you play that with?"

"Some of the ladies from tennis."

"That's that Chinese board game, isn't it?" he asked.

"Yes."

"How many of you play?"

"Four of us. It's good with four. Sometimes, three, but I don't find that as good. One of the ladies has six different sets! Very beautiful tiles. She bought one set back from Hong Kong last month. I'd love to go there."

"You should," he said, scooping more than a mouthful of cake and placing it all in his mouth.

"One day, I might."

"I didn't tell you ... I visited Dad."

"When?" she asked.

"A few months back."

"Why did you decide to do that? After all these years."

"I don't know why, exactly. It just ... the timing seemed right. I guess I was curious to see him. To just reconnect ... not hugely. Just to see where he lived and that sort of thing."

"And what did you think?"

"I thought he seemed to be doing alright. I mean, I knew you'd told me he hadn't long retired. You talk with him much?"

"Occasionally," she said.

She boiled the kettle and made some tea. Tom got a toothpick. The lazy Saturday afternoon that he hoped would arrive did so, and he took his cup into the lounge room.

For a second, Mr Casper entered his head when he saw the old stereo in the corner with its ancient radio. Rosemary came in and sat down with her cup and saucer. Some gentle rain was falling outside. He was very glad to be in his old home, once more.

"Does that thing still work?" Tom asked, as he sat on the couch.

"What, the turntable?"

"No, the radio."

"Yes. Why do you ask? Do you want it on?"

"No. I was just curious."

"Do you think your father is enjoying his retirement?" she asked after a while.

"I think so. He likes not having to get up early."

She took a sip of her tea.

When he didn't say much more and she thought he was a little quieter than usual, she said, "We could turn the radio on, if you want."

"No, not unless you want it on. I'm happy just to chill. I might even have a doze."

"Do you want me to get you a blanket?"

"No, I'm fine. I might get another cup though." He got up. "Do you want a refill?"

"You could bring the pot in," she said.

He put the pot on the low table that sat in the middle of the room. "Pass me your cup," he said. She took a final gulp and handed it to him. He filled it and handed it back to her. "You want more sugar?" he asked. She told him no. He sat down again with his cup half full. He was trying to keep it that way.

"Has work been busy?" she asked.

"Not especially," he said. She waited for any elaboration, but it didn't come.

A minute or two went by without a word.

"Mum, have you ever been to a clairvoyant?" he asked. He had finished his tea and now sat a little bit more upright in the chair. She thought he looked like he had snapped out of some mild trance. This was the last thing she was expecting him to say.

"Once, many years ago. Before your father and I were married. Why do you ask?"

"It's … kind of work related."

"Oh," she said, and paused, partly in fear of breaking the golden rule not to ask too much about his work.

"When exactly?" he asked.

"When did I visit her?"

"Yes."

"Oh, gee. I must have been, I don't know, maybe twenty, even nineteen. I remember, actually, because I went with my girlfriend, Maureen. It was her idea. I didn't want to go."

"Well, what did she tell you?"

"Let me see. It was a very long time ago. I don't know if I can even remember. She told Maureen more than she told me. She told me that I was going to meet a man who worked with his hands."

"Dad's a baker."

"He wasn't a baker then. And who doesn't work with their hands?"

"What else did she tell you?"

She was surprised how interested he was. "Um, she was an old lady. A bit weird, really. But good. She said I would have three children – and I did – and I would enjoy good health for most of my life. I remember she said *most* and I wondered what she meant."

"Anything else? Like, that wasn't right?"

"No. Not to me. She told Maureen that she saw her living abroad. A year later she moved to Paris with a Frenchman. *That* didn't last. She said that she saw a person in Maureen's life who would always be coming and going. She got married three years later. He was a travelling salesman. We still laugh about that to this day."

"Are they still married?"

"No, they got divorced and then about two years later, they remarried, only to divorce again!"

"Huh!" Tom said and sniggered.

"I can't remember too much else, really."

She waited for him to say something more. Maybe ask another question. She dared to ask one herself, even though it was apparently *work related*. "Did you see one? A psychic? Something to do with one of your cases?"

He thought for a moment. She was expecting that to be the end of that topic of conversation. But he said, "I did, actually."

"You interviewed her? Was it a lady?"

"No. I mean, yes. It was a lady."

She knew not to jump in too quickly. "You mean, it wasn't like, you actually asked her about a case you were working on?"

"No, not specifically. Not exactly. Well, actually, I asked her one thing. But she didn't know who I was. I never told her."

"What was the thing?"

"I asked her if we would find her."

"A person you were looking for?" She knew enough about what he did, particularly from one prominent case years ago that had made the news.

"Yes."

"And what did she say?" He seemed ready to talk. Needing to talk. She felt somehow relieved that he was opening up.

He looked away. Like he had to think. "She said ... she said that, it was too hard. But then she said, and I have had a hard time getting this out of my head. She said ... she didn't know *yet*."

"Did you go and see her about yourself?"

"Not intentionally. I *had* to see her."

"Has it upset you?"

"No. Not at all," he said quite quickly.

"It's weird. They keep it general, I reckon, with what they actually tell you. You can read too much into it or whatever you want into it, really. It's very easy to do. They know that," Rosemary said.

"She told me I had a sister called Rebecca."

"Did she? *That* was a clever guess."

"She said her name began with an 'R' and was either Rebecca or Rachael."

"Hmmm, that's odd. That's *really* odd."

"What do you mean?" he asked.

"When your father and I brought Rebecca home from hospital, we had a bit of an argument over names. We had agreed on naming her Rachael, some weeks before, if she was a girl. That was his idea. But I changed my mind and told him she was going to be Rebecca."

CHAPTER TWENTY-FOUR

"I'm sorry I never got a chance to visit your mum when I was in Norwich," Tom told his friend Paddo. "I only stayed the Saturday night and came back. I didn't drop in on Rebecca either."

They were sitting in Paddo's office at the Department for Environment, Food and Rural Affairs in London. It was known as DEFRA, a ministerial department supported by a number of agencies and public bodies. One was the Exmoor National Park Authority.

"This isn't a social visit, is it?" Paddo said, seemingly knowing the answer. "In all the years we've been friends, you've never once visited me at work. You must want to pick my brain. I can feel it," he added.

"Spot on, son. It doesn't mean I don't love you."

"Leave it out, would you. My office might be bugged."

Tom laughed. "Yeah. And I might have been the bugger."

"You're not supposed to do that stuff, are you?" Paddo said.

"No. Private investigators never bug a place. They debug."

"Right. What's on your mind?"

"Official business. And so, I don't mind telling you. Did you ever hear about that young girl who went missing – vanished – in Exmoor a couple of years ago, a girl called Anna?"

"Yes. It's was news at the time. Did they ever find her? I haven't seen anything in the papers about it for ages."

"No. But I've got some work from the father. He's not that interested actually."

"What? Not that interested in finding his daughter?"

"That's not what I mean. I shouldn't have said that. I mean, he's not that interested in having me follow it up. But, he's kind of going along with some friends of his who are very interested that I be involved; they're concerned for him – for his mental health. The father has taken it very hard, as you would expect. It's a difficult one, to say the least."

"I couldn't imagine," Paddo said. "How old was she?"

"Nine."

"Horrific. Have they found anything?"

"When you say *they*, the answer is no. And me, I'm struggling. Totally. Hundreds of people were involved trying to find her."

"I felt for those parents. Like, your worst nightmare."

"Yep. Anyway, I've been back to Exmoor a few times. It just doesn't make sense. I admit, I'm certainly no expert when it comes to the environment and the outdoors and stuff. But there were no tracks. I mean, it's wet underfoot out there a lot, isn't it? Boggy."

"Yes, but it depends. In the open moors there are dry parts. It depends somewhat on the weather too, obviously. I mean, from memory, it happened somewhere around the central area. On the wooded trails. Near the river. I know for sure that's relatively dense in some parts. There would have been *some* tracks. There's quite a lot of open space too."

"There were tracks but not hers. Apparently."

"Sounds impossible."

"Do you think that if I went and had a chat to the Exmoor National Park Authority, they could help, or they might give me something more to go on?"

"In my area, I don't have a lot to do with those guys. As you know, Exmoor covers not just the moors, but woodland, farmland, lots of valleys, coastline. I mean, it's huge. They have a massive job. I think they have about eighty on staff. That's forestry teams, planners, conservation advisers, rangers, of course, and even archaeologists. In fact, I met one the other day. But, when it comes to what you're looking for, it's really a police matter. Sure, they could tell you more than me about the specifics of that environment: the wildlife, known dangers, that sort of thing. I'm sure they would be very helpful about any information within their domain. I'm not sure you would come away with any more clues, though. Didn't the search go on for, like, weeks, with volunteers?"

"Yes. I met someone who was a volunteer. She gave me a pretty detailed run down of what happened with that search. They found nothing. Not a bloody thing. They had those infrared heat-seeking devices that would show up a body. What about the wildlife, though? Would it be possible that somehow something took her?"

"Ah, no. I don't think so. Not unless some wild pony broke with thousands of years of evolution and decided to pick up a small human and swallow her whole. Or a red deer ran away with her on its back, never to be seen again. Or an otter, that hardly anyone ever sees these days anyway, jumped out of the river and dragged her under. Other than that Tom, you might want to look into the evil owls and the dreadfully big butterflies. Some of the fish can get quite big too, but they can't walk. Should I go on?"

"Please don't. You know, you can be so annoying."

"Me? You've received awards for the most annoying person in the world, twice, haven't you? Look, perhaps I'm being a little insensitive. It's very sad, what's happened but what I'm saying is, yes, it's a national park. But it's not like Australia, where there are hundreds of things that can kill you. A crocodile can take you down there and you can vanish without a trace. Or like America, where there are bears and mountain lions."

"And guns," Tom added.

"That too," Paddo said.

"This all happened in silence," Tom said. "If someone shot a gun, you'd hear it for miles."

"You could talk to the rangers. The rangers out there are brilliant. They just appointed a new one the other day. I would love to get one of those jobs," Paddo said.

"You've been here a while now. Why don't you apply?"

"I have. I missed out in the last round. But I'm hopeful when I get a few more years on me, I'll have more of a chance."

"Would make a nice change from this desk job," Tom observed, knowing he was going to get no disagreement.

"I'm ready. The money is better here. But I would trade it any day for a ranger's job."

"I'm sure you'll get it. Would it have to be Exmoor?"

"Preferably. I'd take Dartmoor and probably Yorkshire Dales as well. What have the police said?"

"They didn't give me a lot, other than the obvious. Stuff I already knew. But they don't have much. I think they're waiting for remains to show up."

"Dreadful stuff. Where's your next lead? What's next for you with this?"

"I really don't know. I don't have any leads."

"The parents?"

"They're out. I mean, they were seen with the daughter some half an hour before. He's beside himself – the father. The mother was like, 75 yards away, if that. Anyway, thanks for this. I'd suggest a beer and lunch, but I've got to keep moving."

"Me too. I have to get a report in by lunchtime tomorrow."

"Say hello to Bessy for me."

"Will do. I'll see you out, Tom. Thanks for dropping by."

CHAPTER TWENTY-FIVE

It was on Wednesday of the next week that Tom received the returned call he had been waiting for.

Cathy came in and said, "Travis is on the phone. He mentioned you'd left a number of messages and apologised for not getting back to you earlier. Also, Mr Gordon has just turned up for his appointment. What do you want me to do?"

What he wanted to do was to take Travis's call, for his motivation to continue with the case was still there, despite not having heard further from John.

He knew Audrey would want him to continue.

Anton Gordon was the North London manager of a food retailing company. This was his first appointment. He had got the ball rolling several weeks ago with Tom on the phone but had to wait for board approval to see him officially. Since then, he explained in his last call, things within the company had deteriorated further.

"Tell Gordon I'll only be a few minutes. I'll take the call."

Tom picked up the phone.

"Travis?"

"Yes."

"Thanks for calling back."

"That's alright."

"I understand you were walking in Exmoor that day when the young girl, Anna Brownlan, went missing. I run a private investigation firm and have been engaged by the family to look into the disappearance."

"Okay."

"I was wondering if I could see you or you could come into my office. I'm in the process of finding out as much as possible. Would that be okay?"

"I've already spoken to the police."

Tom was used to that reply. It was natural. He always responded to such a remark in a patient if not positive way. "Of course. And I'm very sorry to bother you about it. Particularly after such a long period. It won't take long."

"I can see you. I'm working shifts at the moment. It might not be for a week or so. I have a couple of days off at the end of next week. Where is your office?"

"I'm in Camden."

"That's alright. What about next Friday afternoon?"

"That would be fine." He pulled his diary towards him. "What about 2 pm?"

"Can we make it 3?"

"Yes. I have no appointments that afternoon," Tom said, and gave him the address. "Thank you very much."

Tom saw Anton Gordon straight after the call and promised to start work on his case soon. It turned out that the company suspected that it had a rat or a 'mole', in Anton's words, in its midst and, because the whole affair was more civil in nature than criminal, the police were hardly interested, or if they were, they weren't going to give it much priority. It wasn't outright fraud or monetary theft exactly but, according to Anton, it was costing the company a lot of money.

Some person or persons within the company were feeding a competitor information, some confidential, and the company was 'bleeding quite badly' as Anton put it. He'd been with the company just under twelve months and despite being only thirty-two, had an extensive background in senior corporate management. He used some economic jargon that Tom didn't quite understand, and again he thought of Mr Casper and how handy it would have been to have him there to explain it.

The company, or Anton more likely, had apparently already worked out some strategies for going about the whole investigation. Working in conjunction with the IT staff was one, provided he sign a confidentiality agreement, which Tom said was no problem, and conducting interviews with certain staff members in the presence of the head of HR was another. It was good paying work at his top hourly rate.

Friday of the next week rolled around and it was time for Cathy to take a long weekend. She was off to Brussels for chocolate, her boyfriend and beer.

Tom had told her about a bar he knew in the city that had well over a hundred beers on tap and over a thousand different bottles. She wasn't impressed. He told her she would have to do her own research when it came to the chocolates, as they didn't get the same attention from him the times he had been there. She wouldn't be back until Tuesday. He told her to take the days as a bonus and he would not classify them as part of her holiday entitlements. It was only fair he thought, given she had worked back often in the last year and never complained once.

Barbara felt a little overloaded by the time Travis Gustafsson fronted at reception. She was looking forward to 5 pm and intended on being out the door at 5.05, hoping Tom was not going to be upset if he would find her gone when he came out after spending two hours with Travis.

But he had no intention of spending that much time. He did, however, have a slightly different approach planned than normal for this meeting, and a manner unlike he had shown Travis on the phone.

"Please, take a seat, Travis," he said, pointing to the couch rather than the chair in front of his desk.

This was always going to be a couch interview. His idea was to start casually. He already knew what Travis looked like, yet was still surprised by his height, well over 6 foot 8 inches, and his incredibly slim build. His blond hair was a similar colour to Tom's, but longer and straighter. He could have been a male model, if he wanted, Tom figured, but he didn't quite carry himself that way.

Tom had always wanted to be taller, but not that tall. He noticed how Travis bowed his head and tilted it slightly when he was standing, even lower than when he had come into the office. Like he was used to having to duck everywhere he went.

Travis didn't know where to sit, even though there was plenty of couch space across two chairs. "Here, is okay?" he said, in a noticeable accent.

"Please, sure," Tom said and sat down. Once seated, Travis seemed to relax and he stretched his long legs way out. He wore some very trendy-looking low-cut sneakers, showing some brand Tom didn't recognise.

"Look, thanks so much for coming and seeing me," Tom said with a very big smile. "The family really appreciate it." The truth was 'the family' didn't even know about it.

"No problem," Travis said.

"It's been a very dreadful thing, as you know," Tom began. "It's approaching three years since Anna went missing."

"Yes," Travis said.

Tom noticed his eyes were light blue. He had trained himself to notice such things, then test himself with recall later. "It's been a total mystery to all involved. I understand you and your friend were on the trail that day. That you actually saw Mr and Mrs Brownlan and their young daughter."

"That's right," he replied. He had a neat stubble of whiskers under his chin which he rubbed with his finger ever so lightly. He shifted his gaze towards the bookcase and then back at Tom.

"Do you remember when, exactly?" Tom knew precisely when he had seen them, as reported to the police at the time.

"Oh, it would have been about 4 o'clock. Maybe a bit after."

"Did you both see them? I mean, you and your friend, Astrid?"

"Yes."

"You don't mind if I ask you a few questions? Nothing personal. Just about that day."

"No, not at all."

"Good. Because I have some of your personal information anyway. Like, I know you were with Astrid. And had been for a while. Anyway …"

"Yes, I was with Astrid. What do you mean, *personal information*?"

Tom was pleased that he'd picked that comment up. He took a moment to see its disruptive effect. "Well, I know you went back to Sweden a week later, after that day. That isn't really relevant, I suppose. At least, the police didn't think so, when they looked into you."

"Yes. I had to. I said I would go back with her." Even though he had an accent, he was very clear, almost careful, in the way he articulated his words.

"I know you're originally from Sweden. I know you have British citizenship."

Travis straightened up a little. He wasn't expecting this. "My British citizenship is because of my father."

"I know that," Tom said. "I know your mother's name is Lovisa."

"How do you know that?" he asked.

"It doesn't matter. And I know your father was born in Manchester. That you were born in Gothenburg. But I digress. My apologies," Tom said, dismissing himself, watching Travis sit up even straighter. Tom could tell he was thinking that this was now somewhat uncomfortable. "There's nothing pleasant about this whole investigation, I'm afraid. What were you doing on the trail that day? The walk, I mean. It was for pleasure, I assume?"

"Of course it was," Travis said.

"And what time did you actually stop walking?"

"We got stopped by the police. Before dark. They told us a girl had gone missing."

"Just a girl. Is that what they said?"

"I think so."

"Not a child?"

"Oh, maybe. Maybe they said a young girl."

"And that was the first you'd heard of it?"

"Yes."

"What did you think, when they told you that?"

"I don't think we thought anything. It sounded like it wasn't that serious. They asked us to wait for a minute and we did. Then, some rangers arrived, near dark."

"What happened then?"

"We walked back to where we had seen them. It was not convenient for us to do that, but we did."

"Right. I'm sorry to go over stuff you've told the police. I need to though, you understand."

"Yes. I understand. I don't understand why you found my personal information."

"It's part of my job. It's what I do. There's a missing child. What happened then, after you walked back?"

"Oh, well, it got dark. I remember we waited around for a long time. We were back showing the police where we thought we'd seen them. There was a valley and a river. It was hard to remember. I just showed them. But it was hard to remember as the light wasn't good then."

"You came back the next day, though?"

"Yes. We did. It was a bit easier, but still not … we could not pinpoint exactly the spot. It was also … there were also, um, lots of people there, then. Lots of shouting. Men came with dogs."

"Did you meet Mr Brownlan later?"

"Once."

"And Mrs Brownlan?"

"No. We saw her. She was very upset, crying. We never spoke."

"And this walk you were on. It was part of a longer walk?"

"Not really … maybe. I can't remember. We'd been walking in that area in the park for about three days. We had changed our minds a few times. Astrid wanted to do some other longer walk, the whole of Coleridge Walk or something."

"The Coleridge Way?"

"Yes. But me, I wanted to do little walks; different ways on different days. Not just one long walk."

"I see. And did you see any other people that day?"

"No, because we started late. Like they did. We didn't see anyone but them. That's why we remember."

"Sounds a bit odd that, apart from them, you didn't see anyone."

Travis shook his head.

"Did you say hello as you passed them?"

"I think so. I don't know."

"What do you remember about the daughter – Anna? Was she walking with them?"

"I wouldn't ... she was a young girl; that's all I remember."

"I asked you, was she walking with them?"

"Yes."

This was never meant to be about giving Travis a hard time. It was going to be about testing him though. To rule him out.

"Did you participate in the search?"

"No. I wanted to, but Astrid, she had a sore foot. Her ankle was hurting."

"So, you stayed close by?"

"We went to Porlock after that."

"For how long?"

"One night."

"After that?"

"Then we went to Bath."

"Do you mind if I ask where you stayed? You stayed overnight?"

"In Bath?"

"Yes."

"I can't remember. Close to the city."

"The police took you to the area she went missing, is that right?"

"Yes, that's right."

"Did it look like an area where someone could get lost?"

"Oh, maybe. But not for long. I mean, like there were some trees around. But, maybe just for a while."

"Was it possible that she could have fallen into the river?"

"If you go down to the edge. But, it's not very deep. Not on the edge. It's possible, I think. But ..." He shook his head.

"And then you went to Sweden?"

"Yes. Astrid had to be back for her mother's birthday. I went to visit my parents."

"Right." Tom paused and wrote some things on a pad of paper.

Travis looked at his watch. "Has anything been found?" he asked.

"No. Not that I'm aware of." Tom kept writing. After a moment he placed the pen on top of the pad and looked up. "You're living in London permanently at present?"

"Yes. I'm studying."

"What are you studying?" Tom knew the answer and where.

"Graphic design."

"Just one more question, if I may, Travis. And thank you for your time. It's very much appreciated."

"What is it?"

"What do you think happened to Anna?"

"I don't know. I really don't."

CHAPTER TWENTY-SIX

The time was soon approaching when Tom would have to talk to John again. He wasn't doing it all for free. There was that, of course. Never forget *that*, he reminded himself. This was a business. Wages needed to be paid. Outgoings, rent.

Looking into John's background brought no surprises. He was unquestionably successful in his work, before it happened. And wealthy. Everything that Richard and Alex had told him was evident.

Born to British parents who had moved to Australia, he was schooled in Sydney and had gone on to the University of New South Wales where he had completed a degree in computer science with honours by the age of twenty-three.

Samantha studied law at the same university. It was possible that is where they met. She never practised and, earlier on, had worked in a range of jobs, mostly in public relations or related fields.

He had spent substantial time in England working at very senior, highly paid levels. They had travelled frequently back to Australia and still had a house in Sydney, where Samantha now lived.

It didn't seem like he was putting up much opposition to the divorce, *or* to the division of assets she was proposing.

Anna had not been interested in sports, it would seem, but she loved the outdoors, despite her apparent lack of co-operation on the day it happened. She loved animals. Birds seemed to be her favourite. She would not hear of having a bird in a cage, though. It was the birds in their natural environments that she adored.

They had spent a little time north of Sydney in the hinterland of Byron Bay in the immediate months leading up to their last return to the UK. They had been house sitting for one of John's business friends and his property was a haven for birds.

Tom sat down with Richard and Alex, once more.

Richard spoke of those happy days, for he had travelled from England and visited them at the time. He told Tom about Anna's love of butcherbirds. That it was a clever little bird, with a varied and beautiful song. One bird used to fly into the yard almost every day. Anna could hand feed it, and she was so thrilled, so proud that she could.

Tom listened carefully.

When Richard said that sometimes you could hear the butcherbirds singing on moonlit nights, it took Tom's mind back. Back to his own trip to Australia, and camping under the stars with his friends Paddo and Bessy, listening to the sounds of the outback on a still evening.

Richard told him that where John, Samantha and Anna had stayed that time was not the outback. Not the 'lonely' outback, 'where the songs of the birds drift away into the darkness of the never ending distance.'

It was a good idea to visit John, he was told. Important.

So Tom did, the next day.

But when he got there, there was no talk of Anna's love for birds or Australia. It was not a good day, for John … and words came out of his mouth that Tom did not want to hear.

You DAMN well come here, with your reports of NOTHING! I don't care what you have to tell me about that Swedish fellow, Travis! That … you've spoken to Sam. Do you think I might have actually had enough … of nothing? That I'm OVER IT? Well, do you? ANSWER ME!

Tom waited for him to calm down. And then he asked him, did he want him to stop.

John told him he didn't care anymore. To do just do whatever he wanted … do whatever Richard told him to do. He was then asked to leave. To see himself out.

CHAPTER TWENTY-SEVEN

It took Tom a week to report to Richard what had happened. It only came about because Richard called him, one afternoon.

Richard told Tom that John had gone into a 'facility' and he had been given power of attorney. "He's okay. He's not insane. Otherwise, I couldn't have been given that responsibility. Nor would I have accepted it. It's more rehabilitation. With his money, he can afford the best. He's getting the best of care. We're all hoping he's bottomed out. That this is a turning point."

"Let's hope," Tom said. He had his doubts. A turning point. Turning where? "There was a terrible look in John's eyes that last time."

"I know the look, Tom. It's one Alex and I have seen often and had to deal with, many times. I'm sorry you had to witness it."

"There's no need to apologise. I'm just telling you what I saw."

"I know you are. And we appreciate it. Please, keep going. Only if you can, though … if you think you can."

"I'm pretty close to pulling out, Richard. I was a bit worried that I should have done it earlier. It's not that I'm not motivated. I am. To be honest, I'm just running out of avenues. I know who the police interviewed. The police working on the case are brilliant. The people who live in that area are salt of the earth. It's almost overwhelmingly difficult."

"That's why we came to you. Send the bills care of me. I will ensure they're paid."

Tom was having trouble getting Anna out of his head as he sat listening to one employee after the other in his latest case.

Anton had introduced him to Tahlia Barron from the human resources division of the food retailer that morning. They had a brief discussion about the interviewees. It was review time for the lucky ones and Tom was being asked to sit in and to 'assist' with ongoing enquiries about some 'concerning breaches of confidentiality by staff' and to offer some advice.

"This is Mr Greer from Thomas J Greer Investigations," Tahlia would say to each employee as they nervously entered the room to commence their review.

Tom's mind flitted between Anna and counting the sleeps to when Audrey would be back in the country. He'd even told Marzena about Audrey; not everything, but that he was very much hoping they could continue what they'd started. Audrey was going to be very disappointed, he feared, when he told her there had been no progress in finding Anna. And that her father had gone into a mental health unit.

"Now, why would you think that was a good idea? To hide someone's lunch!" Tahlia said. Her voice was deadly stern. Tom could see she was a formidable cross examiner. She was originally from the West Midlands and more than a little intimidating: tall, well dressed, confident, and pounced like a panther at the first sign of vulnerability.

The young lady seated opposite her and Tom was visibly shaking. She was petite, rather plain looking, not at all confident, and certainly not the culprit of some sophisticated corporate espionage.

"I didn't ..."

"Stop!" Tahlia said. "Three of your colleagues have informed management that you did." The girl went to speak again. "Tut, tut!" She held out her hand like a policewoman commanding traffic. "It's just not acceptable."

"I was going to say, Ms Barron, that I did it ... as a joke."

"Rhani, it's not *a joke* when someone can't find their lunch box and they have fifteen minutes and they have to get back on their feet and out on the floor or on the registers. Do you understand what I'm actually saying?"

"Yes, Ms Barron."

"I'm not certain you do. Mr Greer, do you have any questions?"

He smiled at her. "I think Rhani understands there's a right time and place for a joke, and she will not be doing it again."

"Oh no, I won't, Mr Greer, I won't! Never. I'm very, very sorry."

"Well, I hope not, Rhani," Tahlia added abruptly. "I think management will let it go this year. I had to do quite a bit of convincing. Have I been clear that it's also very dangerous? Some people are diabetics and it's very, very important they eat. Not be stressed!"

"Yes. I wasn't thinking." She looked at the floor.

"No, you weren't."

Tom felt like saying to Tahlia that as young Rhani was obviously remorseful, best not to kick her in the guts and knock all confidence out of her. But he refrained and kept smiling.

"Alright then. As I said before. Keep your mind on the job and your little hands off other people's things." She shuffled some papers. "Since you *say* you don't know anything about this breach of confidential information, I think it's time for you to go back now."

"Thank you, Ms Barron." She stood up, her face red with shame, and shot out the door as fast as she could.

"I don't think she's involved," Tahlia said to Tom as soon as she had left.

"I'm certain of it," Tom said. "Who've we got next?" Although, he wanted to say, 'Who are you bullying next?'

"Ronald Goodenough. He's been with us a year now, but this is his first review." She pressed a button on the desk and said unnecessarily loudly, "Next!" It reminded Tom of the headmaster's office at school, a place he had spent quite a bit of time in.

"Take a seat, Ronald," she said. "Now, let's see here." She flicked over a few pieces of paper. "Hmmm," she said. "Right," then she looked up with a huge smile. "How have you enjoyed your first year, Ron?"

"Well, it's been good, actually," he said, awfully slowly.

Tom thought this was going to take some time, or more correctly, waste some time.

"What was so good about it? What was the highlight, do you think?" she said, the smile slowly fading.

"Aw, um, well, I think, that um, aw, I can't think of one thing, like … it's been, just been all good."

"Right. You've been from the registers, then to out the back, in deliveries. How're you finding that?"

"Yep, really good."

"And Mr Donellan said you got in late once, last week. Why was that? An hour late, it says here."

"Oh, well that's because I lost me keys. I eventually found them, but I missed the bus. Well a few buses, really."

"Look, I think it's your only misdemeanour for the year. It's no huge issue. We've otherwise been quite happy with your work, Ron. How old are you now?"

"I'm twenty-two. Oh, sorry, twenty-three. I had a birthday the other day. I forgot."

"And you've heard about some of the trouble we've been having with some suspected breaches of confidentiality?" she asked.

"What?"

"You haven't heard that?"

"Sorry. What did you say?"

"Breaches of confidentiality."

He looked at Tom. Then looked back at her. "I um, don't … think so. I don't know what you—"

"Sorry, Ron. You don't think you've heard it? Or you don't know anything about it?"

He looked at Tom again, more confused. "Ah, um, I just don't know. Am I supposed to know? I don't … know exactly what you mean."

Tahlia wrote something on the paper she held. "That'll be all, Ronald. I hope this coming year is as good as last year."

"I can go now?"

"Please do," she said.

He got up and left.

"We've done a few," Tom said. "When were you thinking of lunch?"

"Let's do one more before we take a break," she said. She pressed the button. "Next!"

"Joy Farooqi, this is Mr Greer. He is assisting the company with the investigation into the suspected breaches or disclosures to our competitors of confidential trade secrets. You've had a very good year, Joy. How long have you been in accounts now?"

"Three years."

"Are you enjoying it?"

"Yes. Very much so."

"Good. Look, you'll be receiving a discretionary pay rise in the next quarter. I just want to go straight to this issue if we can. It's almost lunch and Mr Greer and I have been going all morning. You okay with that?"

"Yes."

"Has there been anyone who has caught your eye? Like, doing something they shouldn't be doing?"

"Well, Rhani took my lunch box and put it under the—"

"No, I don't mean that!" Tahlia shook for a moment, like a mini earthquake. "I mean, accessing files, other people's computers – that sort of thing – being in records, going through invoices. Being seen after hours in places they're not normally seen?"

"I saw Ronny going into a strip club last Saturday."

Tom snorted, trying not to laugh.

"You're missing my point, Joy! I mean, after hours, as in, in *this* office! I have an office. In my office, for example. Somebody snooping around. I know you work back. Have you seen anything? Security cameras are going in everywhere next week."

"No. No, I don't think so."

"Do you have a password on your computer, Joy?" Tom asked.

"Yes."

"Who else knows that password?"

"My supervisor. Bill."

"Bill Robertson," Tahlia said to Tom in a frustrated tone. "The senior accounts manager."

"And how often does the password get changed?" asked Tom.

"It's never been changed."

"We're changing all the passwords next week," Tahlia said.

"Do you have any suspicions at all about who might be doing this to the company?" Tom asked.

"No, I don't, sir."

"And you would tell Ms Barron if you did?"

"Yes, sir. I would."

"Very good," Tom said. "Well, I don't know about you, Joy, but I'm hungry. It must be all this food around here. I find it hard to focus when I have an empty stomach. I don't think you'll have to worry about your lunch box going missing again." He turned to Tahlia. "We good to excuse Joy?"

"Thank you, Joy. You may go now."

He knew he *had* to keep busy.

APERTURE OF THE EYE

CHAPTER TWENTY-EIGHT

"The police are in reception, Tom," Cathy said.

A few weeks had passed since his last visit to the company's head-quarters and he knew so much more now about food retailing. When Cathy made her announcement, he was putting the finishing touches on his report. It seemed a bit redundant as he never was able to identify the 'mole' and the situation seemed to have cooled. There had been a large number of resignations and what with the added security mea-sures and changing passwords on all computers regularly, it seemed the secretive behaviour had stopped or the person had left.

He was now glued to the screen and eager to get out a final account. "What did you say about the police?" he said, looking up from the laptop.

"I said, they're in reception. Two of them."

"What do they want?"

"They asked to see you. Asked if you were available."

"Right, well." He looked at his watch. "I'll be out in a second." He went back to finish the sentence he was typing about Tahlia, hinting, but not suggesting, she too should come under some form of review.

When he got out to the waiting room he found the police officers were both female. He had been expecting men. "Good afternoon," he said. "Did you want to see me?"

"We just need a moment of your time, Mr Greer. Do you have a moment for us?" one of the constables said, standing up. The other one was talking on her phone.

"Yes. Not a problem. Come in."

He motioned them to the two seats in front of his desk. It didn't quite seem suitable to be sitting on the couches. "Nice office," the same constable said. They both had their hats off now. She introduced herself as PC McGuire and her colleague as PC Starling who was now off her phone.

"How can I help?" he asked with a smile. PC Starling pulled out a pen and small pad.

"Do you have a client by the name of Mr Donald Creighton?" PC McGuire asked.

"I did. I don't anymore," he replied. He was a tad disappointed but not surprised that the police were here about Creighton and not Anna. But that would have been pure fantasy: '*We thought we would just let you know, we've found her safe and well.*'

"You heard his factory burnt down, did you?" she asked.

"Yes. His vacant warehouse, you mean?"

"The one at Harrow."

"Yes. He informed our office about that."

"When did he do that?" PC Starling spoke for the first time.

"I can tell you when, *exactly*, in fact. Because I was coming back from Exmoor. It was a Monday, the day it happened, I believe." He stretched forward to see his diary. "A bit over two months ago." He watched her write that down.

"And were you aware of his insurance? His policy?" PC McGuire asked.

"I may have been. It may have been something he'd told us as part of the background of our brief."

"And what was your brief, Mr Greer? What did Mr Creighton come and see you about?" McGuire asked.

"Well, hang on a minute. I don't think I'm all that comfortable with this sort of questioning. No disrespect intended, Constable, but ..." He smiled and shifted his gaze from one to the other. He felt he didn't need to elaborate, as they should know he wasn't at liberty to discuss why his client had engaged him.

"Why is that?" Starling asked, holding his gaze directly.

"I don't want you to get me wrong. I'm always happy to help the police. I mean, I work with the police all the time. But when I take on a case, I assure all my clients – I actually make a promise to them, a contractual promise – that I'll keep their information confidential. That includes what they have come to see me about. I need to honour that, no matter who it is."

"When you say *no matter who it is*, are you suggesting that Mr Creighton was not *exactly* your favourite client?" It was Starling again, and she said it with such sarcasm, he felt she thought that he thought he was being clever, when he used the word *exactly* before in describing when the firm had been told about the fire.

It dawned on him that they also knew of the fractured relationship between him and Creighton and were hoping he might spill some things.

"No, that's not what I'm saying. I'm saying ... that you should not assume that I'm deliberately avoiding giving you information about Don. It's irrelevant what I think of him. I would be telling you," he paused, because he nearly said *exactly* again, "... *precisely* the same thing no matter who you were asking me about. It's not information I can give, I'm afraid."

"Right, well, let me understand something, Mr Greer," PC McGuire said, with a slightly less friendly tone now. "You just gave us some information, not long after we sat down. But now, you are deciding not to co-operate with us? I'm not following."

They were annoying him now and he was no longer in the mood to smile. "No, no. There is a difference, and—"

"What is it, Mr Greer?"

"Let me finish, please, and I'll tell you. I *can* tell you facts that are part of the record of events. For example, you asked me if I knew the warehouse had burnt down. Right? I said yes. I also told you how I came to know and *when* I was told. That's got nothing to do with confidentiality. It's got nothing to do with why he engaged me. That's his private business."

"Fair enough, Mr Greer. We don't want to bother you with some sort of witness summons or formal court procedure."

"That's different. If it comes to that, I have to comply with the law. I have a provision in my agreement with all my clients whereby they acknowledge that the confidentiality obligation does not override any obligation to disclose information if I'm required by law to do so. So, if that's the path that's followed, then you might get what you want. But understand this: I can't break my client's contract, with you or anyone, unless I'm legally compelled to do so."

"What do you think of Mr Creighton? That's not confidential is it? It's just an opinion."

Tom realised they were working as a team, taking turns. "I could ask you the same thing," he said.

"We're the ones asking the questions. It's our job. We also are obliged *by law* to do our job."

"Again, it's irrelevant, what I think of a client. Whether I like them or dislike them is of no consequence." When he heard those words come out of his mouth, he knew that wasn't true.

"Come on, Mr Greer. We are just asking you for an opinion."

"I can tell you that unlike a lot of the private guys, I put a lot of things in writing to the clients. If a client chooses to show that correspondence to whoever, that's a matter for them. Have you asked Mr Creighton for correspondence?"

"We have the letter you sent to him, yes."

"Well then, why are you coming and seeing me?"

"We wanted to know if there was anything more to it."

"Again, that's not a question for me. Not at this point. But that's not to be taken the wrong way. That there is *something more*. That's not a conclusion you should draw by what I'm saying."

"Let me ask you this. How many arson attacks have you investigated in the past?"

"None. Not one," he said immediately.

"Why do you think that is?"

"For one, they're not that common. I might get one in the future. But, I haven't had one to date, apart from that one. I'm not investigating that arson attack, if that's what it was. I mean, it's outside my expertise. It's a job for the police and for forensics. The fire authorities."

"Missing persons are your specialty? We've heard that you've been looking into the Anna Brownlan case."

"I've had a few missing persons cases. You can see from my website the types of things I do."

There was a general consensus that the brick wall Tom had put up was not going to crumble, no matter how long they sat there and which way they put their questions. Tom was annoyed to be put in this position because of Creighton. If he was going to defend a client's personal business and put his own reputation of being helpful to the police at risk, at least it could be for someone he liked.

He suspected Creighton lit the fire himself, or got someone to do it more likely, and the whole silly engagement of him was a ruse, just like the constables obviously thought. But he couldn't say that, *exactly*.

He also realised that for the sake of his future, he had to prevent the two constables from returning to the station and saying, "Well, next time Greer wants something above and beyond the call of duty, screw him." There would be no more phoning Stanley, for example, and asking him to fast track a trivial thing like a stolen radio, even if it did belong to a blind man. He thought about trying the old, 'I'll just mention this off the record' thing but he already had a letter from the solicitor acting on behalf of the dodgy and untrustworthy Creighton. Besides, that wasn't his style. He knew who he could trust and having just met these two young ladies, he couldn't be certain they would keep his confidence. He also appreciated they were just trying to do their job.

"Thanks for seeing us, Mr Greer. It's been, what would you say, *illuminating*?" PC McGuire said.

"Very," PC Starling added, as she closed the notepad and placed it in her pocket.

Dangers everywhere, Tom thought.

As the police officers rose from their chairs, Tom said, "No problem. You know, you have a hard job. Day in day out. It's hard here too. I sympathise."

"Thanks, but we have to be going. We don't want to be wasting any more of your time."

"No. I really do. Sympathise, I mean. You wonder who *is* on your side at times. I mean, just *generally* speaking. And whether it's all a big waste of time, even when your *gut instinct* is telling you it's not and that you should keep looking, provided it's in the right places, of course. Going down the court procedure route to get documents; the lawyers love it. But it doesn't always reveal everything, of course. If someone actually wants to hide something, it's usually hidden carefully, has been my experience anyway."

He saw they had resettled a little and were not so eager to be seen to the door. He continued. "Doubts, I mean, well, I have them all the time. Whether I've been looking in the wrong places, you know, if I could be missing something. I don't know what I would have done with some of my cases without the tremendous help from the police. The Met in particular. I want you to know that. I um, I'm a big, big believer in gut instincts. If I don't like someone, and suspect they are a bit, you might say, *dodgy*, I consider the position carefully. But, that's just me. Good luck with your investigations, ladies. Keep up the good work."

Starling smiled. "I didn't take any of that down, you might have noticed," she said. "You talk quite quickly, sometimes. Care to give us any more *general* information?"

"Oh, not really. I mean, I sound like I'm a bit of a know it all. Actually, I really don't *know* anything. I'm just a person who's learning and I suppose I'm a bit careful. It pays to be careful or you can end up paying for it. I'm kind of wary due to being from the school of hard knocks, if you know what I mean. But I do trust gut instincts, as I said. Sometimes they kick you in the guts and prove you wrong. Sometimes, they're spot on. I'm sure you both know what I mean."

"I think we do, Mr Greer. Thank you again, for your time."

Of course Cathy wanted to know all about what they wanted as soon as they left.

"Creighton, for Christ sake! I wish I'd never agreed to see him in the first place," he said.

"What about him?"

"What do you think? They suspect he's burnt the bloody joint down and it's insurance fraud!"

"What did you tell them?"

"Nothing, of course."

"They were in there for a while. That's a lot of nothing to be telling them. Were you chatting them up? They seemed pretty happy when they came out. One actually laughed about something on the way down the stairs. Had a good old cackle. That's usually what happens when you chat up a girl."

"What do you mean, laughed?" Tom said.

"I heard her. So did Barbara."

"Right. Well, I wasn't trying to make them laugh. It was probably something totally unrelated."

"Did you tell them Creighton was an arsehole?"

"No! Not ... *exactly.*"

CHAPTER TWENTY-NINE

Tom threw a Christmas party for his staff the week before Christmas. Everyone was in fine spirits and both Cathy and Barbara brought along their boyfriends. Marzena made an appearance as Tom's companion for the second year in a row and Cathy still had to convince Barbara that there was indeed nothing more to the relationship than good friends. No other benefits, she said. "He's waiting for another girl to arrive back in the country!"

The restaurant had been good and also quiet, but they were now in a noisy pub on the top floor, sipping cocktails. "Who?" Barbara asked.

"Some girl called Audrey."

"Really?" she said. "Have you met her?"

"No. He only mentioned her a little while back."

"Where is she?"

"She's currently in Thailand. But she's been all over Asia, apparently."

"Travelling or work?"

"Extended holiday. She's a pre-school teacher."

"How did he meet her?"

"You know that weekend he went to Exmoor? Then."

"When is she back?"

"Middle of January."

"Maybe she'll be at next year's party!"

"Maybe indeed! He seems very keen."

"Have you seen a picture of her?"

"Barbara! You're such a nosy person," she said and laughed, touching her arm. "He said he didn't have one. But I tracked her down. Here," she said, taking out her phone. "Don't let him see me show you."

"Don't worry. He's half blind, already ... Hmmm. Very nice. She looks like a good girl."

"She does, doesn't she. Rather wholesome," Cathy said. "He doesn't think I've noticed him chatting with her online. Silly bugger. He doesn't do it a lot. I think she's only just started to reconnect with him. It's improved his mood. It's about bloody time. I wish he would just get rid of the Anna Brownlan case. I know it's tragic and all. But if she hasn't shown up by now, I mean, it's not looking good."

The two girls were standing at the bar and Tom was sitting at a table making Marzena laugh about some tale he was telling. The two boyfriends were chatting about something at the other end of the bar.

"I've been expecting him to tell me to close the file. I don't think he's done anything on it, not for ages," Barbara said.

"What *can* he do? The father, John, he's turned into a basket case. We can't get any instructions. He's never even really given any. They've come from that Richard fellow. He's a nice enough guy and he's been very good to his friend. Very loyal. But, not intentionally, I'm sure, he's put Tom under a lot of pressure. Emotional pressure ... to keep the file open." Cathy shook her head and twirled the glass of strawberry daiquiri in her hand.

"He should just render a final bill," Barbara said. "That's what he normally does when he hits dead ends."

"I know, but there's something about this case that's different. Like, I don't know sometimes if he's telling me everything."

"What do you mean?" Barbara asked.

"I don't know. It's weird. He normally tells me everything. I just get the impression there's something there that's keeping him motivated to stay on it. Like he doesn't want to give up and miss some huge breakthrough that everyone has been waiting for. I can't see it myself. I think his gut instinct from the beginning is going to turn out right."

"What was it?"

"That he's not going to be able to solve this mystery. He can't solve them all."

Tom came over and interrupted the conversation by sounding them out about dancing at a nightclub. "After a few more here, say around 11?" he said.

"Sure," Cathy said.

Barbara nodded and said she'd check with the boys.

It was close to 11.30 pm when they left, taking their good cheer down some alleyways and side streets, eventually finding their way onto a dance floor where they partied well into the early hours of the next morning. The next day, they all woke up with sore heads but still in good spirits.

On Christmas Eve, John was discharged from the rehabilitation facility. Very early on Christmas Day, he had a cocktail of his own – sleeping tablets with various drugs. Then he sat in his car in the garage attached to the house and left the motor running.

CHAPTER THIRTY

Tom was in Norwich, sitting on the floor in the lounge room with his mother and Rebecca. Rosemary was running through the rules of mahjong. They were just about to start a game, when he got the call.

Almost switched that phone off, he thought. He was so tempted. Boxing Day or *friends day*, he'd always thought. The day he caught up with friends, so best to leave it on. So, when it rang, he expected it to be a friend – Paddo perhaps. He was also in Norwich, staying with his mother. It was usually a relaxing time of the year. *Usually*.

"Hello," he said.

"Hello … Tom. It's Richard Smith. I'm … very sorry to be calling you. It's just that I felt I had to. It's about John."

For a split second Tom was slightly annoyed. Richard's name hadn't appeared when he'd taken the call, either on the screen or in his mind. He was the last person he expected to hear from that day.

"Oh, hello Richard. That's okay. What is it?"

He knew that John was getting out of the rehabilitation unit, or whatever it was, sometime before Christmas. In a way, he was thankful there had been no contact in that last week. No doubt sometime early in the new year he would be given an update. Not today. *Couldn't it wait?*

"I've some very sad news. I left it until this morning to call you." He paused and cleared his throat. "Yesterday morning, I went to John's place. I'd made arrangements with him. It was to see him … to pick him up, so that he could spend the rest of the day and the evening with us. Alex and me. Overnight. So that he wouldn't be alone. When I got there, I found him in the garage. He was in his car. He'd decided he'd had enough." His voice broke. He was trying to hold it together, but couldn't.

Tom heard those words *decided he'd had enough* just before he heard the tears.

Tom glanced at his mother and sister and went into one of the bedrooms where he slowly closed the door. "Sorry, Richard. You're saying ... that?"

"I'm saying that ... when I got there, he was already gone."

"He was ... dead?"

"Yes."

"Oh, Richard. That's ... I don't know ... oh! That's dreadful. I'm so sorry to hear that."

"I had to switch the car off. I still had his spare set of keys. They were in my hand. In my hand, Tom, to give them back to him!"

More tears than words now, and then a silence.

"Richard? Richard? Are you still there?"

"Sorry, Tom ... I can't. Hang on."

"Tom. It's Alex."

"Hello Alex. I'm so sorry to hear. That's just ... I didn't think that he would ..."

"None of us did, Tom. None of us. Not after the rehab. I thought he was a little better. That ... the whole, you know, care and help and support they gave him ... that it helped. He was still down – very down, but he wasn't ... he just didn't seem to be, you know, as bad as when he went in."

"I never saw him. I would have come and visited him," Tom said, still shocked. He could feel his heart pounding.

"No. No, you did the right thing by not. It needed to be about something else while he was there. Not what you were doing. So, that ... when he was out, he could deal with it. Equipped to deal with it, in some sort of clearer way. That was the aim. Always the aim. To equip him. To give him that ability. It failed."

"That must have been terrible for Richard. Were you with him?"

"No. I stayed at home. Cooking. I wish I'd been there. That I'd gone to the house as well. I got there straight after Richard called me."

"My God. Just awful. I'm so sorry for your loss."

"Thank you, Tom. Richard is very upset. He's very upset with the facility John was in."

"Is he?"

"Yes. Not that they didn't do their best. But he can't see that at the moment. It was just extremely poor timing. Why they let him go ... let him out on Christmas Eve." Tom could hear the pain, the frustration as Alex continued. "We wanted him to stay until *after* Christmas. To come out after New Year's Day. Even that day. Just not be by himself, even for one night, at this time of the year. Christmas was always going to be hard. It was too hard for him last year. Far too many things, and memories, to remind him. It would have been better if he stayed there. But he convinced them he was fine."

"Oh ... of course, I see what you mean. That's ..."

"We should have done more, to say, no, *that's* what's happening. He *has* to stay. I should have said something, Tom. I feel like I could have done more to keep him there, just for a few more days."

"Alex. You can't think like that. You can't blame yourself. *Must* not. None of it was your fault."

"I know, but Richard's going to be angry."

"It sounds, if I can say, that no matter what you did, in fact, no matter what *they* did, or we all did, and how much everyone tried, he was going to do what he wanted. He possibly planned it. Telling them he was ready to leave."

"Yes. I think that's right. He certainly convinced that doctor he was ready. He did a good job on him. On all of us, really. He probably used his ... I don't know how you would describe it. He possibly used that time there to think, in a way, and a sense of calmness masked what he'd already decided. He was showing us that calmness, when I think about it. I don't know. We had our doubts. It was still a horrific shock."

"What about his ex? Has Samantha been told?"

"Yes. I rang her late last night."

"And is she ... will she ...?"

"She's leaving on the 28th. She'll be here in a few days."

"Is there anything I can do? That I can assist with?"

"No, thank you, Tom. I don't think so. There's a lot to be done, though. That car, for one. We need to get rid of it. I can't even look at it."

"The car he used?"

"Yes. It's old. It was expensive. It will probably be worth a lot of money one day. Although, maybe not now. He bought it at Richard's suggestion years ago. When things were different and he was interested in things. He was looking into joining a vintage car club back then. Taking his family on Sunday drives in it. He never got the chance. Not once. How things change. How things *can* change ..."

"I will be back in London before the new year. Will there be a ... gathering?"

"Funeral?"

"Yes."

"We have to discuss it more with Sam. But most likely, a small gathering. He wasn't religious. He was an only child and his parents have long since passed. It would only be very small."

"I would like to come. If you and Richard think that's appropriate."

"Very much so. Of course. You knew him. I'll be in touch about it, when we know more. More likely me than Richard, I think."

"Thank you, Alex. I didn't say to Richard that my thoughts are with him. And you."

"Thank you, Tom. I'll pass them on. We're sorry to have ... had to ... at this time of the year. You must be with your family."

"Alex. Thank you for letting me know. And letting me know, when you did. I appreciate it."

"Goodbye, Tom. I'll call again in a few days when plans are in place."

"Goodbye, Alex."

It would be discourteous to his family if he did not share this bad news with them as it would so obviously affect him for the rest of his stay. His childhood home, in the company of loved ones, was no place for pretending otherwise, regardless of confidentiality. But he kept it simple. They didn't need to know all the details, for that would be discourteous too.

And so, he said that it was a work-related call and yes, it was bad news. Unexpected news. That he had a client and it was a very sad case about a child who had disappeared. A mystery to all that he had been engaged to help solve, but he couldn't. He had tried hard but felt that he hadn't done enough. His mother found that hard to believe. She told him he always did his best and worked so hard. Too hard. And that he shouldn't take it personally.

He told them that the father had never been the same.

That he'd … *decided he'd had enough.*

CHAPTER THIRTY-ONE

It was a small gathering. Perhaps twenty people. Instantly, when Tom saw her, he knew it was her.

She wore a black veil that extended just to the bottom of her top lip. The thin mesh was of squares angled to form diamond shapes to match the sparkling diamond earrings. Her hair was dark brown, almost black, the colour indistinguishable from the colour of the band of material that she wore on her head and that slightly covered the top of her ears. Her hair was tucked and shaped underneath it, but the locks were still shiny and visible and hung just below the earrings. Her dress was an olive green, with a paisley-like pattern in a creamy yellow. She was tall and still and stood clenching a little matching handbag.

Everyone sat down and Richard got up to speak. There was a little lectern and he placed something on it. Alex sat in the front row, next to Samantha.

"Is that his wife?" Cathy whispered.

"Yes. I think so," he said.

Richard composed himself and gave a short eulogy about a man he loved. Afterwards, the coffin was wheeled behind a curtain and it was all over. It was time to go.

He felt he needed to go over to her. She was standing silently with Alex. "Come with me," Tom said to Cathy.

"Alex. Hello," Tom said.

"Tom. Thank you so much for coming."

"You remember Cathy?"

"Yes. Hello," he said, and kissed her on the cheek.

"I'm so sorry," she said.

He nodded and smiled ever so briefly in acknowledgement. "Sam," Alex said, and turned. She turned towards them. "This is Tom. Tom Greer and Cathy."

"I'm very sorry for your loss," he said. It was always going to be dreadfully difficult.

"Thank you, Mr Greer," she said.

He didn't know what else to say to her. Maybe nothing. Maybe just saying what he said was enough. Just being there, was enough.

"Would you like to come back to the house? I mean, our place, Tom?" Alex said, after he could see there was in fact very little conversation happening.

This was indeed a tricky one. He was in two minds about that. He had given it some thought on the way there and before that, as he put his tie on that morning. But he still had not resolved what he was going to do *if* the invitation was extended. What he would say, when asked. It was going to be very intimate, and now he knew just how intimate a gathering it would be. He wished he'd mentioned it to Cathy and got her opinion.

"We're just having a small celebration of his life," Alex added.

Tom saw Samantha look away.

His life. Richard had done a very good job in describing it in the most glorious and positive way. Anna was his greatest love, his greatest joy. That is all he said about her. That, he had a stellar career in his chosen field. That, everyone admired his work. Looked up to him. He was inspirational. And he was a good man. A man who loved deeply and powerfully and with passion and dedication and spirit. That he'd been there for him, as much as he could be. *As much ... as he would let me.*

Samantha's name was absent. Not mentioned once.

"Do you have to get back?" Alex said. "To the office?"

"We ... Cathy, I don't have any appointments, do I?"

"No. We cleared them for the day."

"We would be honoured," he said.

Cathy was relieved that he had chosen what was the brave thing to do.

On the way to the house, he said to her that he was not certain he had made the right decision. "She's so cold. I don't think she will want me there."

"I think you would have regretted it later, Tom, if you didn't go back to the house. We don't have to stay long."

Tom followed Alex's BMW and pulled in to his large circular drive-way. It was a two-storey residence. There was enough room to park four cars. Inside, a lady who looked like a caterer was in the kitchen. There was a spread of sandwiches and cake, tea and coffee, and opened bottles of red and white wine.

A few other people arrived and after Alex spent some time chatting with them, he asked Tom and Cathy, "Something to drink and eat?" as the caterer approached with a silver tray.

"Oh, thank you," Tom said, taking a sandwich, as did Cathy. Alex was called away and Tom and Cathy both helped themselves to white wine from the tray of drinks the caterer offered them.

It seemed like all of the twenty or so people had come back. "Do you think most of these people were business associates? Work colleagues?" Cathy asked Tom.

"Probably. Mostly, maybe. I don't know. Some are friends, presumably."

They chatted and stood. Most people were standing in small groups. Cathy remarked that the house appeared to show signs it had been renovated somewhat, giving it a more open plan feel. It worked very well, they observed, as they continued to talk.

"I think Richard and Alex must entertain a lot. It's lovely," Cathy said, admiring the room and the décor.

Tom noticed Samantha was talking with someone while she ate a tiny sandwich. She held a glass of red wine in her other hand and had removed her veil.

"I should try and have a chat with her, I suppose," he said.

"Don't leave me alone," Cathy said.

He saw the person Samantha had been speaking with leave. "Let's go over," he said.

As they approached, Samantha turned towards them.

"Richard and Alex have a lovely house," Tom said, breaking the ice.

"It's very beautiful," Cathy said to her, looking around as if she was in awe.

"Yes. Well, I was here the day they first inspected it. I told them not to pass it up. That they would be fools if they did."

"I can see why you would say that," he said.

"How many bedrooms does it have?" Cathy asked.

"Five," she said.

"Are you staying with them?" asked Cathy, simply because she couldn't think of something better to say. It wasn't perhaps the wisest thing to ask.

"Ah, no. I'm staying in the house. *My* house."

Tom thought he had observed a slight shake of her head. But perhaps not.

"When did you arrive, Samantha?" Cathy asked.

"Last week," she said.

When an awkward silence followed, Cathy decided: no more questions.

The caterer arrived with the tray of sandwiches. Tom and Cathy both took another one.

"No, thank you," Samantha said.

After a moment, a moment when Cathy took the opportunity to look around and see if someone else might be best to approach, perhaps someone a little more friendly, like Richard, Samantha took a sip of her wine. "Mr Greer," she said, holding her glass. "I was going to send you an email."

"You were?" he replied.

"Yes, I was, but I never got to it," she said.

Tom thought that he had never heard such a dainty way of speaking, if that was the right description, for an Australian. Posh, almost. It wasn't bad, just seemed a little forced.

"But since you are here, I suppose I could mention it in person. I can confirm it in writing, if you wish."

Since I was *here*? Charming, he thought. Like, since I had perhaps *invited* myself, and that it was out of place? Maybe he just took it the wrong way. That it was just her way, and he was merely feeling uncomfortable, as it was.

"I would like you to formally cease your investigation," she said. "My understanding is you haven't."

Cathy had lost focus on the conversation, but she heard that, and looked at Tom.

"Well, no I haven't actually. But I haven't done anything active on the case for a while."

"Understood. Render your final account and wrap it up," she said. It wasn't a request, it was a directive.

"Have you spoken to Richard about that?" he asked.

"I have spoken to him, yes. About you, but not about, what I'm telling you."

Now it didn't bother him that the investigation was at an end, necessarily. It *did* bother him that it was coming from *her* and how she was saying it. He felt like reminding her that she had told him not to send her the invoices. That she hadn't wanted anything to do with it. But he needed to be careful; show respect. He looked at Cathy and she looked at him. A momentary pause to regain his composure was indeed called for.

"My apologies, Samantha. But ... didn't John appoint Richard as his attorney? His power of attorney?"

"That's finished now. My husband is dead. The power of attorney has therefore ended. The estate, and all matters pertaining to it, have devolved to me."

"I see," he said.

"We never divorced," she added, taking another sip of wine.

"Right. Well ... that's fine. You don't need to put it in writing, unless you feel it's necessary," he said.

"I just thought it was appropriate I inform you. I wasn't expecting to see you today, *here*."

There it was again. Cutting him like a knife.

Perhaps she saw his reaction. "I appreciate what you did. That ... you tried."

"I never... I feel in the end, I didn't do much."

"I know," she said. "I know you didn't do much. I've seen your bills."

If she had softened, it was but momentary.

"Did you think it was a waste of time and money?" Cathy asked.

Careful, Tom thought. *Careful*.

"No, I wouldn't say that. I wouldn't put it ... that way. It's just that, a line in one's life has to be drawn somewhere. Otherwise, well, we're here today, aren't we? You can *see* what can happen."

A man and a woman came over and gave her a kiss. They said something to her, ignoring Tom and Cathy. And Samantha turned her back, excluding them further. So they politely excused themselves after a brief conversation with Richard and Alex, and left.

On the drive back to the office, Cathy didn't hold back. "Doesn't she want to know what happened to her daughter? I nearly said that, you know. I felt like spitting in her eye!"

"I'm glad you didn't," Tom replied. "Look. People react differently to grief. It's not for us to judge. She seems to have moved on, somehow."

"She didn't seem to be too upset to me. What with her fancy veil and get up! Dressed like a ... That poor man. What he must have had to put up with."

"He's free now."

"He may be, Tom. I'm not certain you are."

CHAPTER THIRTY-TWO

In two days, Audrey would be back. Tom hadn't heard from her in almost ten days, but the calendars were marked. Every calendar in his office.

The email had come through from Samantha. All very formal and polite. He understood. That, she was a certain type of person. That she would have no problem in using words like *move on* and *closure*, even if others couldn't and there wasn't. Even though, it was her daughter. No, he understood. Absolutely, he did. He had moved on from her reaction *and* her comments.

He knew it was not that easy for some people. Some people had to do different things, special things even, to move on. He thought of what Audrey had done with the tattoo. How the simple act of being a volunteer, in a search party, had profoundly affected her. And how she was so very, very different from the woman John had married. And while Tom had moved on from Samantha, in order for him to move on from the case, he needed to do one more thing.

One thing that had been bugging him.

This time it was in the morning. Cat's very first appointment.

Nothing had changed. Still the same waiting room and still the same bare walls. He said on the phone yes, he had seen her before. He wondered whether she would recognise him.

The same glasses, the same shoes and the same hat. He didn't wear the ring, this time.

"Come down," she said.

He knew where to go. But this time, he wondered, where she would take him.

"I want to tell you, this time, not my name, if that's okay. But, something you said to me ... something I've been thinking about ever since and, what I do, for a job, I mean. Would that be okay? I mean, if I told you that?" he asked.

"Of course," she said. "I don't have rules about what people tell me."

"Thanks," he said.

"No problem."

"I'm happy to pay your full fee. But, I'm only after a short visit, like a mini consultation. It's quite specific, what I want to discuss."

"Fine by me. By all means. Don't be nervous," she added, with a smile.

"You can tell?"

"Relax. It helps if you relax, if you can. You seem excited."

"I don't know about *excited*."

"Yes, you do," she said. "You're excited about something. Something you've been looking forward to."

"Maybe you're right. What am I excited about?"

"Ha! It doesn't always work like that. Slow down. Tell me what you do. You said you wanted to tell me that, this time."

"I'm a private investigator."

"Are you just? That makes sense."

"Why?"

"It suits your personality, except for some things."

"Like?"

"Like, you take things very seriously; you *feel* a lot. But you don't show it to everyone. You have a good sense of humour, but sometimes, it gets you into a little bit of trouble. But it actually saves you most of the time. It saves you from that *other* side of you. I feel there's a constant battle going on there."

"Still no crystal ball?" he asked.

"No. Don't need one."

"Have you ever worked with the police on cases?" he asked.

"I have."

"Private investigators?"

"No. My fiancé hired one once, a while ago, though."

Wow! He proposed, he thought. *Stay clear. Don't go there. Concentrate*, he silently counselled himself. *Don't end up breaking that rule he said never to break. Change the subject quickly.*

"I've had a missing persons case. Well, I've had a lot of them. But, it's now finished for me. This particular case. She has never been found. Never."

"Go on," she said.

"Well, I thought we touched upon it, when I first saw you. It's a girl, she was, is, a child. And, you said to me that you saw a girl. That she was connected to a man. I asked if we would ever find her. And you said you didn't know. That it was hard. And, you didn't know *yet*."

"Hmmm," she said. She sat back. Took a moment. "Give me your right hand."

He knew the routine. She closed her eyes. She turned his palm up. She held it in the air, just above the table. She squeezed it, pressing her thumb right down in the middle. It almost hurt. She opened her eyes. She released the pressure, lowering her hand and his to the surface, resting her hand softly on his palm. It felt good. Sensual. He waited. She began to say something but stopped, like she had changed her mind. He waited some more and she closed her eyes again. She seemed to be trying. Her eyelids flickered. Then they opened.

"You're going to be seeing me again," she said.

"I am?"

"Yes. I see a girl. One who is coming to you. She's on her way."

He thought of her … of Audrey. But that wasn't his question. That wasn't his concern.

"Her name … I can't quite. It begins with an 'A'," she said.

Oh, what was it with the bloody names! he thought. *She's done it again!* It was so frustrating.

"But will she be found? Do you know? Please. If you could just … so that I can…"

"Move on?" she said.

He nodded, excitedly.

"I can't go *there*."

"Where. Go where? Exmoor?" he said, feeling desperate for more information, ready to give her much more.

"I just can't go there. Not now. I'm sorry. I can't."

"What do you mean?" he asked. He thought he could ask her anything, but he could see she was retreating. That she'd lost it, whatever she had before. He wanted to pull her back. "Is there anything, *anything* at all that you can see, about that girl?"

"I'm sorry." She took her hand back.

And on the way out he didn't speak. He wanted to, but he couldn't.

"You'll see me again," she said at the top of the stairs.

No, I will not, he thought. He had to move on.

CHAPTER THIRTY-THREE

The date of Audrey's return came and went, and suddenly ten days not hearing from her turned into three weeks. Then four.

When it hit the fifth week, Tom became worried. When he couldn't look at the calendars anymore after six weeks, they all went in the bin.

What a lot of nonsense Cat must have been speaking. Audrey had changed her mind about seeing him upon her return. *It was obvious!* He had to pull back. It didn't sit right with him to use his skills and track her down. And even though he knew people changed their mind all the time, and had every right to about these sort of things, it still kept him awake at night. That chance that he thought he had, was no longer a chance at all.

He reasoned that it would have been better if she'd just said, "Look, I've moved on." *It was fun meeting you, and that night we had, but …*

Cases no longer mattered as much to him. He'd clearly misjudged the whole thing, and as each day went by without as much as a text message from her, that thought was reinforced. His confidence took a hit. *What else am I missing?* But whenever he asked that question to himself, he also felt that it all didn't seem to make sense. He was tired of things not making sense.

When Cathy saw his growing despair, she tried searching for Audrey online. "I can't find her," Cathy said. It was late in the afternoon. A Monday. Another week. "I don't think she lives in London anymore. I've looked."

"Cathy. Leave it alone, will you just? I'm sorry I told you. I really am! It's none of your business."

When he saw her face, he knew he'd gone too far this time. She stormed out of his office abruptly.

He picked the phone up. "Can you please come back in?" he said.

She slammed the phone down in response but appeared at his door. "Why don't you just fuck off!" she said. "You're such a cranky bastard. Here I am, trying to help you! Trying to be *so* bloody patient. And that's how you treat me. Like, you're sorry I care. Well, sorry I annoy you! Do you ever consider people might care? Or are you so self-absorbed?"

He'd never seen her quite so upset. He was shocked he had driven her to that point.

"I'm sorry," he said.

"Things better improve, Tom. Or, quite frankly, I'm out of here."

"Is that right? Sorry is not good enough?"

"No, it's not!" She stormed out for a second time, grabbed her bag and flew out the door.

It went on like that for another two weeks, more or less. She was professional in her dealings with him, but hardly sympathetic. He gave up hope of ever seeing Audrey again.

Cathy still felt sorry for him, despite the difficulty of being around him. She thought it was so cruel of Audrey to just cut him off. So without Tom's knowledge, she kept trying to track her down. Eventually, she discovered she was back in London from a random post related to the pre-school. But she couldn't bring herself to tell him.

It was time for everyone to just move on.

Things had slowed over the winter as they usually did and then picked up as the weather improved. She could see he had picked up.

The cases were boring, but profitable and plentiful.

He threw himself into the work and started working very long hours.

She knew he was trying to get his sense of humour back. She even took to laughing at his attempts, although more often than not, she was just trying to make him feel better.

Maybe some new case would come along and spur him into obsessional activity, as they occasionally did.

And then, one sunny afternoon, absolutely everything changed.

Cathy glanced up from her laptop as she sat at reception. A woman had stopped at the entrance to catch her breath. She stood on the other side of the glass door after ascending the stairs. The door was new, with a heavy timber frame and clear glass. The man was coming tomorrow to etch the firm's name in the middle. Cathy could see the woman was puffing and after another deep breath, she slowly pushed the door open.

The woman approached the counter and gathered herself. Cathy was alone at the desk as Barbara was on her afternoon tea break. "Can I help you?"

"I was wondering if I could see Tom Greer?" she said. "I'm sorry. I don't have an appointment." She flipped the strap of her bag more securely around her shoulder and glanced around to see if anyone was seated and waiting.

Cathy thought she could see perspiration on her brow. Could it be ... surely not? Her hair was different. Her face, fuller.

She looked at the large appointment book in front of her. It was 4.30 pm. His last appointment had gone in at 3.30 and he was still in there.

"I'm not sure," Cathy said. She was about to ask what her name was, just to confirm that her first thought couldn't be right, but just at that moment Tom's door flew open and he came out talking loudly. Like he was on a roll, as he often was.

"As I said," he was saying to the client. "If you leave me with that, I should be able to get back to you, most likely in a week. Certainly not more than ..."

He stopped dead mid-sentence when he saw the woman at the desk. "Um ... as I say, err ... would that, that ... um ... be okay?" he said to the man who was with him, while still looking at the woman standing at reception, then refocusing back on the man.

"Yes. That's perfectly satisfactory. Thank you, Tom. Good day to you now," the man said. They shook hands. He turned to Cathy.

"Goodbye, thank you," he added with a wide smile as he left the office. He seemed delighted with his consultation.

Cathy didn't respond, because she didn't hear it. She was staring at Tom who seemed unable to speak. She looked at the woman a little more carefully and realised why she might have stopped at the top of the stairs.

"Audrey!" he said. He shook his head in utter disbelief.

"Hello, Tom," she said. "I'm sorry I didn't call."

"What … what are you doing? I mean, what are you doing *here*?"

She didn't respond.

"Do you want … to come in?" He was utterly stunned. Cathy had never seen him look so surprised.

"Are you busy?" Audrey said.

"No, no! Come in, please, please," he said, without taking his eyes off her.

Cathy watched the door of his office close and she looked at the clock on the wall. *Damn*, she had arranged to meet Connor, her new boyfriend, just after 5 for drinks with friends.

The phone rang and she switched it straight to message mode. It was right that 'we' can't take your call right now, as your call was in fact *not* 'important to us.' Not right at this moment, anyway.

"Connor," she said, leaving a message on his phone. "I might be a little late for drinks this afternoon. I have to stay back at work. I should be there by 5.30. Just thought I'd let you know, babe. Sorry. Bye … See you there."

If she didn't get there until 6 it was going to be worth it, as there was no way she was going to miss this.

The first thing Tom said was, "I'm so glad to see you," and then he said, "I can't believe that you're here …" followed almost instantaneously by, "Let's get out of here! Let's find a café."

He didn't sit down. He didn't offer her a seat. And she didn't disagree with his suggestion – not that she was given any opportunity. "You okay with that?" he asked and grabbed his coat. He hardly took much notice of anything else, including Cathy, when he walked past her on his way out. He almost raced out like he was going to a fire. "I'll see you tomorrow. Close up when you want. Switch the phone off. Have an early one."

Barking the orders, he didn't stop to hear Cathy say, "But ... but," as she watched him open the door for Audrey and start walking down the stairs.

When Cathy got to the pub before Connor, she realised it wasn't worth explaining it to him and he wouldn't have been interested, anyway.

When they got out on the street Tom said, "There's a place just up here." He was walking fast, pounding the pavement with a spring in his step that he'd thought had vanished for eternity.

"Tom," she said. "I can't walk that fast."

"Oh, sorry," he said, slowing his pace. "It's just up here," and he picked up his pace again.

When they got there, he opened the door for her and they walked into the tiny café. There was only one other couple inside. "Good," he said. It was quiet and intimate and it wasn't his office.

Audrey was relieved they had stopped walking.

He pulled a chair out for her. Then she sat down and then, he sat down opposite her. She placed her bag on the floor. It was a largish brown bag that he didn't notice she had carried over her shoulder. But he wasn't noticing much at all, still in a state of amazement.

He had already taken his coat off and put it on a rack behind him. "How was your trip?" he said. This wasn't the question he wanted to ask. He wanted to say a lot more. But any anger that he harboured because she hadn't responded to him since her return, had vanished on that short walk. He was just happy to be looking at her face. He couldn't take his eyes off her face.

"Good," she said.

He waited for something more. "Just good, yeah?" he said, trying to slow himself down and process her being in front of him.

"Yes. It was good."

"How have you been?" he asked.

"I'm good now. I still feel a bit, not so good at times," she said. "How have *you* been?"

"I've been good. Busy. Good."

The waitress came over and said, "Hello, Tom. The usual for you?"

He was so focused on Audrey, he hadn't seen her approach. "What's that? Oh, yes. Thank you, Jo."

"And for you?" she asked.

"What are you having?" Audrey asked. Tom didn't care what he was ordering. He had to think what Jo meant by 'the usual'.

"What am I having again, Jo?" he said.

"A large Americano."

"Oh, that's right," he said.

"That's fine," Audrey said. "Two."

"Do you want something to eat?" Tom asked.

"Are you having something?"

"I could eat," he said. "I'll have a slice of banana cake."

"Two," Audrey said.

"Okay," Jo said. "Anything else?"

"No," they both said simultaneously.

The café had seating for about fifteen people. "You come here often?" Audrey asked, looking around to see just the other couple.

"Probably once a week," he said. "Why didn't you respond to my messages?"

He'd said it now. He spent his whole life asking questions. But he'd come to the conclusion this was one question he would never be able to ask her. He felt he needed to get it out of the way, as abrupt as it may have been, before she left again.

She scratched the top of her brow. Then she rubbed her eye. "Sorry," she said. "I think I have something in my eye." She rubbed it again. "Is there a bathroom?" she asked.

"Just behind you. That door," he said.

She got up. "Excuse me," she said. He noticed for the first time that she had left her long dark coat on. He should have offered to hang it up with his own on the coat rack. The café was always warm.

When she returned, he said, "There's a coat rack over there, if you want to take your coat off," he said. "I can hang it up for you, if you like."

"I'm okay," she said.

"So, did you get my messages?" he said. "I mean, I haven't sent any for a while. I figured you … that … you didn't want to hear from me."

"It wasn't that, Tom. I never meant to ignore them. I just didn't …"

He waited before saying, "Didn't what?" when she didn't finish.

"Didn't know what to do."

"You didn't know? Didn't know that … that, it was just … I'm not following. Sorry. Is that wrong? I mean … to say that actually, I don't understand." Some frustration had resurfaced now.

She waited to see if he was going to say something more. But he didn't. "No. You're not wrong, Tom. *I am.*"

"I know we only had *that* weekend together. But you did say that we would see each other again. So, I just naturally thought … I'd hear from you … you messaged me from Thailand. What happened? It's had me beat."

"I'm pregnant, Tom."

Very rarely stuck for words, she waited again for him to say something. Anything.

"I thought you might have noticed," she said, seeing his lip drop and his eyes widen. "When I walked into your office."

"Pregnant?" He paused, with his mouth open. "You mean … with a baby?"

"Yes. That's what pregnant means, Tom. *With a baby.*"

"That's why? Is *that* why … you didn't return my calls? You've met someone else? You could have told me *that*. It … I would understand. It makes sense, now. I'm not that—"

"No, Tom. I haven't met *someone* else. There *is* no one … *else.*"

"What?"

"There's no one else, Tom. The baby … it's *our* baby."

"That's …WHAT? It … it's, what? That's … impossible. I mean …"

She smiled, but then shook her head. "Think, Tom. It's not … impossible."

"But, hang on."

At that moment, Jo brought over the two coffees and the banana cake.

"Thank you," Audrey said to her.

He was in some sort of daze now and hadn't even noticed the cups had been placed in front of them.

Audrey calmly peeled off the top of the sugar sachet and poured the contents into her cup and proceeded to stir. "Are you upset?" she said, placing the spoon down on the saucer without meeting his eye.

"Upset? No, no," he said. "But … how do you know?"

"How do I know I'm pregnant?" She stood up and opened her coat. "*That's* how I know," she said, before sitting back down and sipping her coffee.

"Oh my God!" he said. "I mean, Audrey! How do you know it's mine? Ours?"

"Simple really. I haven't been with a man for more than four years, except you."

"But didn't we …"

"Be careful? Yes, we were," she said. "Not careful enough, obviously. I was very worried that you were going to be upset."

"I'm not upset. I'm just … surprised!"

"I'm sorry to give you this shock. Look, Tom, I was shocked as well. Then I got quite sick. My parents – I told you how they worry. You can imagine. I couldn't work when I got back, I was so sick."

"When you mean sick, like, what sort? Do you mean morning sickness?"

"Yes. I had that pretty bad. Very bad, really. But then my blood pressure went up. My heart started to race. It was a bit much. I thought about contacting you, but then I couldn't get out of bed, I was so sick. My feet were swollen. I didn't want you to see me like that. I didn't feel I was capable of much at all. I moved out to my parents for a while. So, it just became a bit overwhelming for me." She sighed heavily and felt as if the blood was draining from her face. That she had now done what she had set out to do.

"Audrey. You should have contacted me. I would *never* be upset with you. Never. I ... wow! Oh, God! I need more than a cup of coffee ... a baby!" He sat back in the chair and ran his hands through his hair. "I just can't believe it!"

She saw a smile take over his whole face. She burst into tears and started to sob uncontrollably.

"Don't cry. Why are you crying? Please, Audrey! Please don't cry." He leant towards her.

She picked her bag up and took a tissue out. "Sorry," she said.

"No, Audrey, please. I don't want you to cry. We can do this. We can. We can! You and me!"

That made her cry even more.

Tom held out his hand and took hers. It was shaking. "Hey, hey ... please," he said, slowly and softly as he looked into her eyes. "It's okay. It really is." He waited until she calmed. "You're here now. Oh my God ... with me. That's all that matters. That's *all* that matters."

CHAPTER THIRTY-FOUR

Cathy enrolled in an investigation course not only because it seemed a natural progression, but because there was going to come a time soon, Tom said, where she would need to run the practice. It wouldn't just be a matter of him taking two weeks off here and there, like he was now about to arrange. It may very well ultimately involve six months or more. Possibly even a year or two. Audrey may want to go back to work at some stage and he would be the full-time caregiver. He would join a father's group or, if there wasn't one nearby, the mother's group. He would take her to the park.

For it was going to be a *her*. And everything was going to be about her. Not the client. Not some deadline.

Audrey had known that it was going to be a girl for some time. And when she asked him if he wanted to know the sex of the baby, he had said, "Yes, of course I do. That way we can turn my spare room into her room. We can do it now. Both of us."

When Audrey expressed concern about his business, he told her Cathy was excited about having him out of the office for two weeks when he took some time off, that it was all taken care of, and she need not worry about anything at all.

Audrey moved into Tom's place three weeks after the double shock of her appearance and the good news. Yes, it was good news, really, it was, and he told everyone – everyone that was close to him, once he had fully digested it. Whether he completely understood all the implications was another thing, yet to him, it didn't matter. It became like some magic shot in the arm, a fresh beginning, a new burst of energy and optimism. He felt invigorated. That it had liberated from somewhere deep within him a wonderful feeling that was actually there all along, just waiting to be felt.

He'd changed – with her. And the day he called his father to tell him he was to become a grandfather, he recalled the advice he had given him. "I'm so happy, Dad. I can't wait for you to meet her."

He held Audrey tight in bed at night, wrapping himself around her warm and sensual and beautiful body. A body that he was in awe of, that was growing another life, part of both of them. He told her that he had totally convinced himself that he would never get the chance to ever hold her again, not after that first time. That he was destined somehow only to have that first time, and no other. To have lost a person, or thought you had, and to suffer the grief, only to find her again, that was truly something. That was unlike anything he had ever felt before.

What happened about that? About Anna, and that poor man? You haven't mentioned it. I still think of her, a lot. A lot.

And he told her.

"What are you going to do when your mother wants to come and stay, Tom?"

Audrey watched him fill a box in the spare room. He lifted a pile of photography books off the floor and put them inside.

"What are *we* going to do, you mean," he said.

"Yes."

"She will either have to sleep on a mattress in the lounge room or check into a hotel. Simple as that."

"Or, we could get a bigger place. One with three bedrooms. That's all we'll ever need."

"What do you mean, that's all we will ever need?" he asked, as he strapped some wrapping tape over the top of the box.

She had been to the doctor the previous week and he remained concerned about her blood pressure.

"I'm not sure I'll be able to have more children, Tom. I'm not certain my doctor thinks I should."

"Why?"

He pushed the box across the floor to the wall with the bottom of his foot, ready for the next one.

"I've had blood pressure problems all my life."

"Sounds like your doctor is a bit conservative. Don't lots of people with blood pressure issues still have babies? I'm sure my blood pressure has gone through the roof at times." He found another book and started skimming through it. "This can go," he said.

"I suppose," she said, leaning against the door.

"Besides, it's expensive to move. This will be fine. I'm not buying a new house just for one-off visits. I think the solution is we visit her, more than she visits us. She has plenty of room."

"It's going to be difficult for your mum to sleep on the floor. I would be concerned about that at her age."

"Your parents are older."

"Yes, but they're not likely to come to London very much or want to stay overnight."

He picked up the box and moved it to the hallway where another three sat stacked on top of one another. "Well, let's just cross those bridges when we get to them. What do you say we start thinking about colours for this room? Don't say pink. I'm not a fan of the reds. What about apricot or yellow? Yellow, a pale yellow."

He was almost done with the packing and clearing of the room of his smaller things. The desk and the bookcase and the bed were next. "I think we need to start painting next week. And have it done by the time I have to go back," he said.

Paddo came and took the bed. Cathy's boyfriend, Connor and his strapping rugby union playing friend came and got the desk and the bookcase and took them both on the back of a utility to the office for Cathy. The carpet was steam cleaned after everything was out of the way and the drop sheets went down.

Neither apricot nor yellow met with her consent and a very light shade of pink with dark red accent ended up on his roller and brush.

On his hands and knees cutting in and complaining at night about sore muscles, it took three days, with Audrey's help with the roller, to do a proper job. That left just a little bit of time to shop for a cot and a changing table and a host of other things, some of which he had heard of, but others he thought she was just making up.

A freshly painted empty room provided a bare canvas for his photographic eye. He convinced Audrey to allow him to set up some lights he still had from his university days and to pose for some 'artistic shots' as he put it. Luckily for him, her interest in photography allowed him to indulge his desire to test his skills. "Just to see if I still have it," he said.

He put the drop sheets back in the room, now splattered with colour, and made her drape them over her naked body. He changed cameras and took colour digitals and black and white negatives. He suggested she wear her hair out first, and then, after a few dozen photos, up. Then she went out of the room and returned wearing an almost see-through night gown. He positioned the lights so that they silhouetted the gown and he stepped back so he could admire the beauty of her shape in the subtle atmosphere. He took shots with the flash and without, and he fiddled with his lenses. They both posed for silly shots and laughed, and talked about where the cot would go, and what should hang from the ceiling, and what wall hangings should go where.

They stayed in the room for a long time, kissing.

"You know, I wanted to do this that night we stood under the stars on the top of Dunkery Beacon," he said. "But that ranger was there."

"He walked down the hill and left us there, Tom. I thought you might have taken your chance then."

"I should have. You don't get many opportunities to kiss a beautiful girl for the first time there. Not in that location."

"Hey, maybe we could get those stars you stick on the ceiling that shine in the dark. You could kiss me under them and pretend it's on the hill," she said.

"Yeah. That's a great idea! Then, when she gets older, we could tell her we met under the stars. Just like these ones, and show her."

"Yes. But we actually met the night before."

"We can skip that bit. We keep saying *her*," he said. "What are we going to name her?"

She ran her hand through his hair before stepping back slightly. She looked down, running her hand slowly over the front of her gown and felt her belly. "I've given it some thought. Have you?" she said.

"Actually, no. Not until just now."

"I think we should get an envelope," she said, "and both write down a name and put the names in it. Then, we should keep our choices secret until she is born. Then open the envelope."

"What if we choose different names? That's likely, isn't it?" he replied.

"Then, we toss a coin. Heads, you get your choice, tales, I get mine. What do you say?"

"I say, that sounds good! Really damn good. Fair, even," he said. "Easy! And, when I think about it, no possibility of an argument."

"Let's do it soon. I think this girl is going to be here soon. I think she's going to be early."

CHAPTER THIRTY-FIVE

She made her way into the kitchen and opened the fridge in the dark.

He hadn't heard her get up.

She lifted out the jug of water and placed it on the counter.

She switched the light on.

When she reached up to take a glass from the shelf, she felt the pain again. She winced and sat down on a chair. The clock on the microwave oven said 3.12 am.

She touched her belly. It felt tender. She stood up again and felt something trickle down her leg. Her first thought was that her water had broken. When she looked down, she saw blood. And more drops on the floor in front of the fridge.

"Tom," she whispered, sitting on the edge of the bed. "Tom," she said again, her hand placed gently on his chest. When he failed to open his eyes, she switched the bedside lamp on.

He opened his eyes. It was a dream that he had been in, and they were holding hands, walking. But now, she was sitting there, looking right at him.

"Audrey ... What ... what ... are you doing? What time is it?"

"It's just after 3, Tom."

"Is it, oh ..." The brightness of the light hurt his eyes and he put his hand up to shield them as they adjusted to it. "What's wrong?"

"I don't know," she said. "Something's wrong."

"What do you mean?" he said, as he sat up a little.

"I'm bleeding."

"Bleeding?"

She pulled the top sheet away and examined the bottom sheet. "See," she said.

"Oh my God!" he said and sat bolt upright. "Are you … are you alright? I mean, are you in pain?"

"My belly is sore."

"Like you're in labour? Is that what's happening?" he asked, panic more in his voice than hers.

"I don't know. I don't think so. But we should go to the hospital."

He jumped out of bed. "Yes! Yes! Shit! Shit! Of course," he said, pulling his trousers on.

Audrey got out of her night gown and noticed more blood. She tried to calm herself, but her heart was now racing.

"Tom, can you please pass me that … oh," and she bent over quickly in pain.

"Audrey!" he said, rushing to her aid. "What do you want me to do? Should … should I call an ambulance?"

"I don't think … oh!" and she lowered her knees to the floor, her arm stretched out, her hand gripping the edge of the bed. "Get me that, that … those clothes, over there."

"What clothes? Where, where?" he said.

"Just clothes, Tom! On the rack! And get a bag and put more in, quickly. Get a bag, fill it!"

"Am I calling an ambulance? I should call an ambulance!"

"I don't think I can wait for an ambulance; let's … just get in the car!"

As he threw some clothes in a bag, she forced herself up and into the clothes she had asked for.

"Leave everything! Just leave everything else," he said. "Let's go. Let's go! Can you walk? Are you able to walk?"

"I have to. Take my arm."

They were out of the house and in the car in a matter of seconds. She held her belly like she was holding everything in, but it hurt. "Where am I going? What hospital? Christ! I should have … thought about this," he said, his hand shaking as he put the key in the ignition.

After she told him where it was and how to get there, he said, "Yes. Yes, I know where it is!" He backed out onto the road and sped off.

Soon he was hurtling down Chalk Farm Road and when he saw a red light and no one around, he went straight through it. He got further onto the A502 and told her they should be there soon. In peak hour the trip would have taken much longer. "Hang on, please. Just hang on! I'll have you there in minutes …"

He pulled straight into A and E, stopped the car, got out and raced around and opened her door. "Just … can you get up? I can go in and get help. What do you want me … what do you want to do? Can you walk? Let me help you …"

"It's all right. Get the bag. Just get the bag, Tom. Don't forget the bag."

He lifted the bag out of the back seat, put it over his shoulder and helped her slowly step out of the car and walk the few steps into the hospital.

"Please, nurse, can you help us?" Tom said, seeing a lady in a uniform behind a counter. The nurse rushed over.

"I need to sit! Please, I need to sit!" Then, the wailing began. It started slowly, only for it to rise and rise and permeate every corner of the room.

The nurse may have said labour and asked where it was hurting, but he couldn't be sure. He held her, trying desperately to comfort her.

"I'm BLEEDING!" she shouted, and started to fall. He held her up, and then his foot slipped and he almost fell with her on top of him, but the nurse grabbed her arm and supported her. "I can't …" Audrey said, and her head went back. "I CAN'T," and she passed out in their arms.

Another nurse paged a doctor, then grabbed the phone at the counter. "Patient at the front! Urgent. We need a bed asap. Porters. Now! Just … stay where you are! Don't move her…" she said to Tom.

"Hang in there, please, Audrey, please …" Tom said. "What's happening, what's happening to her?" He was now sitting on the floor holding her on top of him, the nurse supporting her left side.

"Stay calm, sir, help is coming."

Two men in white gowns arrived with a bed on wheels. It was immediately lowered to the floor. "Lie her back gently, please sir!" one said before taking over from Tom. A third man appeared and within an instant they had raised her. Tom softly stroked her red cheeks and before he could speak, they whisked her through a set of doors and away.

He stood there, and watched, as the doors swung back and closed.

"Am I able to ... go in there?" he said, still staring at the doors. "I don't want her to be ..."

"There's a place over here, sir," the nurse said calmly. "Come with me and sit down." He stood for a moment, unable to take his eyes off those doors.

"Your bag, sir," she said. He turned and saw it lying there on the floor. He picked it up and went with her.

She led him to some seats. "Let's sit you down here for a while. Would you like some water?"

"No."

"Where did you travel from?"

"Camden. The car ... it's parked, out there. It's ... it would be in the way. I need to move it ... Where did they take her? Will she be alright?"

"Yes. You will need to move the car. Luckily, we have a very quiet night. She will be seeing a doctor immediately. The doctors will look after her. We will get to the paperwork shortly. Best just to be calm, take your time for a minute. We need some details. Tell me what happened. Just, very briefly. Are you her partner?"

"Yes, yes. My name is Tom Greer. Audrey, her name is Audrey Brockwell. We were in bed. I was ... she must have gotten up. She said she was in pain and bleeding."

"Did you see the blood, Mr Greer?"

"Yes."

"How much blood, and where?"

"Some, a lot. I don't know. In the bed, on the floor."

"Anything else, before or after that?"

"Her blood pressure has been an issue. That's all I know."

"Who is her doctor?"

"I can't remember. My head's spinning. She did tell me, but … oh, God, I'm sorry. I couldn't even remember which hospital!"

"Okay. Look, you've done well Mr Greer. Thank you. I'm going to be speaking with the doctors now. Normally, it's something you could have done direct, but our priority was to move her quickly so that they could attend upon her."

"I should move the car!"

"Yes. It's important it be done. Are you able to do that now?"

"Yes. Should I come back here?"

"Yes. Come back here. Can you do that?"

"Yes. Thank you."

He took the bag without thinking to suggest it be left for her, moved the car to a parking spot, and returned to the same seat. The nurse was not there and more people were now in the waiting area. He waited and he looked at his watch. It said 4.38 am. He thought about making a phone call. Should he call his mother or Audrey's mother? He decided neither, that it was too early, and that he didn't know what to tell them.

He looked to see if he could see the nurse he had spoken to, at the counter. Different nurses now. Then, she came back. There are some admission details, they needed some information he was told. "This way," she said again.

After that, she led him to another area. "This may be more comfortable," she said.

"Where is she?" he asked. "Can you tell me what's happening? How she is?"

"Wait here, Mr Greer. Someone will be with you as soon as possible," she said.

He sat and he waited. No windows. No natural light. He was alone. It seemed to be some sort of private waiting room. A coffee machine was nearby. Maybe he should get one, he thought, as he got up and stared blankly at it. But he decided to wait. Then, when another half an hour passed and he felt light headed, he got one, and sipped it slowly, thinking, worrying. Still no news.

Again, he thought about making a call. He could call Cathy and tell her where he was, at the very least. That he would not be coming into the office today. That's all he needed to say. Better still, send a message. Then he wouldn't have to explain. If he did it now, that would be out of the way. He took his phone out and sent it off. *Not coming in today. Will call later.*

And when more time passed, he grew cranky and even more worried.

But just as he was about to get up and try to find someone to ask, a man with grey hair appeared in the doorway. He wore a surgical gown and stopped outside to chat with a passing nurse.

A doctor, Tom thought and hoped he was there to see him and tell him what was going on. The doctor met Tom's eyes. "Mr Greer?" he said as he walked towards him.

"Yes." Tom stood up.

"I'm sorry that you've had to wait so long."

"Yes. What is … what's been happening? Is Audrey alright?"

"Mr Greer, please, let's sit."

"Alright."

"My name is Dr Brinley Sloane. I'm one of the specialist surgeons here in the maternity unit. A little while ago, your partner, Audrey, gave birth to a little girl."

"Oh my God!" he said. "Is she … okay?"

"Your daughter is doing very well, in the circumstances," he said, slowly. "She is premature and we'll have to keep her with us here for a little while. That's normal, when babies are a little early. But she's fine. She will have to stay with us for a bit? You understand?"

"Yes. Yes, of course," he said, with a welcome sense of relief. He exhaled, and shook his head.

"We believe Audrey was about near on eight months," the doctor said.

"Yes," Tom said. "I think that's right."

"Okay. Now, you'll be able to see the baby a bit later. But I wanted to speak with you about Audrey."

"Yes. Is she okay?"

"Now, what's happened is something called placental abruption. It's when the placenta comes away – detaches – from the wall of the uterus. This can cause bleeding. And pain. Once that happens, and we don't always know why it happens, it's not possible to reattach the placenta."

"Is she okay, Doctor?"

The doctor blinked and closed his eyes for a moment, before opening them again.

"At the moment, she's in surgery. I will explain. It was crucial that we performed an emergency caesarean section, because when this happens – what happened to Audrey –which was quite severe, it can cut off the baby's supply of oxygen and nutrients. It was a very good thing you brought Audrey in immediately. It's quite possible that an ambulance may not have got there and back in time. Now, at the moment, she has lost quite a lot of blood. Sometimes that happens and the body can go into shock. So, while immediate delivery was the safest and best option, in fact the only real option, we've had trouble stemming the bleeding. That can occur in severe cases, as can the necessity to perform an emergency hysterectomy. We've had to take that step." He paused. "Sorry, I know this is quite a bit for you to take in."

"You mean, she's in surgery now?"

"Yes. We had difficulty controlling the blood loss and she is undergoing an emergency hysterectomy."

Tom didn't speak. Couldn't speak.

"The removal of the uterus," the doctor added for clarity, when he saw him struggling to digest it all.

"Will she be okay, after that?"

"We are very much hoping so, Mr Greer. She's in very good care. The finest, I wish to assure you of that. But we won't be able to report much more for just a little while."

"Should I be worried? I mean … you're saying … is it … very serious, her condition?"

"What she has experienced *can* be very serious. I can't say, you know, that it's not. Her body has suffered a great deal in a very, very quick space of time."

"Why? Why would this happen?" Tom asked.

"We don't really know a hundred per cent for certain why it ever happens. Sometimes there are triggers, like a sudden trauma. A car accident, for example. Where some sort of impact has occurred. There has been nothing of that sort, I assume?"

"No."

"Substance abuse is another."

"No! Not at all. No, Audrey is very health conscious. Very much so."

"Hypertension is thought to play a role."

"She's had high blood pressure. Is that what caused it?"

"Listen, whatever the cause, the focus now is on Audrey's current position and her recovery. That's the important thing at this point. We're getting her files transferred from her doctor, but we have some information already."

"Yes, that's ... When, when will you be able to tell me more?"

"Later today. But it will be a few hours more, at least. You've been in since very early this morning. Like me. If you haven't had breakfast, that might be something you could do, to help the time to pass. I'm sorry, I can't tell you much more at this stage. You have a beautiful little girl," he said with a smile.

"I have two. Two beautiful girls."

"Indeed," he said as he stood up. "It will be one of my colleagues later today. I'm next in tomorrow. Congratulations."

"Thank you, Doctor. Thank you so much."

CHAPTER THIRTY-SIX

"Mr Brockwell?"

"Yes, who's calling?"

"Tom. Tom Greer."

"Who?"

"Tom Greer. From London. Audrey's ... partner."

"Oh, oh, yes, yes."

"How are you, sir?"

"Well, thank you."

"Listen. I apologise for calling at this early hour. I'm actually at the hospital. Audrey, she has ... I'm calling to let you know that, well, she gave birth to a little girl this morning! You and Mrs Brockwell have a granddaughter! Congratulations."

Normally, when he said congratulations, there wasn't this pit of worry in his stomach. He didn't want to inflict the same thing upon them. Before he called, he could almost hear Audrey's voice saying, *You know how much they worry.*

"Did she! Oh, that's marvellous! But, she ... didn't she have a month to go?"

"Yes, she always said she thought it would be early!"

"Doris. Doris! Pick up the other phone! Hang on a minute, son." It was the first time he had called him that.

"Hello," she said.

"Congratulations, Mrs Brockwell. You have a granddaughter."

"Oh, my dear!"

"Yes. It's … very good news. It was this morning. Early."

"I never expected it *this* early. Is everything alright?"

No time for a pregnant pause. But it was inevitable. "Actually … there is one bit of a complication. I've just seen the doctor. It's … that she had some bleeding, this morning. It was all a bit of a rush to get in here, actually. But we made it. The doctor said the baby is fine. Premature, but in good—"

"A complication?" Audrey's mother said.

"Yes. With the bleeding. Something to do with the placenta coming away," he said.

"An abruption!" she said. "That can be very serious. Life threatening!"

"What, dear? What did you say?" Mr Brockwell asked, on the other phone. She didn't answer him.

"What did the doctors say?" Mrs Brockwell snapped at Tom.

"They said, well, I only saw one. Dr Sloane. He said she had lost a lot of blood and that *can* happen and … they had trouble stopping the loss. It—"

"WHAT!" she said. He was losing control of the flow of information. "When was this? What else did they say? What else?"

"As I say, I've only *just* found out. You are the first I called. She's in surgery. They are performing urgent surgery."

"Surgery?" Mr Brockwell said.

"Yes. For a hysterectomy."

"WHAT!" she said again. "We need to get there! Where are you? What hospital?"

In between the cacophony of words exchanged by Mr and Mrs Brockwell, he gave them the name of the hospital and where it was and how to get there.

"Tom! Errol, get off the phone! Now! We need to get on the road!"

"I didn't want to worry you, it's—"

"Tom, pray for her! She has a very weak heart." Mrs Brockwell started to cry.

"What do you mean?" Tom said. "A weak heart?" His stomach plummeted at those words.

"She's had it for years! Oh, God! Didn't she tell you?"

"Tell me? WHAT?"

"Cardiomyopathy!"

"What is it? What is that?"

"I don't have time to explain it, I'm sorry, Tom! Weakness of the heart muscle. She must have told you!"

"No! I mean, she didn't tell me. But the doctor would have known!"

"Tom! I'm hanging up now! We'll see you at the hospital in how many hours it takes us to get there. Goodbye!" Bang went the phone.

A nurse had been watching him and waiting. She approached him soon after he got off the phone. "Mr Greer, would you like to come and see your baby?"

He had been contemplating ringing his mother next, but his head was now spinning again and he was staring at his phone. He looked up from it and saw the smiling face of the nurse. "Yes," he said.

"It's this way," she said. She walked him through a door and into another ward. She took him to the end of the corridor and stopped in front of a glass panel. "She's the good looking one to the right, just at the back there," she said, waiting until he spotted her.

"That ... that baby over there?" he said. He touched the glass with his finger, pointing to the one he thought she meant.

"That's her. We've already had an enquiry from a modelling agency, wanting first option on her," she said with a huge smile. "I'll leave you to admire her from a distance for now," she said and wandered away.

Tears welled in his eyes. How beautiful she looked. But, why was she so red? And all the wires and the tubes; they looked so scary. Her tiny arms looked like tiny little sticks. The incubator was so strange looking. He had never seen anything like it. And so many babies. How could they tell them apart? He looked at the tiny little band around her wrist. The words said 'Brockwell' and something else he couldn't make out. What were they going to call her? He'd forgotten all about that envelope. He stood there and looked at the other three babies. Were they all born today? This morning? Wow, it was just amazing! All just amazing.

The nurse returned. "The tube?" he said.

"Yep. Looks pretty weird, doesn't it. A bit freaky. Don't worry about that or those wires either. They might look scary but they're just there to keep an eye on her. So we know everything that's happening, that's all. She's just fine."

"Why is she so red?"

"Because she's normal. Normal for her age, that is," the nurse said and smiled as she continued on her way.

He knew now was the right time to tell his mother. That he had seen her granddaughter and, she was healthy, and, she was beautiful.

Back in the waiting area, he needed to hear her voice. He told her everything, from the moment Audrey had woken up to what Audrey's mother had said. And that he hadn't had a chance to really think about it, what Audrey's mother had said, but it worried him greatly.

Rosemary told him not to worry about that for now. And try not to worry at all, as impossible as that was. "I will beat her parents there," she said. "I can be by your side. Soon. This afternoon. Leaving now. Ring me, keep me informed. I love you."

"I love you too …"

Tom went outside and took in some light. The day was overcast and he remembered that rain had been forecast for the afternoon. If he'd had a cigar, he would have inhaled it, not for pleasure and the celebration of the birth, but from stress. But he didn't smoke. He shifted the car again and realised he hadn't eaten since the night before. He decided to head back to the hospital cafeteria and get something … anything, and to eat there. He thought he should ring Cathy too.

He ordered a toasted sandwich and a black coffee and looked at a newspaper as he ate.

Nothing was sinking in. Merely words on a page that could have said anything but meant nothing.

The caffeine failed to work and he felt sick. It was a feeling that he couldn't shake. He got some chewing gum and he decided to walk, to see if it would relieve the nausea and to keep moving. He needed to go outside again and see and breathe. To look at the sky. The sun, it needed to shine. But the same grey clouds.

Why couldn't it just be easier? Why was this all so hard? He thought again of their little girl. He started to cry when he thought of Audrey lying on some operating table. A nurse passed him, perhaps on her way to start her shift, and saw him crying as he walked. She gave a nod and a sympathetic look. They must be used to that, he thought. *Pull it together, you fool. Stop it!*

He called Cathy, if for nothing more now than to remove himself from his thoughts, as he continued to walk. "I just thought I would let you know. I don't want to talk long. I'm outside, just wandering aimlessly. I'm so worried, Cathy. I'm going to go back in soon ... No, you stay, if you can. I'm okay. No point in being here at the moment. We just have to wait. I'll call you later ... Yes. Yes. I know. I know ... Thanks, Cathy. Thanks."

He looked at his watch. 10 am. How that time had flown. How time had flown altogether, since she had come into the office that day.

How he loved her so much. But he hadn't told her that. *Or have I?* He was confused now. He thought hard about it, as he walked and walked. He needed to fix that. To tell her, with all of his heart. It was urgent. He needed to hold her hand. To be with her.

He was now a mess. He sat in the gutter outside the hospital. *A weak heart? How could she say that?* She *had the best heart*, he blubbered to himself. *It was strong and caring.*

His nose started to run. He wiped his face on his sleeve. He thought of the tattoo under her heart. For a person, a child, she had never met. But she still cared. *That's how good her heart was! Don't say my Audrey has a weak heart. Don't ever say that about her!*

The tears continued to pour out as he got up. He shook his head. *Stop worrying! Go in. Go back in. Get another paper. Sit. Wait. Everything will be alright. Everything.*

CHAPTER THIRTY-SEVEN

Tom sat in the same chair in the waiting room. He pulled open the pages of the newspaper and started to read. After perusing several short reports, he turned the page and looked over the top of the paper at the nurses who had come into his view. There were three nurses, then four, standing in the hallway. The latest arrival said something to the others. He returned his attention to the paper. One broke from the group and approached him. "Excuse me, Mr Greer," she said. "I'm sorry to disturb you. Would you mind coming with me? It's just a short walk."

"Alright," he said. He got up, folded the paper and put it under his arm.

The nurse showed him to another small room that he hadn't been in before. She closed the door as she left.

A lady was seated at the round table, her arms resting on it with her hands clenched together.

She was staring at her hands but rose when he came into the room. "Hello, Mr Greer," she said. "Please, sit down. I'm Dr Shana Banistock."

They both sat.

He placed the paper on the table. "Is there an update?" he asked.

She didn't answer, but held his gaze.

He blinked and looked at her and knew.

Knew, that she had heard the question.

"What is it, doctor? What is Audrey's update? Is she out of surgery now?"

"I'm sorry," she said.

Her eyes; he could see something in them that he wasn't expecting, that he didn't want to see. *Sorry? You're … sorry? For what?*

Although he hadn't spoken, she knew what he was silently asking.

Silence ensued. For it was her eyes, once more, that answered.

He shook his head. "No, you … you can't say *that* …" he said, aloud this time. "SORRY!"

It was not possible for him to believe what he felt couldn't be true.

"She, Mr Greer … Audrey went into … she had a massive cardiac arrest in theatre. We tried everything we could, *everything* we possibly could, to resuscitate her. To save her. We had a team and … we didn't give up. But we … it, failed. I'm very, very, sorry for your loss. And—"

"No. No, I said, you *can't* say that. No! That … that can't be right. How can … how can … that happen?" He looked straight through her in utter disbelief and confusion.

"I'm sorry, Mr Greer. I was the assistant surgeon. Her heart … her heart was under *the* most enormous, enormous stress. She tried. She tried … so hard."

She paused.

He couldn't speak. He couldn't move.

"I wish we could have done more. But … it wasn't possible. With the blood loss and what her body had been through, it just … wasn't possible."

He took a deep and painful swallow. "I … ah," he said, shaking his head from side to side. He couldn't even look at her now.

He turned and stared at the wall. *She can't be gone … Again.*

"I … ah," he said, just like before, still staring at the wall. He cleared his throat, deeply and loudly.

She waited for him to speak, when he was ready. When, he was able.

He sniffed and turned his face to her. "I loved her."

She nodded.

"No, I did."

She nodded again, as she saw his tears emerge. Now she had to summon her own strength.

He sniffed again, and the tears fell from him. "I mean … didn't anyone know, just how much … how much *she* loved?" he said. "Did *anyone … anyone* know that? I knew." he said. "I knew how much. I did, you know. She showed me. ME!"

He pressed his hands to his face and covered his eyes.

They sat in silence once more.

He removed his hands and stared at her, shaking his head. "You know, I never told her," he said. "I NEVER told her I loved her," he added, bursting into tears. "And now … now I can't! Oh, my God!" he yelled.

Dr Banistock couldn't fight it any longer. And she allowed herself to cry with him. Softly. But in his agony, he didn't see her tears.

"I'm so sorry, Mr Greer," she said, gathering herself.

He put his shaking hand up and then drew it back slowly and placed his fingers across his lips and held them there. "It's … not fair. She didn't deserve this. She needed to be with her child."

"Yes," she said.

"Did she get to hold her daughter, Doctor? DID SHE?"

"No, Mr Greer, she didn't. I'm sorry."

He hung his head and looked down. Down into the darkness of his closed eyes.

"I need to go," he said, getting up so suddenly, the chair he had been sitting on flipped back and onto the floor.

"Where are you going?"

"I don't know."

"We can arrange someone to be with you. Mr Greer … please, please."

"I don't want anyone to be with me. NO ONE!"

He rushed out of the room and down the hallway.

Next minute, somehow, he was in his car. The sounds of the traffic were blocked out as there was no outside world. Then, he was in their bedroom. How did he get there? He would never, ever remember. He tore the sheets off the bed, ripping the bottom one apart as it caught on the edge of the mattress. He threw it to the floor, then into the garbage.

He collapsed on the bed face down. He could hear the sounds outside now: the hum of the city, the trains and traffic, somewhere off in the distance. He listened and felt he was the only one who could hear that secretive tone of desolation and isolation and … nothingness. He closed his eyes but it only made the sounds of the outside world unbearable. So he got up and went into the kitchen where he stopped short when he saw the blood on the floor. He collapsed onto his knees, not caring that they hit the floor with force. He wished the fall had cracked his knee caps, so maybe the physical pain would take away his anguish but he just rolled on his back and cried, like he had never cried before.

Up on his feet, again. *What time was it?* It was *no time to be a coward*, not now, he thought. Her parents would be there soon. No one was going to tell them.

No one, but him.

But before he got in the car, he went into the nursery. He sat on the edge of the chair and pulled open the drawer in the tiny table beside the cot and removed the envelope. His hand shook as he took one last look before running his finger underneath the seal. He held it upside down and two little pieces of paper fluttered to the floor. He recognised the one he'd put inside. The pink paper she had used was folded in two. He picked it up and unfolded it. In her beautiful handwriting she had written, 'Anna'. *We agreed.* He closed his eyes and tilted his head back. When he opened them, the stars on the ceiling came into view, and he cried again.

CHAPTER THIRTY-EIGHT

Six months later. A sunny day …

The sound of a car pulling into Tom's driveway meant that it was time to go.

A knock at the door. "Who might that be?" he said. "Let's go and see, shall we? Yes, we shall." He took a few steps, moved her to his other hip and opened the door. "Why, look! It's Aunty Cathy! Hello, Aunty Cathy! Hello!"

"Hello, gorgeous! Here, you come to me! I've something for you," she said, waving it in front of the baby, before gently touching her nose with it.

"Cathy, she's already got ten of them. Three, from you."

"No one can have too many teddy bears. Can they, Anna? No, they can't. Not at all."

"I'm going to go," he said, as he handed her over to her waiting arms. "I'm already running late. Her bottle's in the fridge, if you need it. I'll only be an hour, if that. She had a sleep this afternoon. Goodbye darling. Daddy will be back in a little while."

After kissing his daughter on the cheek, he stepped outside.

"You sure this is a good idea, Tom?" Cathy said.

"No, but I've already made the appointment."

He sat in the room for the final time. This time, he knew it would be his last visit. Nothing had changed.

"Still no crystal ball?" he said.

"No. Don't need one."

"I see."

"Do you? No glasses this time."

"No. Don't need them."

"I said you would be back."

"I know. That's why I'm here."

"No, it's not."

"No … it's not."

"Why *are* you here?"

"I want to know if you know, now. I've waited a long time to come back. Do you know, now? You said you didn't know, *yet*. That's what you said."

"I can see your eyes, now that you've taken off your disguise."

"Very good. What else can you see?"

"Let me look into them."

"Aren't you going to ask me for my hand?"

"No. I want to look into your eyes. Let me."

"Okay." He waited. "What do you see?"

"A lost love."

"Very good. What else?"

"I see that you were once a pupil. But now, you're a master."

"A master, am I?"

"And there's something else there. Something … that you have come to see me about. Something … that's been there, from your very first visit. Give me your hand."

"I thought you said no."

"*Give* me your hand."

He knew the drill.

"The girl."

"Yes."

"You've seen darkness. I know darkness, and people who live in it, and they survive."

He looked at her rings. A diamond. A wedding band.

"You know, your pupil – those things," she said, forking her fingers and pointing them towards his eyes. She returned her hand back to her lap but continued to hold his hand with her other hand. Gently. Softly. It felt good. "The pupil, it's the aperture of the eye. It dilates in darker conditions. It dilates to let more light in. You should know that."

"Darker conditions?"

"The ones you've seen."

"Why should I know that?"

"Because you have an eye. A photographic eye. You know that in the dark, you have to open the lens. You have to *let* the light in. You have to let the light dominate the darkness."

"But ... but, what about her? You haven't told me, about her."

"You *have* Anna. You have found your Anna."

"Very good." Tears welled in his eyes.

"You know what else I see?"

"No," he said, unable to control the tears now.

She looked deeper into his eyes. "I see that you've been given permission. You can stop, now. Forever."

"Stop?" The tears fell. He let them fall.

"Stop looking. Start seeing."

"Alright."

"When you go home today, I see that you will see."

"See what? What?"

"You will see the light in your eyes. That *she* is the light."

ACKNOWLEDGEMENTS

My deepest thanks to my wife, Kirsty Spence, for her patience and support. To my daughter, Jessica Spence and my mother-in-law, Alison Caperon, thank you for reading the manuscript and your feedback. Thank you to my son, Shay Spence, for encouraging me to follow a passion.

I also extend my gratitude to Patrice Shaw from PS Editing and Kirsty Ogden from Epiphany Editing & Publishing, Brisbane.

ABOUT THE AUTHOR

Carl Spence lives in Australia and his interests include gardening, sports, responsible fishing, cooking, photography, travel (particularly to the United Kingdom), and the preservation of wildlife and its habitat. He also enjoys a wide range of music, with the occasional ale, but can't play any instruments. And of late, he's taken a liking to early nights.

For more information, please go to www.carlspenceauthor.com.

www.ingramcontent.com/pod-product-compliance
Lightning Source LLC
Chambersburg PA
CBHW020126120726
47903CB00007B/2132